Wolfchild

A Young Adult Novel

Robert U. Montgomery

RUM Publishing

Wolfchild

Robert U. Montgomery
RUM Publishing

Project Management and Book Design: DavisCreativePublishing.com

Publisher's Cataloging-in-Publication
Names: Montgomery, Robert U., author.
Title: Wolfchild : a young adult novel / Robert U. Montgomery.
Description: Bonne Terre, MO : RUM Publishing, [2025]
Identifiers: ISBN: 979-8-9884538-2-6 (paperback) | 979-8-9884538-4-0 (hardback) |
    979-8-9884538-3-3 (ebook) | LCCN: 2025901280
Subjects: LCSH: Human-wolf encounters--Fiction. | Kidnapping--Fiction. | Wolves--Fiction. |
    Survival-- Fiction. | Secrecy--Fiction. | Good and evil--Fiction. | LCGFT: Action and adven-
    ture fiction. | BISAC: YOUNG ADULT FICTION / Action & Adventure / General. | YOUNG
    ADULT FICTION / Animals / Mythical Creatures. | YOUNG ADULT FICTION / Girls & Wome
Classification: LCC: PS3613.O54884 W65 2025 | DDC: 813/.6--dc23

CONTENTS

PROLOGUE 1

Part One | DREAM LAND   3

Chapter One. .5
Chapter Two. 11
Chapter Three 15
Chapter Four 25

Part Two | BETRAYAL   31

Chapter Five. 33
Chapter Six .35
Chapter Seven 39
Chapter Eight. 45
Chapter Nine 49
Chapter Ten 53

Part Three | FAMILY REUNION   63

Chapter Eleven 65
Chapter Twelve 77
Chapter Thirteen 85
Chapter Fourteen. 89
Chapter Fifteen 93

Part Four | FITTING IN   99

Chapter Sixteen 101
Chapter Seventeen. 105
Chapter Eighteen. 111

Part Five | LOVE SONG   117

Chapter Nineteen 119
Chapter Twenty 125

Chapter Twenty-One. 139
Chapter Twenty-Two 145

Part Six | DANGER & DEATH   155

Chapter Twenty-Three 157
Chapter Twenty-Four 165
Chapter Twenty-Five 175
Chapter Twenty-Six. 183
Chapter Twenty-Seven 191

Part Six | ESCAPE   197

Chapter Twenty-Eight 199
Chapter Twenty-Nine 211
Chapter Thirty 219
Chapter Thirty-One. 225
Chapter Thirty-Two. 233

Part Seven | FIREWORKS   237

Chapter Thirty-Three 239
Chapter Thirty-Four 251
Chapter Thirty-Five. 255
Chapter Thirty-Six. 265
Chapter Thirty-Seven 271
Chapter Thirty-Eight. 285
Chapter Thirty-Nine 293
Chapter Forty. 303
Chapter Forty-One 311
Chapter Forty-Two 315
Chapter Forty-Three 319

EPILOGUE   329

About the Author   333

PROLOGUE

They ran swiftly and silently under the full moon of June, crossing streams, climbing hills, leaping fallen logs. Their amber eyes showed them the way, but they followed their noses. A great horned owl watched as they passed under his perch. Rabbits squeezed to the backs of their burrows, wide-eyed and fearful. A startled raccoon dropped the crawfish it had been eating and scrambled up a tree.

But rabbits and raccoons were of no interest to the hunters. They were a family, and they needed food, not only for themselves but for three young ones back at the den. Ignoring smaller animals along the way, they followed the ripe scent of deer blood.

Suddenly, the alpha, a large black wolf with gray hair around his nose, slowed at the top of a cedar-cloaked ridge. Two others skidded to a halt behind him. A fourth, the youngest, sped past them, intent on supper. A low growl from the leader stopped him, and his back legs overran the front, sending him sprawling.

Now all four had picked up the new odor. His followers paced nervously about, whining softly and sniffing the air as the leader looked into the westerly wind. He saw a light where, on other nights, none had been before. Food was important, especially now. They hadn't eaten for several days, and his mate's pups were fast-growing and always hungry. But checking out this new danger to the family was more important. He looked over his shoulder at the other three. They lowered their heads and tails and whined, telling him that they would wait for his return.

The alpha ran toward the light, a hurtful noise and a foul smell that his instincts told him to avoid. But a sense of responsibility—along with the curiosity that came with being a wolf—demanded that he investigate. His long legs propelled him down the ridge and through the moon-dappled woods. His well-conditioned heart raced with worry. He had smelled men before, but this was more than man scent.

He was panting heavily by the time he reached a low-lying hill that overlooked the source of the light. The human thunder had stopped, but men still were there. His gold eyes noted that some stood or walked while others lay as if sleeping in the sudden stillness. His keen ears picked up laughter and low voices in the false silence.

The alpha cocked his head and studied the cruel sounds, sniffing intently all the while. Yes, this formerly empty place now smelled of men. Most men, for a reason that he and his kind would never understand, had devoted themselves to killing wolves. They would have to be especially careful when hunting near this place in the future.

But this scent was more than man smell and meant more than potential danger. He shook his head and pawed at his nose. He had breathed too deeply of this place. He would have no appetite tonight, despite his hunger.

He turned and ran away, away from the smell of man, away from the stench of evil.

PART ONE
DREAM LAND

CHAPTER ONE

Kara saw a hawk circling above. She heard chickadees and finches twittering on both sides.

Up ahead, a doe and her spotted fawn stared with enormous brown eyes and then bolted for cover. The yellow wildflowers of summer had begun to mix with the fading purple. The world was bursting with life, and so was Kara.

The bright sun warmed her bare arms and legs as she ran up a steep hill. She wore soft moccasins and a leather tunic that fell about halfway to her knees. She could feel the "thumpa-thumpa" of her heart deep in her chest.

She was running, running, running.

Suddenly, she realized that she didn't know why she was running. Was she going somewhere? Was she chasing something? Was something chasing her? Or was this just a pleasant morning run to celebrate life?

She paused and looked around as she reached the top of the hill. Clouds partially blocked the sun now, and shadows deepened in the thick woods. Sucking in great gulps of air that seemed colder than they should be, she saw nothing in any direction.

As her heart slowed, however, Kara heard someone—or something—charging up the hill behind her. So hard and fast was its approach that twigs on the forest floor cracked like thunder.

She was the hunted! This was not running for the sheer joy of it. Whatever was coming was in hot pursuit and would be on her in seconds.

She could hear deep, ragged breathing, growing louder and louder amidst the crunch of leaves and snap of branches. Not just one was after her, but two or three or more.

Kara ran down the hill, dodging from side to side to avoid cedars and boulders. She ducked under low-hanging branches.

Why are they after me? she wondered. *Why?*

Suddenly, she knew. "It's a game," she huffed, keeping her brown eyes on the way ahead of her. "We're playing a game!"

She nearly sagged to her knees as relief washed over her. Catching herself on a small oak, she smiled and breathed deeply.

"Well, they won't catch me that easily!" she said.

She turned back toward her pursuers.

"You won't catch me that easily!" she yelled.

Now she was happy, not caring at all that clouds had stolen away the sun and ever colder air was blowing into her face. She ran on, enjoying the game.

At the bottom of the hill, she found herself along the shore of a small creek.

"Come and get me!" she called behind her. "I'm waiting!"

Regaining her breath, she dropped to her knees to scoop a handful of water to drink. As she lowered her head, she realized that she heard no one behind her. She stared up the hill, listening intently. She noticed that a morning in early summer seemed to have transformed into the dusk of late winter.

Puzzled but thirsty, Kara turned back for her drink. The liquid in her hand felt like water, but it was as black as a moonless night.

"Ugh!" she said, tossing the fluid away and wiping her hand on her tunic.

More curious than concerned about what had happened to her pursuers, she followed the flowing water upstream. No birds sang, no animals drank, no fish jumped, and no wildflowers bloomed. The day grew even darker and darker as she neared a bend that blocked her from seeing what lay ahead.

It was then that her family called from somewhere back up the hill. She heard their voices but couldn't understand what they said.

The haunting calls turned Kara's spine to ice and made her whole body shudder. Her family was calling her. Warning her. Wrapping her arms about her chest, she looked back toward the hill. She should leave this place.

But, no, she wanted to know why the water was black. She wanted to know what lay around the bend. Patting the right side of her waist to be certain that her bone knife was there, she walked on through a day that was all black and shades of gray.

As she rounded a curve, a dead tree sprawled across the gravel, blocking her way. Stepping over its rotted trunk, Kara looked up and saw life again. But it did not comfort her. All the trees were dead, and their branches were heavy with crows and vultures. The birds were as quiet as death. They looked at her with lifeless eyes.

Her family called again. Were they asking her to come back? Were they warning her not to go forward?

Whatever they said, the girl had decided she would not turn back. She must solve a mystery. She must see for herself. As she walked, gray rock walls replaced the skeletons of trees, and the creek seemed to widen inside a steep valley. Just where the walls were the highest, and the creek turned to the left, she saw white. It was so big and so bright it hurt her eyes, even on a day without sun.

Kara walked more slowly now, her heart pounding and her hand on her knife. Her eyes slowly started to separate the mass of white into smaller pieces. They lay all along the shore and in the shallow water.

Nearing the first of many, she kneeled and looked closely. It was the skeleton of a small animal, a squirrel, maybe. Then she saw one that might have been a raccoon or possum. And another that might have been a deer.

Kara's eyes grew large as she realized that hundreds, perhaps thousands, of skeletons were here. Stepping carefully forward, she now was surrounded by a knee-high sea of deathly white. Her hands shook, and icy sweat rolled down her sides as she struggled to understand what she was seeing.

Then she saw bones that made her legs grow weak. They had belonged to a wolf. Stepping fearfully backward, she felt something cold and hard grasp her foot. She screamed, jumped, and fell among the clattering skeletons.

More and more of them seemed to reach for her now. She felt them plucking at her arms, her legs, her neck. Something tangled in her hair. She pushed herself to her feet and ran for her life.

"Nooo! Nooo! Nooo!" She screamed.

Not only had she seen the bones of wolves, Kara realized. She had seen those of humans! Those bones clutching at her had been fingers!

* * * * *

"Nooo! Noo! No."

The sound of her own voice awakened Pamela Jane Conners, known as "P.J." by friends and family. For a moment, she was confused and afraid. The dream had seemed so real. Then she remembered where she was — the guest bedroom of her grandmother's house. She had just arrived to spend the summer.

She sat on the edge of the bed and rubbed her eyes. She noticed the moon shining through the sheer curtains. Now that she was awake — or halfway awake, at least — the light seemed so bright that she feared she might not be able to get back to sleep unless she pulled down the shade.

Wearing her favorite Garfield tee shirt and shorts, she padded over to the window. The cool hardwood floors creaked slightly under her feet. The shadows of an unfamiliar room lay all about her.

At the window, she looked down at her grandmother's garden and white birdbath, awash in the moonlight. Then she looked out past the yard to the woods beyond. Was that movement she saw among the trees? A deer, maybe. She stared more intently, hoping to see it step out of the shadows. It probably was going to help itself to some roses in Grandma's garden.

P.J. smiled. But not because she would enjoy seeing her grandmother's flowers eaten. She loved nature. She loved seeing wild animals of all shapes and sizes.

Two eyes appeared suddenly in the woods, and her smile disappeared.

No, not eyes, P.J. told herself. *Just fireflies.*

But the fireflies didn't blink. Instead, they seemed to lock on P.J.'s eyes. One was light amber, and the other dark gold.

CHAPTER TWO

Ryan Conners stared intently at the antelope leg tied to an upper branch in the thorn tree. The setting sun on the other side of the tree provided the perfect backlight for a silhouette shot if only the leopard would come. If it didn't show, he would have to return to this blind tomorrow afternoon to try for the photos he needed. For the sake of his aching muscles, he hoped that he would not have to.

This close to the equator, both sunsets and sunrises occurred much too quickly. Another ten minutes and the crimson evening sky of winter would bleed into pale blue dusk.

Ryan carefully bent his knees inside the grass blind and realized that soon he would be shivering. The shorts and vest that had been just right a few hours ago weren't nearly warm enough in the bush after dark.

The idea of being cold made Ryan remember how miserable poor little P.J. must have been nine years ago. Snow, cold, trucks, wolves, sirens, tombstones—many things brought the past to life for thirty-seven-year-old Ryan. The flashbacks seemed to happen more and more lately, though, as did thoughts of P.J. in general.

Maybe I'm finally starting to feel something again, Ryan thought. *Maybe I'm finally starting to feel guilty about not being there for her.*

Ryan smiled sadly and absentmindedly pulled a burr from his khaki sock. He had carried plenty of guilt with him for nine years already.

I really don't need any more of that, he thought.

The guilt that wouldn't go away began to sneak into him shortly after he became a single parent.

Police had found Carrie dead in the car, but P.J. was not there. The temperature was below zero on the day of the accident. Then ten inches of snow fell that night as more than two dozen men searched for his daughter. They finally gave up about noon the next day while fierce winds continued to drive pellets of snow, stinging eyes, and unprotected flesh.

"Mr. Conners, I'm sorry, but I just don't see how she could still be alive. She's been out here in below-zero temperatures twenty-four hours," a highway patrol captain said above the blow. "I wish we could do more but…"

Then he clapped a gloved hand on Ryan's shoulder.

"I'm really very sorry," he said again, shaking his head slowly as he walked away into the swirling snow.

Left alone in the blizzard, Ryan told himself that P.J. might be dead, but he would not leave the body to be ravaged by animals. Besides, he knew on some subconscious level the only way he would be able to cope with the death of Carrie right now was to keep his mind and body occupied.

Yes, P.J. was dead too. It wasn't something that he wanted to believe. But he was a realist. The highway patrolman had been right: No three-year-old child could survive for a day in this weather, particularly if she had been hurt in the collision.

Yes, he would grieve as much for his daughter as he would for his wife when the time was appropriate. But right now, he had to find P.J.'s body.

For two more days, he searched through the pine and spruce forest around the accident site. Blowing snow had wiped out any footprints that P.J. might have made as soon as she made them, so Ryan was reluctant to head off in any one direction. Finally, on the afternoon of the third day, the wind died, and the sun pushed through the clouds.

Ryan paused on his snowshoes and removed his goggles. He closed his blue eyes and let his face bask in the relative warmth.

When he opened his eyes again, he saw a small figure standing under the boughs of a large spruce about one hundred yards away.

"P.J.!" he cried. "P.J.!"

He plunged toward his daughter, falling repeatedly in the deep snow. When he was within arm's grasp, he scooped up the child and squeezed her to his chest.

Tears of joy froze on Ryan's cheeks as he cradled his daughter and looked down into the pudgy red face with brown eyes that were too much like her mother's.

Slowly, he realized that those eyes were vacant. P.J. wasn't responding verbally or hugging him back.

"That's okay, P.J.," he whispered. "You're going to be all right."

Authorities were amazed that anyone, much less a child, could survive for three days in such extreme weather. Except for being starved and a little dehydrated, however, she seemed fine. The doctor couldn't even find one sign of frostbite on her face, fingers, or toes as P.J. gobbled up a third bowl of chicken-noodle soup in the small house that the Conners rented near Superior National Forest.

Ryan had a theory as to how P.J. survived, but he shared it with no one. Carrie, he told himself, would be the only one who would believe him. His beautiful, innocent wife accepted that such things happened in the world. She believed in them, she had often told him, because she was part Cheyenne on her father's side, and Indians know that there is more to the world than the physical.

"There is also the mystical," she had said. "We are as one with the animals on this earth, some more than others."

Ryan never could learn from P.J. where she had been during those three days. She would just say, "I don't remember," and return to playing with her dolls. And Ryan didn't mind that the specifics of his daughter's survival remained a mystery. He was overjoyed that he found P.J. alive and healthy.

Over time, though, Ryan noticed that he was withdrawing emotionally from his daughter.

It will pass, he told himself often.

He went through the motions, hopeful that if he acted the part of a good father, eventually he would feel it too. He played catch with P.J. He took her to movies and zoos and playgrounds. He tickled her and treated her to piggyback rides. He read her bedtime stories and kissed her good night.

And two years after Carrie died, Ryan put P.J. in a boarding school and went on the road.

Now, sitting here in a leopard blind in Kenya, the wildlife photographer realized suddenly that he was on the wrong continent. He knew that huge, empty place in his heart was ready to be filled if only he would go home and embrace P.J. Guilt for not loving the daughter that a miracle had returned to him was being replaced by guilt for abandoning his own flesh and blood.

And it took only seven years, he thought with disgust.

I've spent seven years running away from P.J. What a jerk I am. Things are going to be different when I get back home.

Just then, Ryan heard the wall of the blind shake and looked up just in time to see a snarling leopard charge through.

CHAPTER THREE

P.J. leaned on the kitchen table with both elbows and yawned repeatedly. Then she rubbed her face roughly with both hands and stretched her brown eyes open as wide as they would go. For the second time in four days that she had been here, she had managed little sleep because of strange dreams.

No, more than strange, she thought. *The first one — with all those creepy bones and skeletons — was really scary.*

Mary Jennings, her grandmother, hadn't been around her enough yet to know that this sluggish behavior was unusual for P.J. Normally, she was wide awake and ready to take on the world in about five minutes. Years of boarding school had conditioned her to rise quickly and get going with the day's activities.

The white-haired woman with warm blue eyes sat a pan of hot biscuits on the counter to cool. She returned to frying bacon as she hummed some old-fashioned song that P.J. never had heard before. The rich smell of the bread made the girl's mouth water. Her taste buds were awake and standing at attention, even if other parts of her were not.

Somewhere just outside the open kitchen window, a robin warbled to its mate. The humming, the sizzling, the chirping, and the wonderful aromas slowly combined to bring the rest of her around.

"We're having supper with your Aunt Cathy and Uncle John tonight," her grandmother said as she turned the bacon. "They say that you're welcome to go next door and use their pool anytime you want to, and Uncle John has promised to take you fishing next weekend."

A pool? Oh, yeah! P.J. thought. *I hope there's a place around here for me to get a new swimsuit. Maybe a bikini.*

Fishing? Well, that could be fun, especially if we go in a boat or a canoe. I could wear my bikini then too.

"How about that?" her grandmother said with a grin as she turned from the stove, her spatula poised like a conductor's baton. "You're going to have such a good time here this summer. Maybe John will take us to some Cardinal baseball games too. They get all kinds of free passes at his newspaper, you know."

P.J. smiled.

Baseball games! Yes! Ballpark peanuts and nachos with lots of cheese. Ooh, not so good for wearing a bikini.

Finally, her grandmother noticed the smoky kitchen.

"Honey, turn on that exhaust fan for me," she said.

P.J. pushed long strands of brown hair from her face as she dragged a chair to the back door. At five feet, five inches, she hoped that she was still growing. She loved playing basketball. But even if P.J. had been six feet tall, she couldn't have reached the fan without the chair. She climbed onto it and pushed a button to start the old-fashioned fan.

Back at the table, she pulled her wavy hair back and used a rubber band to put it in a ponytail. She sipped her orange juice and wrinkled her nose at its slight tartness. She rubbed a sore spot on her left ear.

Must have slept on it the wrong way, she thought.

P.J. stared into the deep, dark red of a jar of strawberry jam and thought back to the latest dream. She didn't really want to think about it. She'd rather think about bikinis and nachos. But the dream was fresh on her mind. Also, she needed something to take her attention away from the mouth-watering smells until Mam Ma set the food on the table.

* * * * *

Her right arm poised and ready, Kara stood knee-deep in the shallow stream, looking for a flash of silver. Her callused feet were not bothered by the rough gravel bottom. But the cold water stung her bare legs and forced occasional shivers from her young body.

"Where are you fish?" she said. "One more is all I need for breakfast!"

Just then, she heard a rustling sound on the far shore and then a splash. Turning, she saw a bear eating the trout that she had left there on a stick. Enraged, Kara yelled, "Get out of there!" She flung her small wooden spear. It pricked the bear's skin on the left shoulder and hung there a moment before it fell into the water and floated away.

A fish still sideways in its mouth, the big brown animal looked curiously at the small wound. Then it looked at Kara and again at the bloody hole in its hide. It soon returned to more important business. Scales exploded from its huge mouth and flashed in the morning sun as it munched a second trout.

"Get out of here!" Kara yelled again.

This time she picked up a small stone and hurled it. The rock made a dull "thump" as it struck the bear on the forehead. Again, the bear looked toward the girl, but now its black eyes were intent.

For a moment, Kara smiled. Having gained the bear's attention, she was confident it would retreat when she flung a second rock. The stone flew true and hit the animal on the nose. But the bear did not run. It stood and roared, swinging its front paws madly in the air.

Kara stared in wide-eyed disbelief until she felt the earth shaking as the huge beast charged through the shallow water. Then she turned and ran for her life. Just two steps out of the water, however, her foot slipped in the mud. She fell bottom-first back into the stream. The icy flow stung her private areas, and she gasped. But she knew that she didn't have time for distractions. Far worse pain awaited if she didn't move fast.

In an instant, she was on her feet again and splashing toward shore. Looking fearfully over her shoulder, she saw the angry bear only a few feet away.

I'm dead, Kara thought. *I'm dead.*

But then she was onto dry land, where she could move faster. Maybe she would escape after all. She would climb a tree where the bigger, heavier bear couldn't follow. Looking up into the woods, her eyes searched for a suitable tree.

Yes, yes, I'm going to make it! she thought.

A slap to her head from behind sent her sprawling. When she looked up, the bear was towering over her, shaking its head and roaring. Saliva sprayed Kara's face, and she could smell the musty fur. Fish scales drifted down like snowflakes from the huge mouth. With no place to go, the girl covered her face with her arms and curled her body for protection.

Once more, she heard the bear growl. She squeezed her eyes tight and held her breath. She waited for the first blow. She waited to die.

Her heart pounded, not only in her chest but in her ears. The drumming sound was so loud that several seconds passed before she realized the roaring above her had stopped. Cautiously, she opened one eye and peeked out above her arm. The bear was gone!

Kara couldn't believe her luck. She lay there for a moment, happy to be alive. Then she realized that she had better get moving if she wanted to stay that way. The left side of her head hurt from the bear's slap.

As she pushed to her feet and looked toward the woods, she saw the wolves. They stood in a semi-circle around her, their teeth bared and their hackles raised. Kara turned to run and saw the bear bounding up the far bank.

"Don't worry, Young One. We will not hurt you."

Kara turned back to the wolves as the leader stepped forward. His black coat gleamed in the low rays of the early morning sun.

"Then I thank you for your kindness," Kara said. "You risked your life for me."

The black wolf smiled.

"Your people and mine are friends," he said. "We often have shared food with one another. But we really weren't in any danger. The bear didn't want to fight. It just wanted breakfast.

"You, Young One, are the one who risked her life, and for what? For a few fish from a stream that is rich with them? You should pick your battles more wisely."

Kara brushed leaves and mud from her deerskin dress and bare legs.

"But that bear just made me so mad," she said. "Those were my fish."

Once more, the wolf smiled. "Then they were the bear's, and he is bigger than you, Young One."

"But he is bigger than you also," Kara said childishly. "Why did he run from you?"

The black wolf looked over his shoulder.

"We are many," he said. "Being many often is better than being big. That is why we hunt as a family. And, as I said before, he only wanted breakfast, not a fight."

Kara looked at the wolf.

"Still, you didn't have to help me," she said.

The wolf's strange eyes—one light amber and the other dark gold—bore into Kara's. "Yes, we did. We are family."

The girl looked questioningly. "We?"

"But choose your battles more wisely," the wolf said. "Family may not always be there to help you out."

"We?" Kara asked again as the wolves turned to shadows in the deep woods. "We?"

* * * * *

"We?"

"P.J. Wake up. It's time to eat."

P.J. looked up into the concerned face of her grandmother, who was holding a plate of scrambled eggs and bacon. With her free hand, she stroked the girl's hair.

"Are you okay, honey?" she asked.

"Uh, yes, ma'am, I'm fine," P.J. said, trying to pull herself out of the nightmare and back to reality. "I just haven't been sleeping well lately."

She rubbed the sore spot on her ear. "And I think that I must have slept the wrong way last night."

Mam Ma took off her blue and white apron and sat down across from her with her own plate of food. She passed P.J. the biscuits.

"Don't worry," she said. "It's just being in a new place and all. You'll adjust soon enough. And then you'll sleep just fine.

"I'm so happy that you wanted to come here for the summer instead of going to that camp in Maine like you have been for the past four years."

I'm glad that I wanted to come, too, P.J. thought. *But why? Why did I ask to come here? Even with all of the black flies there—and the goofy boys across the lake—I really did like the summer camp. And what am I going to do around here all summer except have weird dreams?*

She split her biscuit open and spread on a little jam. She didn't have much of an appetite now, and the smell of bacon almost made her sick.

Being clobbered by a bear will do that to a person, she thought.

"Mam Ma, do you know anything about wolves?" P.J. said.

The woman nearly spilled her coffee cup setting it down. Her nearly constant smile disappeared. P.J. thought that she saw fear or pain—or both—in her grandmother's eyes for a split second. Then the woman quickly gained control and forced a grin as she reached for a biscuit. P.J. saw her hand shaking.

"Is something wrong, Mam Ma?" she asked.

"No," her grandmother said too quickly. "I was just thinking about your Pap Pa. He used to say he dreamed about wolves, especially right after your mother died. He said that she had sent the wolves to him.

"He was a crazy old man. But I loved him."

Mam Ma took a sip of coffee and then busied herself, cutting a fried egg into tiny pieces. She avoided eye contact.

P.J. picked up a piece of bacon and pretended to study it. She much would have preferred fruit, yogurt, and maybe some Cheerios for breakfast. Sure, she liked ice cream, chocolate, and other foods that weren't particularly healthful. But she tried to stay away from red meat and animal fat.

Fish is good, she thought. *Hey, just like in the dream!*

Only the bear took them from me. Me? Was that me in the dream? Did the girl look like me? I don't remember.

Still, P.J. could adapt—even if steak were served. She was a guest here, after all. And as her grandmother came to know her better, P.J. would tell her what she liked to eat. She closed her eyes and took a crunchy bite of bacon.

Mam Ma's talk of dreams made P.J. nervous, so nervous, in fact, that she forgot about her grandmother's discomfort. She put the bacon back on her plate, picked up her fork, and played with her scrambled eggs. She had dreamed of wolves back in Pennsylvania, too, but could remember little of them when she had awakened.

Wait a minute! I'm not even sure that I remembered having dreams in Pennsylvania until just this very moment, she realized with a start.

Here in Parkland, the dreams were much more vivid, and she wished that she could talk about them. She wanted to ask her grandmother if she or Pap Pa actually had seen wolves around here. But she knew that her grandmother wouldn't like that. In just a few minutes, she knew that the less said about wolves, the better, as far as Mam Ma was concerned. P.J. would keep what she had seen in the backyard — or probably just what she *thought* she had seen — to herself.

She decided that she would walk over to the library after breakfast and read all that she could about the animals. She would do a Google search too. She couldn't do that here because her grandmother had no internet connection. Maybe, too, P.J. could find something that would explain why she was having these strange dreams. The librarian would help her. She was a nice lady. Growing up with no mother — and an absent father — P.J. often sought the company of teachers, camp counselors, and the like.

P.J. forced herself to take a bite of eggs. Yes, she knew that she shouldn't say anything more. But she just couldn't help herself.

"Dad says that wolves are the most misunderstood animals on earth," she said quietly. "He said that he and Mom spent lots of time up in Minnesota taking their pictures and studying them before… Before… Well, you know…"

Mam Ma's smile disappeared for a second time.

"Before that truck slid on the ice and killed your mother and almost killed you? she finished. "Yes, I know how they both felt about wolves. Pap Pa, God rest his soul, was the same way. Said it was because he was part Indian. I guess that's why Carrie, your mother, was the way she was.

"Her older sister, Cathy, took after my side of the family, thank goodness, and decided to stay right here in Parkland, where it's safe. She married a man who's a real leader in the community too. Some think he might be elected governor or senator one day."

Mam Ma studied her coffee cup, and P.J. waited.

"If it wasn't for wolves, Carrie still would be alive today because she wouldn't have been up in Minnesota studying them," her grandmother said. "I still would have my youngest daughter, and you still would have a mother. And maybe if Carrie were still alive, you'd have more of a father, too."

Shocked by her outburst, Mam Ma swallowed hard and stared down at her plate. With red-rimmed eyes, she then turned away, wiped tears with her napkin, and looked again at P.J. She reached across the table and touched her arm.

"Those wolves," she said softly. "Those wolves. . . You just don't know."

P.J. looked down at her plate and then pushed back from both her touch and the table.

"May I be excused now?" she said. "I'm not very hungry."

"I'm sorry, Honey," Mam Ma said. "I shouldn't have said that about Ryan. He's doing the best he can. Losing Carrie when you were so tiny and then Pap Pa last year, well, it's been really hard for me. I say things I don't mean sometimes."

"That's okay," P.J. said and smiled sadly, leaving unsaid the fact that she agreed with her grandmother.

Ryan hadn't been much of a father to her in the nine years since her mother had died. But she didn't blame her father.

It's my fault, she often thought. *It's my fault and I wish that I knew what to do about it.*

CHAPTER FOUR

The smell of evil was often in the alpha wolf's mind these days, even when he lay on a rocky ledge, his eyes half-closed, on a cool sunny morning. The cabin was miles away, over hilly terrain, but he knew that men wander far from their homes, too.

For safety, he now had two of his family constantly patrolling around their den. Another, a young female, was with his mate and pups down by the stream, bathing and playing.

Just as he started to doze, he heard his mate growl threateningly and then yapping from the pups. He sprang to his feet, gray guard hairs on his massive black back bristling to attention. He leaped off the rock and raced down the hill toward the stream.

Other growls came to his ears as he ran, growls not from wolves. He ran faster. One of the pups shrieked. Its cry stopped suddenly and was replaced by deadly silence as he bounded over a fallen tree. Thorns and stickers tore at his black coat, but he ignored them. Nothing mattered but his family.

Charging out of the woods and onto a gravel bar, he saw his mate and the young female lunging at a bear. One of the pups lay lifeless at the feet of the massive animal. The other two were nowhere to be seen. The black wolf hurled himself at the bear. He grabbed a furry shoulder with his teeth and yanked.

Now it was the bear's turn to yelp. It staggered backward and slapped at his attacker.

The wolf dodged the blow as he released his grip. He grabbed the pup by the nape of the neck and retreated. As he did so, the two females charged the bear. He slapped the younger one away, but the other locked her fangs on his rump and held on.

Enraged, the bear twirled to and fro in a dance of desperation. Twice he lifted the white she-wolf from the ground as he thrashed about, hoping to throw her off. But her powerful jaws remained locked, and she ground them toward each other, tearing fur and flesh.

The young female crawled back to the black wolf, and he left the pup in her care.

Then, teeth bared and ears flat, he attacked the bear again. This time he went for its throat. Using a forepaw, the bear managed to slow the attacker but stumbled and fell under the weight of the big wolf. The she-wolf darted away just in time to avoid being pinned underneath.

The bear's growls turned to bawls now as it splashed through the shallow water for the far side. The black wolf and his mate nipped at its heels until it stumbled on shore and ran up into the woods. Both then turned to look for the pups. The mother whined softly.

They heard their offspring crying before they saw them. Then two gray pups came loping out of the brush. First, they ran in frantic circles of joy. Next, they reared onto their parents' shoulders and licked their muzzles. Finally, they rolled onto their backs and squirmed passionately. Their mother returned their affection by nuzzling them and licking their faces. Their father solemnly watched the other side of the stream, making certain that the bear did not return.

The young gray female gently pushed at the third pup, hoping to see it move. The white she-wolf joined her. She whined, licked the youngster's torn left ear, and nudged it.

Finally, it moved, and the two females squealed in delight. They helped it to its feet with their noses and then nearly pushed it down again as they licked it with huge, rough tongues. To escape this avalanche of affection, the black pup wobbled away, still dizzy from the blow to his head. Blood leaked from a tear in his left ear. He staggered to his father and sat down just in time to avoid being bowled over by his brother and sister. They, too, bathed him with love.

When he was certain that the bear was gone, the alpha pushed his barking children away from their brother and stroked him softly with his muzzle. Then he growled a command, and the family left for home. As they climbed, the black wolf stayed to the rear and kept watch over his shoulder.

*   *   *   *   *

Several days later, and five miles from where the wolves had denied him a meal, the young black bear sniffed something good. It wasn't a familiar scent, but it still made his mouth water.

Lifting his nose into the quiet night air, he inhaled deeply to help him decide where to go. The grainy smell made his mouth water. He didn't need meat to satisfy his hunger, although a wolf pup would have been nice. It had seemed lighter in weight but about the same size of a pot-bellied pig that he had devoured just days before.

Probably he would have eaten all three pups if given the chance. But trying to steal even one of the young wolves from the adults had proven too dangerous. Bites on his backside and shoulder were all he could take away from that encounter.

During his journey north from Arkansas into the eastern edge of the Missouri Ozarks, the bear had eaten honey, berries, apples, and garbage. He also dined on assorted road kills. He liked it best when his food didn't bite back.

The bear snapped at the itchy discomfort of the wounds on his rump and set off for the river. He crossed by swimming most of the way and then entered a shallow area that allowed him to wade. Saliva dripped from his mouth as the scent grew stronger.

A light in the cabin made him step quieter, but the desire for food was far stronger than his fear of man. The noises from inside were similar to those that he often heard when he ventured near humans. They reminded him slightly of bird songs but were harsher and louder.

He climbed the bank and sniffed around in the sand and gravel behind the building, following mouth-watering odor. Something shined in the dim moonlight, but he knew from bitter experience that such objects tasted awful. Also, they hurt his mouth when he bit into them.

The scent, however, definitely was coming from the glittery objects. The bear lowered his nose and pushed the cans around, trying to figure out the puzzle. Suddenly, he felt wetness on his snout, and the grainy smell was overpowering. Food was inside the cans!

He licked the gravel and smacked his lips. Yes, that was it!

As he batted around the cans some more, the bear noticed that they were open a little at one end, allowing the delicious fluid to flow out. But there just wasn't enough for him to eat in these scattered objects.

Not knowing exactly what he was looking for, he rose onto his hind legs and peered into the night. He forgot about the light and noise from the cabin. Much more of the delicious food was somewhere close by, he was sure of it.

Then he saw them, shimmering in the stream like trout! He splashed into the water and swiped at the cans. But they were connected somehow, so they barely moved. The bear cocked his head and studied the cans. He slapped at them again and again and again. Gradually, he noticed that if he hit the cans from just one direction, he could push them into shallower water and even onto shore.

Once he had them on the gravel, the bear discovered that they were much heavier than the cans he had found at first. But these new ones weren't leaking food. He took a frustrated swipe at a six-pack and launched it skyward. As the cans fell all around him, two of them burst, spewing like tiny geysers. Liquid sprayed onto the chest and face of the bear, and he lapped at it eagerly.

He tossed more cans into the air. When they crashed and opened, he licked at the spray, moving his mouth closer and closer to the punctures. Slowly, he realized that he could pick up the cans in his paws and suck out all of the beer inside.

Then, he learned that he could smash the cans open with a paw. He flopped onto his haunches, slapped six-packs, and drank beer. It ran out the corners of his mouth and down his chest. His wounds no longer bothered him. Human songs from inside the cabin sounded more and more pleasing to him. He belched. He scratched. He wanted to cry. Finally, he passed out.

PART TWO

BETRAYAL

CHAPTER FIVE

Her fists held high, P.J. danced around the basketball goal on the outdoor court.

"Yes! Yes! Yes!" she shouted.

She had just swished a fifteen-foot jump shot. Most twelve-year-old girls couldn't even shoot a jump shot, much less make one from that distance.

But P.J. could, and she wanted to become even better at doing it. She intended to make the starting five on her school's basketball team this coming winter. She was going to practice every morning on this court at the Civic Center before the day became too hot and/or other kids came to play. She liked being here alone.

Even this early, though, the Midwest heat and humidity still were uncomfortable. Holding the basketball in her left hand, she wiped her forehead with the back of her right. Starting tomorrow, she would bring sunglasses, she decided.

And, despite the heat, she decided, she had better wear a sports bra when she shot hoops. She didn't like to think about the fact that her breasts were growing. She wasn't even sure if she wanted them to grow. They'd just get in the way.

P.J. had heard older girls talking in the bathroom at school. They liked theirs. They called them "the girls." Heck, some even stuck tissues in the cups to make them look larger. How gross! To get the boys to look at them. Even grosser!

For sure, she didn't want big breasts. They'd just interfere with sports. Maybe one of these days, she would change her mind. If older girls liked theirs, then she…

What sounded like a muffled scream grabbed her attention. P.J. squinted down the hill toward the source. She held her right hand over her eyes to cut the glare and saw a big man holding a child near a van.

Suddenly, a word that she had learned in school popped into her mind. *Pedophile*! A guy in a black shirt had grabbed a little girl. The child kicked and fought but couldn't scream anymore. He had his hand over her mouth.

P.J. knew that he would do terrible things to her if she didn't help. She looked over at her backpack. She could dial 911 on her cell phone. But by then, the guy might have driven away with the little girl.

"Hey! Stop that," P.J. yelled. "Stop that right now!"

Before she realized it, she was running toward the man and girl.

"Stop that!" she yelled again. "Let her go!"

Even though she was left-handed, P.J. played shortstop on her school's softball team. That was because she had the strongest throwing arm. She hurled the basketball as she ran, and it hit the man squarely in the head. The ball bounced high as he staggered to his knees, nearly dropping the girl.

P.J. had nothing else to throw. She saw no rocks. The ball had rolled away. And she was too far from her phone. She did the only other thing she could do: She leaped onto the man's back and pounded on his head and shoulders with her fists.

"You!" Wham!

"Let!" Bam!

"Her!" Wham! Bam!

"Go!"

The man did. The girl ran screaming toward the Civic Center.

With P.J. still on his back and raining blows, the enraged man managed to stand. They spun around twice, nearly falling into a drainage ditch. Finally, the man pulled P.J. forward over his right shoulder with his left arm and knocked her out with a backhand from his right.

"You'll pay for this, you little bitch!" Crater Kendall said as he looked quickly about and then tossed P.J.'s lifeless body into the back of the van.

CHAPTER SIX

Hands on hips, Jackie Novak looked at another crime scene, probably the twentieth that she had seen this morning. This one looked the same as all the rest. The red-haired deputy sheriff made a note about the collapsed billboard, shook her head, and smiled.

"These things are ugly, no doubt about it. And they are getting worse all the time," she said. "But, whoever you are, you're breaking the law."

As the new deputy on the six-person sheriff's force—and the only female—the thirty-year-old woman usually was assigned to investigate less violent crimes, like barking dogs, illegal dumping, and, more recently, billboard vandalism.

But she wanted a career in law enforcement, just like her father. Such work, she knew, was the price that she would have to pay. She accepted it without complaint. In fact, she probably devoted more time and effort to each call than Sheriff Wilson expected her to.

Jackie idly adjusted the small gold hoop in her left ear and smiled again at the fallen billboard. "Looks like we've got our own environmental terrorist right here in Parkland."

She examined a couple of the footprints left in the moist ground.

"At least a 13," she said. "Maybe it's Bigfoot." She also sketched the tread pattern and wrote a reminder to find out what brand of boot might leave those marks.

Whoever he was, and no matter what kind of boots he wore, an environmental terrorist was much preferred to a child molester. The area had one of those, too, evidently. Earlier this morning, before checking out the billboard damage, Jackie had investigated a report of an attempted kidnapping near the Civic Center.

Sitting in her mother's 1lap and surprisingly calm, little Heather Carter couldn't recall much. But she did say that the man was "big and mean and smelled bad" and had some red writing on his arm.

Probably a tattoo, Jackie guessed, and the memory of others who weren't as lucky as little Heather came back to her. She had been a military policewoman at Fort Gordon when several women were raped and murdered. A suspect with a red tattoo finally was arrested. Mysteriously, though, he was free and gone before Jackie ever got the chance to see what he looked like. More women were killed after that, including one that Jackie would never forget. No one else ever was arrested.

"And Heather said that he drove a dark-colored van," the child's mother said.

Jackie nodded and smiled, forcing her thoughts back to the present.

The girl couldn't explain how she had been able to escape.

"I kicked and screamed, and then I ran away," she said. "The man didn't want to let me go, but he did."

"Why did he, do you think?" Jackie asked patiently. "Why did he let you go?"

"Something hurt him," Heather said, holding an Indian princess doll against her chest. "Something made him go 'oof!' and that's when I ran away. That's all I remember."

The black-haired little girl looked up at her mother. "Can I go play now? I'll stay in the backyard, just like you said."

"That's a brave little girl you've got there," Jackie told Mrs. Carter as Heather ran into the kitchen and out the screen door. It slammed behind her.

"Thank you," said the slightly obese woman in jeans and a powder blue Silver Dollar City sweatshirt. "Mike and I have always warned her about strangers. But, still, you never expect something like that to happen around here. Catch him, please, before he takes someone else's little girl."

"We'll try our best," Jackie said, putting on her wide-brimmed hat.

Already she was trying to figure out how Heather had escaped. Some important part of the story was missing. She was grateful that she could keep occupied by puzzling over it. If her mind was given a moment's rest now that she had remembered the nightmare at Fort Gordon, she could be paralyzed with grief.

At the playground near the Civic Center, none of the children she talked to had been there at the time of the attempted abduction, and she could discover no clues. On her way back to her car, however, Jackie did find a basketball in a ditch and took it with her. She would drop it off later at the Civic Center. A radio call to check out vandalism along the interstate delayed that side trip, and she was off to count fallen billboards.

As she drove, thoughts of those horrible days and nights four years ago came back to her, and Jackie fought back tears. "Get a grip, girl!" she said through clenched teeth. She wiped her eyes with the back of her left hand.

The sight of collapsed billboards, fortunately, did much to cheer her up. Pulling off on the shoulder before the first casualty, she dried her eyes with a tissue, blew her nose, and smiled. The Golden Arches had fallen. She had long considered billboards an insult to the beauty of rural areas like Parkland, and someone else obviously agreed.

"If we're real lucky, maybe he will start a trend," Jackie said and then looked around guiltily.

She shouldn't have said that. Then she laughed as she saw that the only witnesses—cows—were far more interested in munching grass than what she had to say.

CHAPTER SEVEN

P.J. ran as fast as she had ever run in her life. Had she slowed in the tangled underbrush to be more careful about how and where she ran, she probably would have fallen a dozen times. But she was like a deer pursued by hounds. Speed was her only concern. Her sneakers barely touched the ground as she flew up and down one hill after another.

At the top of the third hill, she could run no farther. Heart pounding in her ears, she leaned on her knees and sucked in deep breaths of air cooled by the shade that covered her. She had scraped an elbow somewhere along the way, but she didn't even notice. As her breathing slowed, her mind sped up, and her fears mounted.

Was the man still chasing her? How close was he? How would she ever find her way back to Mama Ma's or even the road? P.J. never would forget the sour smell of the man's breath in her face, the dirty thumbnail pressing into her cheek, and the feel of that cold, sharp blade against her throat.

P.J.'s brown eyes twinkled and she managed a small smile. Likely, the man with the crewcut and the scraggly black and white beard would not forget how hard she had kicked him right between his legs. Besides learning about pedophiles at boarding school, she also had learned how to protect herself. It was the first time that the twelve-year-old had used her training, and she was happy that she had paid attention in class. She just wished that she had been better able to defend herself back in town before the man clubbed her unconscious and threw her in the gray van.

But it had all happened so suddenly.

Left alone in the van, P.J. had awakened just as the man went back to close the gate on a large chain-linked fence. She jumped from the passenger side as he snapped the lock.

Kendall heard the door open.

"Oh, no, you don't!" he yelled as he ran around the back of the van.

He thought that P.J. would be running as well. She wasn't. She was waiting. She drove the toe of her left sneaker deep between the kidnapper's legs, and he crumbled to the ground. That had given her a much-needed head start.

The girl rubbed her tender right cheek now as she regained her breath on the shady hilltop.

"Got to keep going. Got to find help," she said as she trotted down the hill.

With her wits more about her now, P.J. noticed that the woods seemed vaguely familiar.

But I've never been here before, she told herself.

Still, this place made her feel more at ease, and she ran on, listening as best she could for her pursuer. She looked up and saw that what she once thought was shade was really clouds. Her white Cardinals' tee shirt was wet with sweat. A cool breeze made her shiver.

I have been here before, she told herself, just before she heard a crashing behind her and realized that the man was still coming.

Reaching a stream at the bottom of the hill, she paused and looked both ways.

"Upstream," she said. "That's where I should go." And she ran on.

"I'm coming for you!" a poisonous voice called from up the hill. "You're going to be sorry you were ever born!"

P.J. rounded a bend and crossed a fallen tree.

Just like in the dream, she suddenly realized. *Oh, my God, I don't want to go there.*

But it was too late. She couldn't go back. If she tried to cross the creek, it probably would slow her down just enough for the man to catch her.

Now she saw vultures and crows in the trees along the stream. They looked at her with lifeless eyes. She prayed that this was just the most vivid nightmare that she had ever had and not real life. But unlike the dream, the birds lifted as she neared them. The crows scolded her.

P.J. gasped for breath now and slowed down. She was nearly as fearful of what lay ahead of her as what was following. Would bony fingers claw at her feet? Would they pull her down into piles of skeletons that rattled and clattered as they grabbed her arms, legs, and neck?

Sure enough, the wooded shore gave way to steep rock walls in shades of gray. The stream widened in a valley as it turned to the left. Still, she kept running. She had no other choice. Wading through a field of clutching skeletons was better than being caught by the man in black.

Behind her, P.J. heard the man fall and curse. She turned her head slightly and saw her pursuer get up and come charging on.

When P.J. looked forward again, she saw the gleaming mass of white, just like in the dream. She closed her eyes tightly and ran on. She steeled herself for that first icy touch.

When I open my eyes again, I'll be back in bed at Mama Ma's, she told herself.

But she knew that wasn't true. This nightmare was real.

The mass of white, however, was not what she feared it would be. Instead, it was her Uncle John's El Dorado parked near a cabin. She was saved!

"Uncle John, Uncle John, there's a man chasing me," P.J. panted as she stumbled into the clearing and fell into her uncle's arms.

The girl then turned in time to see Crater Kendall stagger out of the woods. As she squeezed around behind her uncle, she wondered at the smile that split the man's red face below his crooked nose. She hoped that her uncle, a retired Army officer, could save them both from the madman.

John Stallings pushed P.J. farther behind him and pulled off his dark glasses. At just over six feet tall, his trim but muscular body gave him a commanding presence. Prematurely white hair, a stylish blue suit, and a small scar on his right cheek added to the image. Mam Ma had told P.J. that the scar was the result of a war injury.

"What the Hell do you think you are doing?" he said to the man in the black shirt.

"Just had the itch and needed to scratch it," Kendall said as he gasped to regain his breath.

He bent at the waist, hands on his hips.

"This kid got in my way.

"Let me have her, and I'll make her disappear. No one will ever know what happened."

His smile was pure evil.

"Uncle John?" P.J. said, her heart now beating faster than it had been when she was running full speed.

What was going on here? Her uncle knew this awful man?

"This 'kid' happens to be my niece," Stallings said.

The smirk disappeared from Kendall's face. "Hey, sorry, Colonel. But, like I said, she got in the way. I wanted a little girl."

P.J. let go of her uncle. She looked from one man to the other. This was crazy. How could her uncle, *her* uncle, be friends with a pedophile?

"Uncle John? Do you know this guy?"

Stallings ignored her.

"Now we have another complication because of you, you crazy bastard," he said to the man who had been chasing P.J. "First you shoot a bear, and now this. I never should have brought you into this."

Kendall smiled again.

"You couldn't do it without me," he said. "Your life is too white-bread these days, and you know it, Mr. High and Mighty Newspaper Publisher. Besides, what's a couple of more bodies out here in the middle of nowhere."

P.J. thought about running again. But where would she go? Who could she tell?

Finally breathing easier, her pursuer took his hands from his hips and stood up straight. He pointed a finger at the girl.

"Look, just give me the kid, and I'll make sure no one finds her when I'm through."

For the first time, P.J. felt her eyes grow wet. But she refused to cry. She wouldn't give that creep the satisfaction.

"Please, Uncle John, don't let him hurt me," she said.

She stepped slightly behind her uncle to hide her trembling from the maniac.

The Colonel spoke to her for the first time but didn't look her in the eyes. "He's not going to hurt you.

"Crater, get in my car. We've got business to do."

Stallings then looked up toward the cabin. "Wilson, get out here."

When P.J. saw the man standing in the doorway, she felt a huge surge of relief. He wore a uniform and a badge. It was the sheriff! Sheriff Grizzly Wilson. She remembered how she had laughed when she first heard his name—until she saw the coarse black hair that covered his arms and bushed out of his shirt collar. "Grizzly" was accurate.

With her uncle and the sheriff here, everything was going to be all right. Later at home, Uncle John would explain everything to her, and she would understand. Not a great way to start the summer. But she had saved a little girl, and now she would be protected from that awful man.

The short, thin man flipped down his dark glasses as he walked down the steps. He carried a coil of rope in his left hand.

As she watched him approach, P.J. also saw the dead bear. The sight brought back memory of yet another dream. Only that bear had not died. She felt sadness as she stared at the lifeless animal that lay among beer cans near the creek.

The Colonel paced impatiently along the shoreline for a moment. Then, he stopped and rubbed the back of his head with his right hand.

"All right," he said, looking at the sheriff. "Make sure that the kid's body is never found."

Stunned by those awful words, P.J. couldn't move. It was as if her feet were frozen. And her heart was broken.

Stallings looked down at his niece, at the girl that he had planned to take fishing. But he looked at her forehead, not into her eyes. "I'm sorry. You just happen to be in the wrong place at the wrong time. I won't let Kendall have you, but I can't let you live."

And then the Colonel was giving orders again.

"Get rid of the bear, too. Get a couple of the other guys to help you," he told the sheriff.

"We can't risk having any good Samaritans notice a dead bear next to the cabin. The fence is supposed to keep people out, but we can't take the chance. Someone might follow the creek in here."

Before P.J. could speak, her uncle had pushed her to Wilson, who knocked her to the gravel and quickly tied her hands behind her back.

Shocked by the betrayal, P.J. watched from the ground as her uncle dusted the arms of his jacket. Then he stepped into the El Dorado, put his dark glasses back on, and drove away.

CHAPTER EIGHT

Looking up from her notes about the billboard vandalism, Jackie saw a silver sports utility vehicle with Pennsylvania plates whiz by. It traveled well in excess of the sixty miles-per-hour speed limit.

"A deputy's work is never done," she said as she closed her notebook and headed for her patrol car. "Looks like my first ticket of the day.

Ryan Conners was supposed to be getting bed rest back home in Pennsylvania, but he had decided that he was not going to wait a moment longer than he must to make things right with P.J. Putting his aching and still-injured body into the Blazer, he had driven non-stop to Parkland. It was now just one exit away. In ten minutes, he would be hugging his daughter.

But suddenly, with his good right eye, he saw the flashing light in his rearview mirror.

"Damn!" he said and pulled off onto the shoulder.

The idea of being delayed irritated him more than the thought of having to pay a fine.

He rolled down the window and watched as the driver of the white police car removed her dark glasses and looked in.

"Going a bit fast, weren't you?" the attractive redhead asked. Her throaty voice so distracted Ryan that he missed the words she spoke.

"I beg your pardon?" Ryan said, flustered that a woman's voice could make him so nervous.

And, as she peered in, he realized that he never had seen such an attractive face beneath a cowboy hat. He realized that he had been alone far too long. He studied the vision.

"I said you were speeding," Jackie said, carefully watching this strange man with a patch over his left eye and deep scratches across his forehead and right cheek.

Was he the winner or the loser? she wondered.

Ryan noted the freckles across her small, straight nose. He saw her green eyes and the mole on her lower left cheek. But, again, the words did not penetrate.

"Huh?" he said.

The subtle movement of her right hand to her sidearm got his attention, and he swallowed hard.

"I'm sorry," he said. "I've been driving all night, and I guess that I was a bit road weary. Was I speeding?"

The deputy took her hand away from the pistol and smiled. "Yeah, you were. Driver's license and registration, please."

Ryan handed her the license and paper.

"I'll be right back," she said and turned on her heel.

As Jackie walked back to her car, Ryan guessed her height at five feet eight inches and her weight at one hundred and thirty pounds.

As he sat and waited, Ryan thought about his surprising response to this female. Yes, he always had enjoyed looking at women, and he had dated several since Carrie's death. But rarely had he felt such a powerful attraction to a member of the opposite sex. Perhaps he was just more open to the possibility of a relationship now that he and P.J. would be together again. They would be a family.

Or maybe he felt this way because of the second chance at life that he had been granted. Not many survived a close encounter with a leopard.

Ryan rubbed the right side of his face and yawned. Perhaps he was just delirious from lack of sleep, and anyone with XX chromosomes would seem attractive to him.

"Especially a woman in uniform," he chuckled.

"You find my appearance humorous?" the deputy asked, peering once more in the window.

She had removed her hat while sitting in the patrol car and neglected to put it back on. Her hair, pulled back into a tight ponytail, seemed ablaze in the late-morning sun.

Ryan's one good eye grew wide, and Jackie noticed how bloodshot it was.

This guy is in need of some serious rest, she thought.

She fought back the urge to smile, realizing that she found herself attracted to this dark-haired man whom she could so easily fluster.

"Uh, no, I just…" he began.

"Look, you don't have a record, and I can see that you're practically dead on your feet," Jackie said. "I should give you a ticket, but I won't—on one condition. You get off at the Parkland exit, find a motel, and get some rest. Okay?"

Ryan smiled. The eye patch gave it a crooked quality, and Jackie was even more charmed. She smiled back. An awkward silence followed, and she looked away. He could see the flush of embarrassment fill in among the freckles.

God, she's beautiful, he thought. *And that's not delirium or fatigue talking.*

"That's where I'm going, anyway," he said, his voice sounding strangely distant in his own head and making him afraid that this was a dream from which he was about to awaken.

"My daughter is staying here for the summer with her grandmother, Mary Jennings. Maybe you know her?"

Jackie looked back, her composure restored.

"No, I don't," she said. "But I haven't been here long. You just drive carefully, okay?"

She extended the license and registration to him.

He took them slowly, intentionally grazing her fingers with his. He savored the tingle that contact produced. He wasn't dreaming.

"I will," he said. "And maybe I'll see you around?"

The deputy grinned and, this time, did not look away.

"Maybe," she said. "But it had better not be because I stopped you again for speeding."

"I promise," Ryan said, thinking that life hadn't been so good in a long, long time.

CHAPTER NINE

Grizzly Wilson tossed the bloody tee shirt onto the little metal desk inside the main room of the cabin. The Colonel sat in a folding chair behind it, scribbling something in a small notebook. Crater Kendall leaned back in a similar chair, cleaning his fingernails with his hunting knife. Wooden crates lined two walls. A television set sat against another, with an assortment of chairs around it.

"I did it," Wilson said as he crossed his arms and wrinkled his one long, furry eyebrow. "I did it, but I sure ain't happy about it. When we started this, you never said nothing about killing no kids."

"Let's see your sidearm," Kendall said.

He stabbed the knife in a crate and sat upright.

"Hell, no," Wilson said, backing up and nearly tripping over the muddy boots on his big feet.

Those flat, black eyes boring into him were evil, pure and simple, he thought. He wanted nothing more than to turn and run out the cabin door to his car. He would drive to Arkansas, beg his ex-wife for forgiveness, and never, ever get involved with any more people like Stallings and Kendall.

When the Stallings had helped him get elected a year ago, Wilson had sworn his loyalty. He had been eager to be one of the first to join the Colonel's secret military group. Stallings said it was needed to protect America and Americans from the many problems caused by illegal immigration. Breaking the law might be necessary, he had explained, for the greater good.

They had broken the law too. Many times, in fact. They were doing what needed to be done, however, and they were being well paid for it.

But the Colonel had never said anything about killing an innocent little girl. No amount of money could justify that.

"Hell, no," he said again, putting his right hand on the butt of the police revolver.

The Colonel put down his pen and stood up. His erect stature and strong personality always made him appear larger than six feet, especially for Wilson, who was four inches shorter. Here in the tiny cabin, Stallings seemed an absolute giant. He smiled and put out his hand.

"Crater just wants to make sure that you fired it," he told Wilson. "He wants to make sure you killed the kid."

The sheriff took off his Stetson and wiped his forehead on the sleeve of his sweat-stained shirt.

"Maybe I used a rock or something," he said. "Maybe I didn't shoot her."

"Maybe you didn't kill her at all," Kendall said, displaying a thin smile under his crooked nose. "Maybe you let her go."

"I told you that I did it," Wilson said.

He pulled the pistol out of its holster and handed it to the Colonel. "I just don't want to give my gun to no crazy man."

Stallings cracked the pistol, checked the cylinder, and smelled the barrel.

Kendall smiled.

"Being crazy has its advantages," he said. "You aren't troubled by things like conscience, things that can get in the way of the mission."

Grizzly Wilson made himself look the man in the eye.

"And shooting bears with an M-16 and kidnapping kids are okay?" he challenged. "You're the one who is putting us in danger here, not me."

Kendall pulled the knife from the crate and ran his thumb along its blade.

"Nothing gets in the way of the mission," he said idly. "I just like to have a little fun along the way."

The Colonel handed the revolver back to Wilson.

"It's been fired, Crater," he said. "Satisfied?"

Wilson grabbed the shirt and stormed out the cabin door before Kendall could respond.

"For right now," he finally said.

The two listened as Wilson started his cruiser and zoomed up the gravel road, spinning tires as he went.

"But, I'm telling you, he's a weak link."

"I'm beginning to think that of you," Stallings said as he paced the open area in the middle of the cabin. "Why didn't I ever know about your sexual appetite for children?"

Kendall shaved the hair of his left arm with his knife.

"Just something that happened when I became a mercenary after I got out of the Army," he said.

He admired the now more visible red tattoo.

"Couldn't find a woman sometimes," he said. "Always could get kids in those third-world countries. Sometimes I bought them. Sometimes I just took them. They can't hurt you like a woman can, and their bodies are easier to bury."

Kendall looked at the Colonel and smiled wickedly. "Lots of room to bury kids' bodies out here, don't you think?"

Stallings leaned against the cabin door, his back to the man in the black shirt.

"This isn't the first time you've tried this here, is it?" he said.

"What if it isn't," Kendall replied. "Like I said, there's lots of room out here to bury the evidence. You should know. You picked this place."

The Colonel turned around. His face revealed no emotion.

"I never should have gotten you off on that attempted rape charge down at Fort Gordon," he said. "You said it would never happen again."

Kendall grinned and slipped his knife into its sheath.

"And it didn't," he said. "Not one more woman ever accused me of trying to rape her."

The Colonel shook his head.

"So you were the one," he said. "I always thought…"

"But you didn't want to ask," Kendall smiled.

"And I won't ask now," Stallings said. He walked back to the desk, where he stood over his former master sergeant.

"What I'm concerned about now is continuing this operation. We've got a good thing going here. We're all going to be rich. Can I depend on you?"

Kendall leaned back again in the folding chair.

"You know you can, as long as I get my share," he said. "And whatever fires I start, I put out. But, you got to remember, I'm used to action. A little target practice once or twice a week just ain't enough for me, no matter how well it pays."

Stallings sat back down behind the desk. He rubbed his chin.

"The Fourth of July is coming up. Our nation's birthday. I've been thinking of doing something big to celebrate. And I can see now that I need to give you more to do," Stallings said.

He slapped one of the two boxes that they had just brought into the cabin.

"You remember how to use one of these?"

Kendall smiled.

"Oh, yeah," he said and mentally pictured the death and destruction that he could cause with such a weapon. "Oh, yeah."

CHAPTER TEN

The state was Missouri instead of Minnesota, and the season was summer instead of winter, but Ryan Conners still felt the same deep loss that he experienced nine years ago. Despite a brush with death, he had been happy for more than a week, thinking about becoming a real father again to P.J. Then, so close to seeing his daughter, he had met Jackie, who made him even gladder to be alive. He had been thinking how wonderful it would be to go on a picnic with the two of them when he fell asleep just three short hours ago.

Now it was all snatched away for a second time.

Damn it! he thought as he sat on the merry-go-round and looked through a teary eye at the playground near the Civic Center. *I was right to be living my life the way it was. I never should have opened myself up to this.*

Then he realized how self-centered he was being, just as he had been since Carrie died.

P.J. needs me right now, he told himself. *P.J. is the one that I have to worry about, not my own selfish feelings.*

Ryan pulled back a sob and wiped his nose with the back of his hand. His throbbing head made it nearly impossible for him to think. *But what am I going to do?* he wondered. *And where do I start? I'm alone and exhausted and…*

Jackie sat down beside him and put her arm around his shoulders. Ryan resisted the urge to shrug her away. He barely knew the woman, and she was seeing him at his weakest.

"Are you okay?" she asked.

"Yeah, sure," Ryan said finally as he stood up. "A lot of it is lack of sleep, you know? Lack of sleep makes you much more emotional."

"I'd be pretty emotional too if my daughter were missing," Jackie said.

She saw the agony on Ryan's face. The combination of the wounds, the patch, and the pain was nearly more than she could stand. She wanted to take him in her arms, but she resisted. She barely knew the man.

"But you're right," she said, picking up the basketball from the merry-go-round and standing beside him. "You only got two hours sleep. You almost didn't get that either. Mary was in such bad shape after she saw the shirt that I decided to take her over to her daughter's house before I woke you up.

"John was there too, thank God. He's good in a crisis."

* * * * *

After stopping Ryan for speeding, Jackie had headed back toward the Civic Center to return the basketball that she had found near the playground. But as she picked up the ball from the backseat, she saw the name "P.J. Conners" written on it in black marker. The "o" had a smiley face inside it.

Ryan had said that he was coming to visit his daughter, Jackie thought eagerly. This was her excuse to see him again.

But she knew that he needed sleep, so she decided to wait until after she was off work at 5 p.m. to take it by. A call came in from the Civic Center as she sat in the office, shoes off, writing reports about the toppled billboards and attempted abduction. Someone had found a backpack on the basketball court. It had P.J.'s name on it.

Ryan's daughter lost *both* her basketball and her backpack? Sure, it was possible. But could anyone, even a child, really be that absent-minded? Suddenly a chill ran down her spine as Jackie remembered what little Heather had said:

"Something hurt him. Something made him go 'oof!'"

Could P.J. have made him 'go oof!' by hitting him, maybe even with her basketball? Could he have taken her instead? That creep could be brutalizing Ryan's daughter right now.

As the deputy struggled to stay calm and decide what to do, Sheriff Wilson came in. He brought a bloody tee shirt. It was a child's or young teen's size. He said that he didn't know who it belonged to, but Jackie knew. She had no evidence, but she knew. Suddenly her whole world spun out of control. What seemed a bright future just an hour ago suddenly turned bleak.

Now Jackie had no doubt. P.J. Conners had stopped a man from kidnapping Heather Carter. He had taken her instead. Probably he had killed her. Such men leave no survivors, no witnesses.

Only bloody shirts. And lifetime scars on the loved ones of the victims.

*　*　*　*　*

Ryan took the ball from Jackie and looked again at the name on it. The smiley face in the "o" nearly made him break down. He swallowed hard to hold back the sobs.

"P.J. stopped him and got killed for her trouble."

Jackie took his arm.

"We don't know that she's dead," she said.

"Mary said that was her shirt, and it was plenty bloody," Ryan said. "What else am I supposed to think?"

Jackie walked him back toward her car.

"Mary might be wrong," she said. "She was hysterical.

"Before I told her anything at all, she started blaming wolves. Said her family was cursed and told me that wolves had caused her daughter's death, her husband's, and now they had come for her granddaughter. She said that P.J. had just been asking her about wolves.

"She felt real guilty because she didn't warn her, didn't tell her that there were wolves around here."

Ryan stopped suddenly and let the ball fall. It bounced once, twice, three times. As it rolled away, he grabbed Jackie by both arms.

"Wolves? You said 'wolves'? There are wolves around here?"

"Calm down," Jackie said, pulling free. "Of course not. If there ever were wolves around here, I'm sure they're not here now. They would have all been killed or driven out long ago. Even if there were, I don't think for a moment that they killed P.J. or whoever else might have been wearing that shirt."

Ryan was very nervous now, pacing back and forth, and Jackie feared that he was losing control.

"Please, calm down," she said.

He stopped then, saw the worried look on her face, and smiled. "I'm sorry," he said. "And how do you know wolves wouldn't do something like that? Most people believe they would."

"I'm not most people," Jackie said.

She stood silently for a moment, mouth slightly open.

This man is losing it, she thought. *First, he was beside himself with pain for the loss of his daughter, and now he wants me to talk about wolves?*

Ryan gently closed her mouth with his left hand.

"Please," he said. "It's important. Did she say anything else about wolves? Did she say that she or P.J. had dreams about them?"

Jackie sat down on the end of a sliding board, cautiously studying the exhausted father before her. She raised her eyebrows and cocked her head. His daughter had been kidnapped, and this lunatic pirate wanted to know about wolves.

"That's all she told me," Jackie said softly, now nearly as worried about the man in front of her as the missing child.

Her green eyes then locked on Ryan's one good, although bloodshot, eye as she stood up. He looked away, almost guiltily.

The man seemed totally disconnected from what was causing him such pain only a few minutes earlier.

His brains are mush, she thought. *He needs eight or ten solid hours. At least.*

"Look," she said. "You should get some rest. Let me take you over to the Medical Center, and we'll get a doctor to prescribe something to help you sleep."

"Yeah, sure," Ryan said as he wandered back toward the cruiser. Jackie went after the ball.

If Jackie hadn't reminded him of wolves, Ryan never would have agreed to get more sleep right now. He would have searched relentlessly for P.J., just as he did years before. But the wolves changed things.

Ryan smiled at the symmetry of life.

I wonder how much of this is reality and how much is caused by lack of sleep and stress overload? How can I feel so confident about this? Am I going crazy? he thought as he reached for the door handle and collapsed in the street.

*   *   *   *   *

Ryan Conners crushed his daughter to his chest.

"I'm so sorry that I've been such a lousy father to you," he said. "I'll make it up to you. I promise."

He rested his cheek on the top of his daughter's head and felt the thick, wavy hair tickle his face. He squeezed and squeezed. He hadn't been this happy since Carrie was alive. Never, ever, would he leave P.J. again. They were a family now.

Grasping his daughter gently by the arms, then, he stepped back and bent down, so that he would be eye to eye with her. But before their eyes could meet, Ryan's attention was drawn to the red stain on P.J.'s tee shirt.

Ketchup, he thought. *The kid eats too many French fries.*

But, no, this stain was much too thick and large to be from ketchup. And it smelled of copper, a scent that Ryan had encountered once before, near the body of a man mauled by a lion.

Blood! P.J.'s shirt was drenched in blood! Ryan's heart thudded like a hammer in his chest, but he couldn't move, couldn't release his hands from his daughter's arms. Slowly he began to raise his head, lifting his line of sight an inch at a time. He didn't want to do it, but he was powerless to resist.

His scrolling eyes followed the crimson stain that stretched solidly from P.J.'s mid-section to the collar of her shirt and beyond.

P.J.'s throat was red, too, and the texture of ground meat. Her chin dripped scarlet.

No! Ryan thought. *I don't want to see any more! No!*

But his eyes keep moving up his daughter's face. Up and up, until…

"No!" Ryan screamed. "No! No! No!"

* * * * *

"Shhh. Shhh. It's okay. You were having a nightmare," Ryan heard a familiar voice say as a cool washcloth moved across his brow.

Slowly he opened his good right eye and looked into what had to be the face of an angel. She smiled at him.

"Who are you? Where am I?" Ryan asked. "Where's P.J.?"

Then Ryan recognized the eyes, the freckles, the ears that stuck out just enough to be attractive. And the mole on the left cheek. She was so beautiful, with her red hair hanging loosely to the shoulders of an emerald green sweater that matched her eyes.

He smiled back weakly.

"Come to arrest me, deputy? Was I speeding again?"

"Hardly," Jackie said. "You've been asleep for more than twelve hours. I brought you here to the hospital after you collapsed at the Civic Center."

Ryan suddenly remembered the real nightmare: P.J. was missing, possibly even dead.

"Have you found my daughter?" he asked.

Jackie shook her head sadly. "No, I'm afraid we haven't, and nothing to report so far. But I filed a missing person report with the Highway Patrol and personally called every police and sheriff's department in six counties. Sheriff Wilson has the rest of the deputies and a big bunch of volunteers out searching in the area where he found the shirt.

"Also, John Stallings is offering a $10,000 reward for information. He's P.J.'s uncle, I understand."

The deputy yawned and stretched in the straight-back chair, pushing her arms down the legs of her jeans.

"What about you?" Ryan asked. "Have you gotten any sleep? What time is it anyway?"

Jackie took his left hand in both of hers.

"It's a little after six in the morning," she said. "And, yes, I got some sleep at home. Just thought that I should be here when you woke up."

"That was kind of you," he said, putting his right hand on top of hers and gazing into her eyes. She looked away shyly.

"Good morning. Good morning," a heavyset nurse with dark blonde hair said as she bustled into the room carrying a breakfast tray.

Embarrassed, Jackie pulled her hands back, stood up, and backed out of the way.

"How's our patient this morning?" the nurse asked.

Not waiting for an answer, she continued, "The doctor will be in soon, and if everything checks out, you should be able to leave right after that."

The nurse left as quickly as she entered, and Ryan smiled.

"I appreciate you looking in on me," he said.

Jackie sat back down again.

"May I ask you some things?" she said, declining his offer of orange juice and coffee.

"Fire away," Ryan said, setting the tray on a side table.

"First of all, what happened to your face?"

Ryan ran his hand lightly across the scratches on his forehead. "I got a little too close to a leopard," he said. "I'm a wildlife photographer. Doctors say that my left eye probably will be as good as new in another week. Probably don't need this patch anymore, but I suspect that it's still pretty ugly underneath it. Anything else?"

Jackie nodded.

"Why did you get so excited yesterday afternoon when I mentioned wolves? Do they have something to do with P.J.?"

Ryan folded his arms across the hospital gown that covered his chest. He looked away from Jackie and out the hospital window. Finally, he spoke.

"That's not an easy question to answer," he said. "And I barely know you, so that makes it even more difficult."

Jackie reached out and gently moved Ryan's face back toward her.

"Extraordinary times call for extraordinary actions," she said. "I want to help. But, for me to do as much as I can, you've got to trust me. Tell me everything."

Ryan continued to look out the window. "I'll tell you what I can right now and more later. It's too hard to do all at once. Okay?"

Jackie nodded and he saw her agreement as a reflection in the window.

"P.J.'s mother and grandfather had a special relationship with wolves," Ryan explained. "When Carrie died nine years ago in a car wreck, P.J. somehow survived three days in below-zero temperatures.

"No one could explain it, but I knew what happened. Wolves took care of her. They kept her warm and alive until I found her.

"Then, when you told me what Mary said about wolves, it suddenly made sense why P.J. wanted to come here for the summer. "The wolves were calling her. I haven't been a very good father since Carrie died, I'm afraid, and she needed a family. The wolves won't let her down the way that I have.

"If there are wolves here, then P.J. is okay. They will see to it."

Ryan kept his head turned so that Jackie could not see the tears in his good eye. But his reflection in the window betrayed him. She moved silently to the edge of the bed and put her arm around his shoulders.

He stiffened and tried to pull away, but she held on.

"No!" she said. "This is not just about you needing someone to help find your daughter."

Ryan looked questioningly at her. "It's not?"

"No, it's not," Jackie said and pressed her lips to his.

CHAPTER ELEVEN

Grizzly Wilson spent as much time looking at the rearview mirror as he did the highway in front of him. Even with the air conditioner turning the cab into a deep freeze, he felt nervous perspiration running down his sides. His bloodshot brown eyes seemed to show the same fear he used to see in the eyes of the deer that he and his brother Ernest spotlighted.

He just hoped that he didn't end up the same way those deer did—dead by the side of the road, a gunshot wound to the heart or lungs.

He was running out on Stallings, and he was scared to death that the Colonel would send that crazy bastard Crater Kendall after him.

Besides making him stink, fear also made Wilson have to piss. His teeth clenched in pain, he pulled off at the first opportunity, a rest stop on the interstate about 75 miles south of Parkland. With dawn just beginning to break, the area was deserted except for a couple of tractor-trailer trucks, their drivers probably still sleeping inside.

Stepping down from the pickup, the sheriff glanced in back to make certain the tarp covering his few possessions still was tied down. Then he headed on up to the bathroom. Once more, he thought about yesterday.

* * * * *

As soon as Wilson led P.J. away from the cabin, he had taken her shirt and given her another.

He didn't want to remove clothing from the body of a child. It was bad enough that he was going to have to kill the kid. But he was not going to touch the body afterward with his bare hands. He would just pile rocks on top or push it with his foot into some cave on the side of a hill.

He would do the killing with his pistol, from a distance. Maybe he could put the shirt on a stick and poke it against the body to get some blood. That would be his evidence for the Colonel and that lunatic Kendall.

With the oversized shirt from the trunk of the sheriff's car on her skinny little body and her hands retied, P.J. stumbled forward as if she had been drugged. Walking close behind, Wilson grabbed her shoulder to keep her from falling.

Kid's in shock, the sheriff thought. *Can't say that I blame her. I would be, too, if my uncle had just told someone to kill me.*

As they trudged up a trail into the woods behind the cabin, Wilson stared at the frail little shoulders and the bright pink flesh at the back of P.J.'s ears.

Can't be much older than my daughter, he thought. *What in the Hell am I doing?*

Just then, Wilson heard a twig snap off the right. He grabbed for his gun with his right hand and P.J. with his left. "Hold on!" he whispered.

An icy chill ran down Wilson's spine, and he cursed under his breath. Not trusting him to do the job, the Colonel had sent Kendall to kill both of them. Well, he wasn't going to let that happen. He would have a much easier time putting bullets into Kendall than he would this poor little girl.

P.J. heard the crunch too, and it slowly brought her back to reality. She had been a zombie for a while, she realized. Her mind had shut down. Her uncle's betrayal had been even more terrifying than her pursuit by the man with the black shirt, big knife, and red tattoo.

Her mother was dead. Her father had abandoned her. And now her uncle had ordered her killed. She had no one. She could trust no one. She was alone in the world.

The rope hurt her wrists.

But she was still alive. Once again, she could feel her heart beat. And she didn't want to die.

For a reason she couldn't explain, P.J. visualized the dead bear by the creek and then the sheriff — Grizzly Wilson — walking toward her. Something important teased around the edge of her memory, but she couldn't grasp it.

Wilson pushed P.J. behind a fallen cedar and crouched beside her. His eyes searched fearfully for any sign of movement among the oaks and evergreens. Trying to ignore his hammering heart, he rested the pistol against his thigh to keep his hand from shaking — until he saw movement straight ahead.

Taking a deep breath, he leveled the revolver in that direction and waited.

Another twig cracked off to the left, just outside Wilson's vision.

"Stallings is with him!" the sheriff said angrily. He spun in that direction.

Bear. Grizzly. Family. Dream. Incredibly, P.J. felt not just determined to live but hopeful. Her heart slowed as she willed her breathing to resume a normal pace. Still, she couldn't figure out how or why she was gaining strength.

Wilson swallowed repeatedly to keep his pounding heart out of his throat. He continued to scan the forest.

A warm breeze rustled the leaves of early summer. A cardinal twittered, and somewhere in the distance, a hawk cried. But nowhere on the ground could the sheriff find life. Maybe the breaking twigs were nothing. Maybe he had just imagined movement in front of him.

A sigh of relief had barely escaped his lips when Wilson heard a rustling to his right. He turned just in time to see a flash of black.

"Kendall!" he cursed under his breath, remembering the color of the crazy man's shirt.

But Stallings had not been wearing gray, and that was the color that the sheriff saw next. Or did he? It seemed like a wisp of smoke.

Both of Wilson's hands shook now. Fearful that his cowardice would be seen, he glanced at the girl. Mercifully, she lay quietly with her eyes closed. Much more of this, Wilson knew, and he would go over the edge.

He wanted to run. He wanted to empty his gun at his invisible enemies and then go. To Hell with the girl. He didn't want to kill her. But he didn't want to die for her either.

P.J.'s eyes, however, weren't closed completely. She saw the sheriff's fear, and she knew why he was afraid. Her family was coming for her. Just as in her dream, her wolf family would protect her from a bear. In this case, a Grizzly bear.

P.J. smiled, but Wilson didn't notice.

"What do you want?" he yelled out to his tormentors. "I'm going to do what you told me to. I swear!

"And I won't tell anyone!"

Wilson waited. Nothing moved. No one answered. He waited some more, willing his pounding heart to slow down. Only the wind stirred.

Finally, legs shaking, the sheriff rose, pulling up P.J. with him. He breathed a deep sigh of relief. No one was following. Stallings trusted him! He would do what he was ordered to do.

They walked for another mile.

P.J. never spoke, never looked up at her executioner, never attempted to escape. She knew that she didn't need to. When the time was right, her family would chase away the bear.

Wilson fought to keep his confidence. But still, he jumped at the shadows and sounds that he knew were the products of an over-active imagination.

I'm a coward, he thought. *I'm a coward who got greedy, and now I'm going to die for it.*

Without the freedom of her arms to help keep her balanced, P.J. fell on a steep slope. She scraped her knee and tore her shorts on a rock. Yet she didn't moan or cry out. She silently regained her feet and limped on. That was more than Wilson could bear.

"Hold up, kid," he said. "Sit down."

Wilson looked at the wound. It was bleeding but not deep. There didn't seem to be any swelling.

Like it really matters! the sheriff thought. *The kid will be dead soon, anyway.*

He pulled P.J.'s shirt from his back pocket and wiped the blood off her leg.

"Let's go," he said, pulling the girl back to his feet. "We're almost there."

They were heading for a wet-weather creek. Wilson knew the area would have enough rocks to hide the body until vultures, crows, and coyotes had taken care of the evidence.

In five minutes, they stood on a small cliff overlooking the dry streambed. Wilson pulled the pistol and backed away.

"Sorry, kid," he said. "Just following orders."

P.J. stood still, her head down, not bothering to look back. Such meek behavior was difficult for her. She wanted to say something, anything, to stall Wilson. She had a way with words. Her teachers often told her that. And from playing sports, she had self-confidence. She knew that she could be cool in a crisis. She wanted the basketball with the score tied in the final seconds. She wanted to bat with the bases loaded and two outs.

She would just talk and talk until she figured a way to outsmart the sheriff.

But P.J. knew that her family was near and closing fast.

Suddenly, the ghostly sights and sounds that Wilson thought that he had imagined returned. Only this time, they were more forceful. He saw blurs of gray and black rocketing down the hill toward them. He heard brush breaking and feet pounding.

Wilson couldn't tell what was coming at him through the thick woods, but something sure was. Panicked, he fired twice and backed up, pushing P.J. over the edge. The ground crumbled, and the sheriff followed, falling ten feet to the dry creek below. He untangled himself from the girl and ran, never stopping to look back.

Up and down the Ozark hills, the sheriff ran as far and as fast as his tobacco-damaged lungs would allow. Finally, he staggered to within sight of the cabin a hundred yards below. His size twelve feet felt as if they weighed one hundred pounds apiece.

Hands on his hips and gasping for air, he braced himself to confront the Colonel and Kendall again. He pulled the shirt from his back pocket to wipe the sweat from his forehead as he pondered what he would tell them.

He saw the blood on the shirt. He had forgotten he had wiped her injured knee with it. His flushed face broke into a smile that revealed yellow and broken teeth.

"I can still tell them that I killed the kid, and here's the shirt to prove it," he said. "I shot her."

Wilson edged himself sideways down the steep path to better control his trembling legs.

"Maybe the kid really is dead, too," he mumbled as he slid and stumbled. "Maybe the fall killed her."

Deep down, Wilson didn't think so. And he was glad of that. He thought of his daughters, living with his ex-wife down in Arkansas.

No one should hurt kids, he thought.

His conscience had created those sights and sounds at the creek, he decided. It had kept him from doing something that he knew was wrong.

But he would be in a world of hurt, he realized, if Stallings found out that he had failed in his mission. Well, he just wouldn't find out.

Wilson wiped his hands on his pants. He wanted no more of this. He took a deep breath, strode up on the porch, and stepped inside.

Although the palms of his big hands were sweating profusely, Wilson had been able to pull off the bluff. He drove away from the cabin in his cruiser, confident that Stallings did not suspect. But as he drove toward Parkland, doubts began to creep back.

What if Stallings was only pretending to believe him? What if the kid found her way back to Parkland? After putting on some dry clothes, Wilson dropped P.J.'s shirt off at the office and talked to Jackie Novak briefly. She had found the girl's basketball and backpack.

He didn't like the idea, but he organized a search for P.J. and her attacker. He didn't want her found—at least not right away. Her testimony could send them all to jail. He lied about where he found the shirt and sent volunteers and deputies miles away from the cabin.

Wilson then spent the rest of the day in Granny's Tavern, drinking beer and considering what to do next.

He liked the burn-down-the-cabin-with-Kendall-in-it option best. He would truly enjoy that, but it was not very realistic. Also, it would make him guilty of murder, a crime that he was trying his best to avoid committing.

Yes, he had broken the law in working for Stallings. But he hadn't been one of those who pulled a trigger. He was, at worst, an accomplice—a well-paid accomplice—although some bleeding-heart liberals might not see it that way.

He could resign publicly. But if he did that, the Colonel wouldn't let him live. He knew too much.

Leaving town seemed the best thing to do. That would provide even more proof that he was a coward. It also most likely would make him a fugitive.

Wilson looked at himself in the mirror on the other side of the bar. Well… he was a coward, and he could live with that. But, as a coward, he wanted to avoid, at all costs, becoming a hunted man.

He emptied one bottle and called for another. Maybe more beer would help him come up with a way out of this mess.

Garth, the bartender, raised an eyebrow as he watched Wilson chug beer after beer.

"Tough day, huh?" he asked.

"The worst," the sheriff said. "Ever kill anybody?"

The fat bartender stroked his beard and considered the question.

"Only my ex-wife," he said finally. "And only in my dreams.

"You kill somebody today?"

The question stunned Wilson, and he strained to clear his muddled brain. What had he said to make Garth ask such a question?

"Yeah, right," he said. "About a dozen."

When he arrived home around eleven o'clock, he found that he couldn't sleep. He paced the floor until 2 a.m. Then, without even realizing that he was doing so, he started packing. He was jolted back to reality by a sudden fear that he was being watched.

"Still spooked from that walk in the woods," he told himself.

He closed the curtains, popped the tab on the last can of beer in his refrigerator, and kept packing. By three o'clock, he had his clothes and furniture in the back of the pickup.

"So, it's the skip-town-and-hope-for-the-best option," he said as he closed the tailgate. "I guess that I'd better get used to looking over my shoulder."

He tied a tarp over his possessions and went back inside, deciding to wait until daylight to head south. As he sprawled on the stained sofa, wishing that he had one more for the road, fatigue and alcohol combined to knock him out for nearly two hours.

* * * * *

Wilson sighed deeply as he pissed out the last of the beer from the night before.

"Next stop, Arkansas," he said and started to turn around.

"I don't think so," said a voice that he knew all too well. If Wilson could have peed his pants, he would have.

Now he felt an arm go around his neck and the tip of a knife against the skin above his right kidney. The red words on the arm were too close and too blurred for him to read them. But he knew what they said: "Death Before Dishonor."

"You're not going anywhere, Wilson," Crater Kendall said through clenched teeth. "Except maybe to the cemetery."

He released the sheriff and pushed him up against a concrete wall. Wilson's foot slipped on wet tile, and he fell roughly to the floor. As he tried to rise, the Afghanistan veteran kicked him under the chin, and he collapsed into the urinal that he had just used.

Kendall flushed it, soaking Wilson's head and back.

Just as Kendall reached for his neck, the sheriff managed to regain his senses enough to counter-attack. He rammed his head into Kendall's stomach, sending him sprawling. The knife spun away under a stall.

Wilson watched the weapon revolve under the fluorescent light, blade glittering.

This is not happening, he thought as the knife twirled. *This is not real.*

But he knew that it was, and he dived for the weapon. His fingers were only inches from it when Kendall's boot came crashing down on his hand. Wilson shrieked and thrashed about on the floor. In a flash, then, Kendall had the sheriff's arm and damaged hand pinned behind him. He sat down on his back.

"Now, talk to me, Grizzly," the man with the salt and pepper beard said. "You didn't kill that kid, did you?"

"Yes, I did, dammit," Wilson grunted. "You saw the bloody shirt."

Kendall bent a finger back and twisted. Wilson yowled in agony as the pain brought tears to his eyes.

"Then why are you running away?"

Kendall grabbed a handful of hair with his left hand, raised his victim's head, and slammed it on the concrete. Blood splattered the floor, and a drop stained the knife's shiny blade.

"I asked you a question."

Wilson tried to answer, but his words, mixed with blood and broken teeth, were garbled.

"Speak up," Kendall said coolly as he pulled the sheriff's head back again. "I can't understand you."

Wilson spit out teeth and gore. "Just let me go. Please. I won't tell anybody anything. I promise."

Kendall released the sheriff's head and picked up the knife. He pricked Wilson's cheek, and a dark line of red ran down his face.

"Just tell me what I want to know, and it will be all over," Kendall said. "You didn't kill the kid, did you?"

"No, no, I didn't," Wilson sobbed. "Now, please, don't hurt me anymore."

Kendall released Wilson's arm, lifted his head again, and pulled the blade smoothly across the exposed neck.

As life gurgled and poured out of his flopping victim, he rose and walked to the row of sinks. He leisurely rinsed his hands and knife. Stepping carefully around the puddle of blood, he removed the sheriff's wallet from the now lifeless body and dragged it into a stall, where he propped it on a toilet.

Finally, he stopped up the sinks with paper towels and turned the water on full blast. Authorities would learn who the dead man was eventually, but washing away some of the evidence would slow them down.

His flat, black eyes nearly showed signs of life as Kendall smiled at his reflection in the mirror. He was glad the kid wasn't dead. Now he could take care of that loose end personally.

He also was pleased that he would be riding back to Parkland in the front of the truck instead of the bed. Lying under the tarp had made him a little stiff.

CHAPTER TWELVE

Birds awakened P.J. Her arms still across her chest for warmth, she jerked her head up and looked around. Dew-drenched daisies and other flowers she didn't know glistened in the morning sunlight. The blue pullover shirt that the sheriff had given her was wet, as were her shorts and sneakers.

Her bottom was numb. She flexed both cheeks in an attempt to restore life and stretched out her legs in front of her. She pushed against the fallen tree that gave support to her back. The left knee that she had injured the day before ached with the exertion, and P.J. felt dried blood on the wound crack apart. It didn't bother her. She was alive, and she had a family who loved her, who would protect her.

The girl staggered to her feet and looked around in search of the wolves.

She stood in a rocky opening on a mountainside above a wooded valley. She had no idea how she got there or how her hands came to be untied. And she didn't care. She cared only about finally meeting the family of her dreams.

The sun pushed above the rounded mountain across the valley from her, and green woods reflected its rays with blinding brilliance. Twin arches of brown rock towered just behind her. She breathed deeply of the clean, cool air.

"I'm here," she said. "Where are you?

"Wherrrre arrre youuuuu?" she yelled, and her voice echoed through the hills.

No one answered.

In the silence that followed, P.J. realized that her behavior didn't make much sense. Her mother was dead, and her uncle—the same man who was going to take her fishing—wanted her dead also.

As she relieved herself, P.J. felt sadness return.

Maybe I just imagined that the wolves rescued me, she thought. *Maybe it was all just an accident that we fell, and I got away.*

Maybe I should be dead. I drove my father away. I don't have a family. No one cares about me. I don't deserve to live.

After pulling up her shorts, she limped down toward the stream at the bottom of the ancient mountain. She had no idea that she was being shadowed.

Suddenly she stopped, scratched her head, and stared at her shoes. A dream. She had another dream last night. And now it was coming back to her. She closed his eyes.

In the dream, she sat on top of the double arches, head in her hands, crying.

"Granddaughter, do not be afraid. Despite the way it seems, you are not alone. There are many who love you. Many are nearby. One more is coming."

P.J. looked up to see a large black wolf. It couldn't have climbed the rock face in front of her, and it couldn't have squeezed around her from behind. Yet it was there, with strangely colored eyes of much gentleness. The wolf's voice seemed oddly familiar.

"Pap Pa Jennings?" she asked incredulously. "Is that you?"

The wolf smiled, showing long, white teeth. Now its eyes twinkled.

"Be brave, Granddaughter," the wolf said in the dream. "And you will be well. Remember that you are not alone. You do have a family. And you do have a home not far from here."

Resuming her slow, awkward walk down the steep slope, P.J. could not remember what happened afterward, but that was not important. What she could recall made her feel better, and she even managed a half-smile.

Still, she was walking in a real world now, not a dream. As far as she could see in every direction, she was alone. She needed more than wolves talking to her as she slept. Much more.

Suddenly the reality of her loneliness overwhelmed her. She was just kidding herself with all that talk about wolves and family. She had no one. No one! And if her uncle and that man in black didn't find her and kill her, then she probably would starve to death.

"I'm tired of all those stupid dreams!" she screamed. "Do you hear me? I'm tired of it!"

She knelt by the stream to wash her face and drink from cupped hands. Screaming had helped, but only for a moment. She looked around her once again, seeing only desolation.

"Where the heck are you?" P.J. said softly. "I need you."

* * * * *

The big, black wolf glided silently through the cedars just a few yards from P.J. On the other side of the girl, his mate, a white female with gray shoulders, kept pace. They had stayed close to her since yesterday, when they had frightened the bad-smelling man away, and P.J. had run and run until she was exhausted. Unknowingly, she had followed them to this place, where they often basked in the morning sun.

As she slept in the shadow of the arches, the black wolf had gently gnawed away the ropes that bound her wrists. His mate had gently licked wolfchild's eyelashes.

The she-wolf had slept just on the other side of the log from the young human. The male had crouched at the edge of the woods surrounding the glade. They were not in the least surprised or disturbed that, since she had awakened, the girl had been moving closer and closer to their den. She was not of their kind, but she was of their family. They would protect her, just as they would their own pups.

They watched P.J. kneel at the stream, rinse her face, and drink from cupped hands.

"Where the heck are you?" they heard her say. "I need you." They didn't understand the words, but they recognized the pain.

Then they saw water fill her eyes as she sat down on the rocky shore and covered her face with her arms.

The male wolf crouched down on his belly and put his gray muzzle on massive forepaws. The posture told his mate that he would stay. The female, silent as smoke, bounded across the stream and disappeared.

The pack leader perked his round ears and wrinkled his forehead as the sound of human sorrow mixed with the gurgle of the stream. His gold eyes reflected the sadness. He wanted to comfort the young one, but standing guard was a more important priority. Survival for him and his family demanded eternal vigilance.

A rustling across the stream diverted his attention for a second, and his heart lightened. Then he resumed his job as sentinel.

*　*　*　*　*

P.J. did not hear her attackers coming, not even as they splashed through the shallow water. Before she knew what was happening, she was pushed onto her back, her arms shielding his face.

Her eyes clenched tight, she heard growls and felt warm breath on her arms. She smelled raw meat. Something tugged on the hem of her shorts. She screamed.

Suddenly, all was quiet, and she seemed alone again. Cautiously, the girl opened her eyes and dropped her hands to see what had happened. Before she could turn her head, however, she was attacked again.

Two gray blurs darted about her head while a black figure about the same size snarled and pulled at her shirt. Just as she was about to kick at her attackers, one of the young wolves licked P.J.'s face with its big, rough tongue.

"Yuck!" she yelled. "How gross!"

As the girl sat up, her attackers backed away, heads low and tails high. Their eyes were rich with mischief.

"Puppies!" P.J. squealed, and suddenly, with the remarkable strength of youth, she was a normal twelve-year-old again. She pushed herself up and scrambled toward the black one with the floppy left ear. It avoided her grasp and ran two quick circles around her.

P.J. clapped her hands and laughed.

"Oh, you're so cute," she said.

A few feet away, the gray duo watched with bright eyes and cocked heads. When their black brother finally stopped and engaged the young human in a staring contest, they attacked from the rear, bowling the girl over.

P.J. sat up giggling. She had found her family, or at least the kids portion of it.

One of the young gray wolves crawled up next to P.J. and rolled on its back. She rubbed its belly.

"Where are your parents, huh?" P.J. said as she scratched the round stomach, prompting the pup to squirm with delight.

The black and remaining gray stepped closer, tongues lolling and tails wagging. The girl reached to stroke the head of the black, but it backed away.

"Hey, come here. I won't hurt you," P.J. said, extending her free hand, palm up.

She continued to stroke the belly of the smallest gray.

The black pup edged closer and smelled her fingers.

"See?" P.J. said softly. "I won't hurt you."

As she lightly touched the head of the black pup, the female gray regained her feet and rejoined her brothers.

All three allowed P.J. to pet their shoulders as their bottoms wiggled wildly. They licked her hand, and the sand-paper texture of their tongues made the girl laugh.

"So, you can't be alone out here like me," she said. "Where are your Mom and Dad?"

Suddenly, her attention was drawn away from the pups by a slight movement. She turned to see a large black wolf, the wolf of her dreams, staring at her. She should be afraid, she knew. A ferocious wild animal stood just a few feet away.

But those eyes — one light amber and one dark gold — told her not to be afraid.

"This is my family," the girl said softly as she once again remembered her dreams.

They made more sense now, as did her grandmother's reaction, when she had asked her about wolves.

As she rubbed the belly of the black pup, P.J. recalled that she had been awakened by her own voice from that dream about the bear. For a moment, she had been confused and afraid. The dream had seemed so real.

And, in a way, it was. The wolves had, indeed, saved her from a bear. Only the bear in real life was a man named "Grizzly."

"Hey, cut it out!"

Another slurpy lick from the tongue of the black pup brought P.J. back from memories of her dreams and that conversation with her grandmother. Laughing at the pups, she forgot her feelings of isolation and rejection. She ignored the realization that the dreams were more than just wild fantasies. She wiped the wolf's kiss from her face and grabbed her black tormentor as it tried to scoot away.

"Ooh, think you're so tough, huh?" P.J. said as she flipped the wiggling young wolf onto its back and tickled its stomach.

It gnawed on her hand with mock ferocity and kicked with its already powerful hind legs.

Without warning, the two gray pups piled on from behind, and the four rolled into the stream, laughing and squealing all the way.

A few yards away, the large black wolf lay with its head on its paws, watching contentedly as his children played.

CHAPTER THIRTEEN

The two men in camouflage uniforms and baseball caps carried their rifles across their chests as they trudged up the steep hill. Twigs snapped under the weight of their black boots. Perspiration stained their backs and shoulders, and they struggled for breath in the warm summer air. Twice, the shorter one stopped, raised his M-16 rifle to his shoulder, and scanned the woods left and right.

"Thought I heard somethin'," he said each time, prompting his companion to roll his eyes.

At the top, the taller and heavier of the two set his rifle down butt-first and wiped his brow. The two watched vultures circling off to the west as their hearts slowed and their breathing returned to normal.

"Christ, man, I didn't sign up for guard duty, especially in this heat," said Fred Walker.

He was the oldest and largest of the six men recruited by Stallings and Kendall for the operation. He was also a sheriff's deputy.

In addition to what they were hired to do, the six alternated guard duty. Every four hours, they checked the ten-foot fence that bordered the compound on three sides. Mostly, though, they patrolled the remote open area in back, especially around the old landfill.

Unlike Kendall, they were content to relax in the cabin, drink beer, and watch X-rated videos when they weren't working or walking the woods. A little time off now and then to go to St. Louis was all they needed. They were making more money than they ever dreamed of, and they didn't want to mess things up.

Still, guard duty was a pain.

"Those damn buzzards will be looking our way and lickin' their chops if we don't get inside pretty quick," Walker said.

He pulled his water bottle from his belt. He then put his back to a cedar tree and slid roughly to the ground.

"No way, man. They like that landfill too much," replied Ben Hartrup, his smaller, younger partner. "But I don't like this heat either. I'd much rather be downing some cold ones back at the cabin until the next truck arrives.

Hartrup lit a cigarette and sucked the smoke deep into his lungs. A deep, wracking cough followed.

"Can't complain about the money, though," he said as he regained his voice. "Kendall was right. This is the best-paying job we've had since we left the Army. A couple of years of this, and we'll all be rich men."

Off to the side, the younger guard thought he saw movement, something large but as silent as wind.

Just tears in my eyes from these damn cancer sticks, he decided. *I've got to quit.*

"Come on, Grandpa," Hartrup said, lowering dark glasses over his eyes. "We've got some more walking to do."

As Walker struggled to his feet, they both heard a distinct "crunch" off to the left.

"See, man, I told you somethin' was out there," Hartrup whispered.

He flipped his cigarette away and raised his rifle.

"It's just a squirrel," the older man said, stomping on the still smoldering butt. "Let's go."

"That ain't no squirrel," Hartrup said. "It's too big. And deer ain't out this time of day."

"Maybe a rabbit," Walker said.

Weapon ready, Hartrup stepped toward the noise just as a "snap" sounded behind him.

"There's two of 'em!" he said. "Walker, you fool, cover my back!"

"Okay, there's two rabbits instead of one," the older man blustered.

But despite his calm voice, he realized that his heart was pounding. Something—make that two somethings—of some size was out there in the woods around them.

Walker saw a flash of gray for a second time but said nothing. *Don't want to excite my trigger-happy little buddy*, he told himself.

But he knew that wasn't the truth. He was scared.

"Hey, you guys! It's us!" Walker shouted. "Don't shoot!"

No one answered.

"Come on. It was nothin'. Just animals of some kind," he said to Hartrup.

Walker tried to ignore the fact that fear had turned the sweat on his back to ice.

What's going on here? he asked himself. *I'm a veteran. I've hunted all my life. I grew up not far from here. I've seen everything there is to see in woods like these.*

He slung his rifle on his shoulder and forced himself to move down the hill.

"Come on, Ben," he said. "We're burnin' daylight."

Maybe you haven't seen everything, a small voice said in his head. *And just because you're a hunter doesn't mean you also aren't being hunted.*

"Hell, I'm too old for this," he said. "Ben, are you coming or…"

Walker's words ended abruptly with the explosion of gunfire behind him.

* * * * *

The two gray wolves that had been following Walker and Hartrup bounded lightly down the wooded hill, unhurt by the blind blast. They were frightened more by what they smelled than the noise. This was the same stench that they had encountered weeks before while out hunting. It meant danger not only to them but to their family.

Wind-blown scent had alerted the pack that the woods were ripe with the smell of danger, and the two males had followed it to investigate. They found men carrying sticks that exploded. The men searched for something—perhaps the family!

The wolves watched the men carefully. They instinctively measured their speed and direction to determine the threat to the pack. Gradually, the two realized that the men were going no place in particular. They were hunting prey, the wolves realized, not a place, not their den with the young ones in it.

Like smoke, they vanished into the Ozark Mountains.

CHAPTER FOURTEEN

Ryan Conners walked along the weedy shoulder of the blacktop road, hands in the back pockets of his jeans. He stopped and kicked a beer can.

Deputy Jackie Novak searched for evidence on the other side of the road, but she also kept an eye on Ryan. She knew what it was like to lose someone you loved. Her recent conversation with the little girl had re-opened an old wound.

Jackie's sister had joined the Army and then the military police with her. One night, she hadn't returned from having a late dinner with friends. No word was ever heard from her. No body was ever found. But Jackie knew that her sister had died terribly at the hands of a serial rapist terrorizing Fort Gordon and nearby Augusta.

Grief nearly killed her father, a retired St. Louis policeman. Her own pain had been directed into dedication to law enforcement. She intended to make the world a safer place by putting such animals behind bars.

Fortunately, her old commanding officer at Fort Gordon had been able to help her get a job in civilian law enforcement here in Parkland. She always would be grateful to him for that.

Jackie bent down, pulled off her sunglasses, and examined a small piece of yellow paper. She hoped against hope that it was something important, a clue of some kind. It was a receipt for building supplies.

The deputy really didn't expect to find anything. Sheriff Wilson said that he had examined the scene carefully after finding the shirt by the side of the road. He noticed it when he stopped a speeder.

She stood up and looked over at Ryan, who was staring off into the trees. She would give him as much time as he needed.

Looking for evidence would at least keep him from going stir-crazy.

Jackie recalled how she and her friends had combed the streets of Augusta looking for Jill or any information that would lead to her whereabouts.

She saw again all those people shaking their heads. No, they had not seen the smiling girl in the snapshot. She remembered the stomach-churning smells that they encountered as they probed trash dumpsters. They found nothing. But searching, mercifully, had helped pass the time.

Finally, Ryan turned and crossed the road. Much-needed sleep helped him look a little less haggard. But his one good eye was full of sorrow. Bright red scratches from the leopard publicly displayed the pain that Jackie knew he must feel inside.

"You're sure this is the spot?" he asked, squinting in the sunlight.

It was the third time that he had asked the question, or maybe the fourth.

Jackie nodded and pointed down the road to a mailbox marked "Prather."

"Sheriff Wilson said that he stopped just a few yards in front of that mailbox," she said.

"And he didn't find any blood stains?"

"Just what was on the shirt," Jackie said.

"Then P.J. might not have been injured here."

Jackie didn't answer. Instead, she seemed to be studying her reflection in the gloss of her low-cut black boots.

"What?" Ryan demanded, grabbing Jackie's arm. "What are you not telling me?"

Sunglasses still in her hand, she looked Ryan in the eye. "I'm not keeping anything from you. I agree with you that P.J. might not have been injured here. She probably wasn't. But..."

"But what?" Ryan said as he turned on his heel and walked to the middle of the road.

"But what?" he demanded, spreading his arms just as a loud blast sounded from his right.

Jackie's scream was drowned out by the roar of a tractor-trailer truck barreling down the hill. Ryan dove toward the other side of the road.

As the truck passed, Jackie raced toward the fallen body. "Ryan! Ryan! Are you all right?"

Before she could reach him, he sat up, looked squarely at her, and said again, "But what?"

Jackie stopped on the highway and put her hands on her hips. "Now you listen here," she began.

As their eyes met, Ryan smiled. "I know. I know that you were being kind, letting me sort things out for myself. I've been through this before, remember? Now why don't you come over here and give me a hand before a truck hits you?"

Jackie pulled Ryan up and hugged him hard. He folded his arms around her. Neither spoke for several seconds as they embraced. Several cars and trucks passed. Most honked their horns at the couple. One driver yelled, "Get a room!"

"I'm so sorry," Jackie said softly. "I'll do anything I can to help. But I just don't know where to start. All we have is a bloody tee shirt that belonged to P.J., along with her basketball and backpack. We don't have a crime scene. We don't have a weapon. We don't have a…"

"A body?" Ryan finished.

He stepped back and gently brushed Jackie's cheek with his left hand. "P.J.'s not dead. I told you that. Don't you believe me?"

Jackie took his hand. Ryan could see her mind working behind those green eyes.

"Of course I do," she said finally. "We still have to find her, though.

"Come on. I have an idea," the deputy said as she started across the road.

Without looking back, she added, "And look both ways before you cross, will you? I don't need a hit-and-run to complicate things right now."

Ryan hurried to catch up.

"I don't know what I'd do without you," he said. "You provide such good comic relief."

"You, too," Jackie said. "Now, get in the car."

"Where are we going?" Ryan asked as he opened the passenger door.

"If the wolves are looking after P.J. like you said, then we are going to find out where the wolves are and go there," she said. "At this point, I don't see anything else that we could do."

Ryan smiled. "You're right. Finding the wolves is the right thing to do. If I weren't so muddle-headed, I would have suggested that already."

He leaned over and kissed Jackie on the cheek. "I really mean it this time. I don't know what I'd do without you. Thank you."

"Not a problem," Jackie said as they fastened their seatbelts. She started the cruiser.

"But looking for wolves isn't exactly in your job description. Is it?" Ryan asked. "Don't you have other responsibilities?"

Jackie put on her sunglasses and looked at the man she had known for just a day.

"P.J. is not only your daughter; she's the niece of the most powerful man in Parkland. He's the man who got Grizzly Wilson, my boss, elected sheriff. He might be governor of this state one day. On top of that, John Stallings and I go way back. I don't think that there will be a problem. Let's go."

CHAPTER FIFTEEN

Mary Jennings looked out the kitchen window and smiled as she saw her husband Frank sitting in the old wooden rocker that was his favorite. He looked so peaceful out there, rocking gently in the low, warm light of a summer sunset. She couldn't see his face because he was facing the woods. He did that often these days, at both dusk and dawn.

She had grown accustomed to finding him there when she entered the kitchen to make breakfast. Sometimes, she would take him a cup of decaffeinated coffee, and he would ask her to sit with him for a while. She always refused, telling him that she had too much to do back in the house.

For the most part, he seemed to be the same old Frank. He was as kind and as humorous as ever. He still helped around the house and kissed her good morning and good night. But, now that he had been weakened by a heart attack, he couldn't go for daily walks. Instead, he chose to sit and look at the woods mornings and evenings.

Mary hated that his life had been slowed by the heart problem, but she was happy that he stayed home now where he belonged. He was too old a man to be out traipsing in the woods, even if he was part Indian.

"I'm waiting for the wolves," he had told her that first spring evening that she saw him sitting in the yard.

She handed his coffee to him and put a blanket on his lap. His brown eyes brightened in thanks for the love offerings.

"It's such a beautiful evening. Why don't you join me? The supper dishes can wait."

Mary stroked his still black hair with her hand and shook her head.

"I wish that you'd forgive the wolves," Frank said. "They didn't kill Carrie. Let me share with you a dream that I had last night. My spirit guide tells me that they even saved…"

"No, Frank. There's a program on that I want to see. Don't stay out here too late. The damp night air isn't good for you."

She turned and went back inside. Frank heard the sounds of running water and then voices from the television set. He sipped the coffee.

For as long as he could remember, many of his dreams had been of wolves. Sometimes they spoke to him.

Dream encounters with his animal totem had come more often after Carrie died. They were even more numerous within the past year. He often had tried to talk with Mary about them, but something deep inside her had changed with Carrie's death. She no longer tolerated his love for wolves. She would not listen when he tried to tell her of the conversations that he had with them.

Perhaps Mary never cared at all, Frank sometimes thought. He was saddened by the idea that she might have pretended interest in his passion for all those years. He wished that he could take away her pain and help her be at peace.

Four months had passed since Carrie's spirit had told him in a dream that the wolves were coming. Real wolves. Not just those of his dreams. He sat facing the woods on a summer's night and waited to see them one last time in this world. Back inside the house, he heard the voices of a situation comedy. For a brief moment, the laugh track deeply saddened him. A light inside the kitchen cast a rectangular square at his feet and then blinked off. Mary had left for the living room.

Frogs in a nearby pond cleared their throats and began to sing as the woods darkened. Crickets came in on the chorus, followed shortly by whippoorwills. Frank looked up to see swallows darting against a pale blue sky and billowy clouds turned fiery by the fading sun. He smiled and closed his eyes.

He wished that Mary would be here with him. He knew the wolves soon would be.

Inside the house, during a commercial, Mary realized that Frank usually had come back inside by now. Rising from her recliner, she walked into the darkened kitchen and peered out the window. A bright half-moon illuminated the backyard enough that she could see a dog sitting next to Frank. It was a large animal, a German shepherd, probably.

As her eyes adjusted, she saw other dogs materialize out of the night as if by magic. She had counted four before the horrible realization struck her.

She screamed, and as she did so, one of the animals looked up at her. One of its eyes was light amber, the other dark gold.

Trembling with terror, Mary snapped on the back porch light, opened the door, and screamed, "Get out of here! Get out of here!"

Pausing for breath, she saw that Frank was alone again.

Had he always been? she wondered. But Mary knew what she had seen. She pulled the door closed behind her and ran to the phone to dial 911.

Back in the kitchen, she looked out the window and saw that Frank still had not moved.

She screamed and screamed again.

* * * * *

"Momma, Momma. It's all right, Momma," Cathy Stallings said as she patted her mother's hand. "You were having a nightmare."

Mary looked up from her hospital bed to see Cathy and her husband, John. Ryan and the red-haired woman who had brought P.J.'s shirt to her were there, too.

"P.J.'s dead, isn't she?" the white-haired woman sobbed, tears staining her pale cheeks. "The wolves killed her."

"We don't know that," said Cathy.

She was two years older than Carrie and considerably heavier, but with the same brown hair and brown eyes.

"She might be alive. Ryan thinks that she is, and he wants to talk to you. He thinks that you might be able to help him find P.J. Do you feel strong enough?"

Mary Jennings nodded. "Could I have a tissue, please?"

She wiped her eyes and swallowed hard.

Ryan knelt beside his former mother-in-law and smiled gently. "I really do think that she's alive," he said. "And I think that wolves might have been caring for her these past two days.

"You told Jackie that there are wolves around here. Do you know where they might be? Did Frank ever tell you?"

"No! No! No! You don't understand," Mary said hysterically. "You've got it all wrong. Wolves killed Frank. I saw them! And now they've killed P.J. too. And it's all my fault. I should have warned her."

As Ryan tried in vain to calm her, Stallings stepped outside to call a nurse.

"She needs another sedative," he said quietly. "Please tell the doctor."

With Mary sleeping once again, the four moved to the waiting room. Cathy and her husband sat on the dark plaid sofa while Ryan paced. Jackie pulled open the curtains to let in late morning light.

"Cathy, please try to remember. Did your mother ever say where Frank went to see the wolves?" Ryan asked, rubbing his forehead above the eye patch.

"We really don't think there ever were any wolves," Cathy said. "Momma's been irrational about them ever since Carrie died. We think that she just hallucinated because of her grief when she realized Poppa was dead. Isn't that right, John?"

Stallings stood up and walked to the window. "That's right, Ryan. There are no wolves around here, believe me. We can keep looking for P.J., of course. But I really don't think that you should pin your hopes on the ranting of a hysterical woman.

"Why in the world would you think that P.J. would be with wolves anyway? All the evidence tells us that she was abducted saving that little girl."

Jackie sank into a cushioned chair. "Trust him, Colonel. He knows what he's talking about. Frank and Carrie had a special bond with wolves. So does P.J."

Stallings turned back and raised a white eyebrow. "That doesn't sound like you, Jackie. Good soldiers don't get emotional."

The deputy stared right back at her former commanding officer, flecks of fire in her eyes. "Sometimes they do, sir. Sometimes they have good reason to."

Stallings nodded. "Point well, taken, Jackie. I apologize. What happened to your sister was a terrible thing.

"Even if this special bond exists, though, I'm telling you that we have no wolves around here."

Ryan walked over to the window and looked nearly eye to eye at the man with such a commanding presence.

"I can understand that you and Cathy and most everyone else don't believe the wolves are here," he said. "But I do. So, accept that, okay? You have lots of contacts. Ask around for me.

"In the meantime, I'll keep looking on my own. I'm not going to give up until I find the wolves and P.J. with them."

Stallings nodded and smiled. "I don't blame you. If it were my daughter, I wouldn't give up either. I'll do everything that I can to help.

"But, please, let's not upset Mary anymore. I'm afraid that her heart couldn't take it. Cathy will stay here with her and if she learns anything she will let you know. I'll talk to some men who hunt the woods around here and ask if they've ever seen or heard wolves.

"If I get any leads, how can I contact you? Cell phone coverage isn't very good in those hills."

Ryan looked out the window.

"I don't know where I'll be," he said. "But I'll check in at the sheriff's office from time to time.

"Jackie is going to help me if it's all right with you and the sheriff."

Stallings nodded his agreement.

He made certain to hide his unhappiness. He didn't know Ryan that well and would have no problem killing him.

But Jackie was a good soldier. Also, he never had known for certain that Kendall had killed her sister, but he certainly suspected it. Guilt about that had been one of the reasons that he made a job for her in Parkland. That, and the fact that she really was a good soldier. Should Crater have to kill Jackie, he would miss her.

PART FOUR
FITTING IN

P.J. pulled a tiny skeleton out of her mouth and wiped her lips with her fingers. Filling her belly made her feel even better than the bath that she had taken in the creek. Even better than putting on the clean and sun-dried shirt, shorts, and socks afterward.

She was certain that she had eaten many better-tasting meals—even at boarding school.

"I won't ever again complain about food in the school cafeteria," she said with a fishy smile. "Not even the creamed corn or the split pea soup."

But these minnows satisfied her hunger as nothing ever had before.

Sure, P.J. knew that almost two days without eating made them seem more appealing than they really were. She was eating bait, for goodness sake!

But a girl in the wilderness had to keep up her strength if she were to survive. And P.J. intended to survive. What she would do beyond that, she didn't know or even think about. Right now, she was content to revel in the fact that someone cared about her.

She carefully pulled the last smoking fish off the stick and kicked dirt into the fire. Those survival lessons at summer camp really had paid off. Otherwise, she never would have known to search for a piece of glass to focus the sun and start her fire or how to trap minnows in a stream.

A little more than two days ago, she hadn't felt so certain that she wanted to survive. But meeting the wolves had changed everything. Her mother was dead. Her father had abandoned her and was off somewhere thousands of miles away, taking pictures. Her uncle wanted her dead.

But her real family—the wolves—had found her and welcomed her with huge, wet tongues. They had brought her to their home and even tried to feed her.

P.J. belched the taste of baitfish in a most unladylike way. Then she frowned as she recalled something even more disgusting. The adult wolves had puked up half-digested pieces of mystery meat to feed their pups and tried to give her some of it.

One had nosed a particularly large and hairy piece toward her.

"Eeeewww! No, thank you," she said.

Nothing, not creamed corn, not split pea soup, not a plateful of worms, was worse than that. Just wait until she told her friends about that total gross-out! And she would tell them when they were eating.

P.J. had giggled at the thought. But the pleasant idea of inflicting mischief on her friends didn't last long.

The sight of bloody, steaming flesh made her want to throw up. In fact, she would have if she had eaten anything recently. Instead, as the pups wrestled for the final piece, P.J. had staggered off into the woods. With her hand over her mouth, her face was as pale as the clouds in a January sky.

Fortunately, the alpha wolves—Arthur and Guinevere, she had named them—didn't take the rejection personally, and no food was wasted. The three young ones were quick to gobble up all that was offered.

The pups, in fact, seemed to be hungry all the time.

"Here, Moe, you can have the last fish," P.J. said as she tossed the minnow to the black youngster with the floppy left ear.

Moe grabbed the fish and bounded away. Curly and Larry chased after him.

The adult gray female, Auntie Em, half-opened one eye to confirm that nothing was wrong. Then she went back to napping in the late afternoon sun. She was the ever-vigilant babysitter, P.J. had decided.

The two gray males—Bert and Ernie—served as hunters, guards, and occasional playmates for the pups. Right now, they dozed on the rocky outcropping above the den.

Guinevere lay with her head on her paws under a cedar at the top of the glade and watched all that happened. Arthur was nowhere to be seen but not far away, P.J. knew.

Although the girl had been with the wolves for little more than two days, she already had learned that each adult member of her new family had a specific role. Also, they all followed a mutually accepted schedule. They hunted by night. They played a bit and bathed in the nearby creek during early morning. Then they took shelter in their den during the heat of the day. Afterward, they lazed around outside before it was time to blend into the darkness again, as silent as a whisper. At all times, however, an adult kept watch, and one of the grays always stayed behind with the pups.

P.J. wasn't yet sure what her role was in the family. She knew that she never could truly live as a wolf. Eating raw and/ or half-digested meat was too disgusting to even consider. Also, she needed people, no matter how much she was hurt by the loss of her parents and betrayal by her uncle.

"Yeah, and wolves don't play basketball, take bubble baths, or hang out at the mall." P.J. chuckled at the mental image of wolves doing such things.

Then, there was "home." Crawling into that den had given her claustrophobia. She had been surprised at how clean the wolves kept it, with only a few bones scattered around for the pups to chew on. The air inside wasn't a problem, with nothing more offensive than the smell of musty dog hair. But she definitely didn't want to sleep there.

Sure, she enjoyed being a tomboy sometimes, camping out and sleeping on the ground. But as a permanent way of life? No, thank you! She wanted a firm mattress, down pillows, soft sheets, and a cozy comforter. A reading lamp was a necessity, too. So were scented candles. And Buster! How could she forget Buster, her stuffed wolf? She loved to cuddle with him. Of course, she was getting a bit old for that.

Now she had real, honest-to-goodness wolf pups, who also liked to cuddle—and lick and pull her shoestrings and push their noses into private places… P.J. blushed at the memory.

The wolves seemed all right with the fact that she slept outside on cedar boughs and wanted to cook her food. Maybe that was because she didn't build too big a fire or make herself too conspicuous. She felt she, too, would be brought back into line if she did something to endanger the rest of the pack. She was a member of the family, after all.

She never would do anything to put them in danger. But what would she do, living here in the woods with the wolves that she had dreamed about and then met? With her belly full, P.J. decided that she would think about that later. She closed her eyes and dozed, under the watchful eye of Auntie Em.

CHAPTER SEVENTEEN

Jackie drew a water bottle from the pocket on her daypack and took a short swallow. She handed it to Ryan as he sat down on a large chunk of sandstone.

He rubbed around the slightly swollen left eye that was no longer hidden by a patch. The eye felt raw and irritated. It was surrounded by scabs and fading scratches. Plus, vision was a bit blurry on that side. But the eye would heal completely, the doctor assured him.

Jackie preferred the "pirate" look but didn't tell Ryan that. She visualized him swinging from a ship's mast, a cutlass in his teeth. She fought back a smile.

"What?" Ryan said. "It's the eye. Isn't it?"

Now Jackie did smile. "Well…The patch did hide most of the damage. But you'll be Mr. Handsome in a couple of days."

"Thanks a bunch," he said as he tossed the bottle back. "Who am I until then? Frankenstein's monster?"

The low sun cast long shadows across the two as they rested to the side of a huge, double arch. It had been carved out of a bluff by millions of years of rain, snow, and wind. Ancient, gnarled cedars pushed out of scattered openings. They looked much like bonsai in an Asian rock garden.

The unusual setting reminded Ryan of a scene from a Western movie, maybe a Western movie filmed in Japan.

"I thought these were granite mountains," Ryan said.

"Yeah, I think that they are, except for this peculiar little area," Jackie replied.

She took off her sunglasses and dropped them into the pocket of her long-sleeve khaki shirt. Much to Ryan's disappointment, she wore long pants, too—to protect her fair skin from sunburn.

Concern for P.J. consumed nearly every waking thought for Ryan. Jackie's presence eased the pain until it was at least tolerable. She made him laugh. She made him forget—if only for a minute or two. And she made him remember. Looking at her now, even all covered up like that, pleased him in a way that he hadn't known since Carrie.

Yes, the sexual attraction was nice.

But if Jackie were not with him as a friend and supporter, he wasn't sure that he could go on. He didn't know if he could continue to believe that P.J. was safe with the wolves. Talking to Jackie about them helped him to believe.

And sometimes, for the briefest of moments. . . When she smiled… He saw how it could be when the three of them were together at last. Jackie wasn't just someone whom he wanted to kiss and caress. She was someone whom he wanted as his wife and mother of his daughter.

"The sandstone and the unique plants that grow here are why Pickle Springs was made a National Natural Landmark," Jackie began.

She stopped when she noticed that Ryan's mind had wandered off somewhere. She sat down and poked him in the ribs.

"Sorry," he said with a sad smile.

"That's okay," she replied. "I've been there."

Ryan's eyes widened as he remembered.

"Yeah, that's right," he said, taking her hand. "I heard what John said back at the hospital. What happened to your sister, anyway?"

Jackie stroked the back of his head with her free hand and stood up. Ryan thought he saw the sparkle of a tear before she turned her back to him. She bowed her head briefly, and the sun turned her red hair to fire.

"Thanks for asking," she said. "But let's talk about that another time. Let's keep our minds focused on why we came here."

When she faced him again, she was smiling.

"Anyway, as I was saying, the brochure that I read when I first moved here said that woolly mammoths and other ice-age animals actually lived in these valleys, eating those plants."

"And wolves ate those mammoths," Ryan said.

He wanted to embrace and comfort Jackie. But he forced himself to concentrate on why they were here.

"No wonder P.J.'s grandfather came here to find the wolves. Look at the history this place has. It's their ancestral grounds."

Jackie sat down again and put her hand on his bare knee. It was a reversal of roles that he didn't mind at all. It had been too long since he had enjoyed the touch of a woman.

"We don't know for sure that he came here on his walks," she said, moving her hand into his. "All we know is that is what he told Cathy, and Cathy told us."

"But it really feels right. Look at this place," Ryan said as he gazed toward the tree-lined creek below. "I'll bet Indians lived here too."

He turned then and looked back up toward the rocky path that had led them to the arches.

"It's wild, but yet it's not so difficult to get to. It would have been a perfect place for P.J.'s grandfather to come until he had his heart attack."

Suddenly Ryan sniffed, stood, and sniffed again.

"I smell smoke," he said. "Stale smoke from an old campfire. It's coming in on an east wind. Maybe it's drifted up from the creek bottom. Or maybe someone built a fire over there."

He pointed across the valley and grabbed for Jackie's hand. "Let's go," he said excitedly. "Maybe P.J.'s there."

Had Ryan been sitting and looking down instead of standing and looking up, he would have missed the slight movement near the top of the arches. That fraction of a second advantage gave him just enough time. He grabbed Jackie and dived away before a boulder crashed down on where they had been sitting.

Their bodies bounced on the bare rock, jarring knees and elbows. Sandstone turned to sandpaper and scraped their hands and Ryan's bare legs. He grabbed Jackie to keep her from rolling downhill into the cedar scrub.

The thunderous impact still echoed down the valley below as they turned to see what had almost killed them. It was big enough to squash an elephant. They squinted fiercely but could see nothing in the glare of the late-day sun.

Jackie looked solemnly at Ryan and said, "It's a good thing you just saved my life. Otherwise, I'd have to arrest you for assaulting an officer."

Then she leaned over and kissed him passionately.

"Better than a pair of handcuffs," Ryan said with a grin as he lifted her to her feet and pulled her close.

"Let's go. We're in real danger here," he whispered in her ear. Then he grabbed her hand and sprinted under the arches.

"Look, I don't think any more rocks…" Jackie began.

Ryan put a finger to his lips.

"Get that pistol out," he said softly. "Someone pushed that rock. I didn't see much, but just enough to know that it didn't fall on its own."

The deputy drew her revolver, and the two peeked out the back side of the arches. Before he could stop her, Jackie was scampering up a rock wall next to the unusual formation. She used her left hand to keep her steady while holding her weapon ready in her right. With no time to stop her, an angry Ryan grabbed a fist-sized rock and followed.

When he reached the top, Jackie was crouched, examining the site where the boulder had been sitting. Ryan looked around nervously.

"We're sitting ducks up here!" he hissed.

"Don't think so," Jackie said. "Whoever did this wanted it to look like an accident. They're not going to shoot us."

"So you say," Ryan replied. "I'd just as soon not give them the opportunity. Come on, woman."

He grabbed her arm and pulled her up.

"Okay, okay," she said. "Point well taken. Let's go."

Jackie holstered her pistol, and the two slid back down.

"There weren't any footprints," she said as they crouched under the arches and looked out into the summer dusk. "But that rock definitely had been pried loose. I could see the scratches in the sandstone."

"Who'd want to hurt you?" Ryan asked.

"What do you mean me?" Jackie said indignantly. "What about you?"

A whole new twist had been added to their search for P.J. Someone didn't want them looking for her.

Ryan and Jackie looked into each other's eyes then and listened for a long moment. Frogs began a chorus in the creek down below.

CHAPTER EIGHTEEN

The creek gurgled. Crickets and frogs chirped. For a change, all was peaceful around the cabin on this summer night.

Then all Hell broke loose.

A cry of mortal agony filled the air as Crater Kendall came crashing out of the cabin. He waved his hands all around his head before he tumbled down the steps. Regaining his feet, he fell twice more as he ran for the creek.

He dived in, hoping to escape an angry swarm of bees that already had stung him more than a dozen times. Unfortunately for Kendall, the water was too shallow to shield him. Bees drilled him repeatedly in the ass.

Stumbling to his feet, he thrashed into deeper water, where he finally found refuge. Nearly a minute passed before he dared raise his head above the water.

The bees were gone. And Kendall was sober, despite a night of drinking beer. Bee stings and near drowning can do that to a person.

Coughing and spitting, he dragged himself to shore. He was very glad that no one was here to see his performance. Four of the guys still were in town. The other two were on patrol. He wondered if those two had put the beehive in the chimney. Maybe they were angry because they had to stay behind.

Just then, he was blinded by headlights. A car came around the bend in the gravel road and stopped just a few feet away.

The Colonel turned on a flashlight as he stepped out of his Cadillac and headed toward the cabin. He stopped suddenly when he noticed the miserable creature in front of him. He saw first the wet shirt and jeans. Then he noticed the angry, red swellings on Kendall's face and arms.

"My God, man, what happened to you?" he said.

"Bees," Kendall said as he paced about. "Someone put a hive in the chimney, and they attacked me when I went inside."

"Oh." Stallings resisted the urge to laugh, but his voice could not hide his merriment.

"Yeah, go ahead and laugh, you son of a bitch," Kendall said as he stopped walking but continued to scratch and flail. "You're damn lucky that I'm not allergic, or this operation would be over. You need me, you know.

"You need me!"

Following the outburst, Kendall stuck both hands into his thin beard and raked furiously.

"Calm down, Crater," the Colonel said. "Yeah, I need you.

"And you're not going to die unless it's because of an infection you get from all of that scratching. When did you become such a whiner anyway?"

Stallings tossed Kendall a small bottle of Jack Daniels whiskey that he carried in the pocket of his suit coat. "Here, have some medicine.

"If it's not bears, it's bees," the Colonel continued. "Let's review, shall we? You killed that bear in front of the cabin. You brought my niece into this. You killed Wilson in a public place. And earlier today, you tried to kill Jackie and my brother-in-law.

"No, more accurately, you failed to kill Jackie and my brother-in-law. Now I've got to think of some way to deal with them."

Stallings shined his light toward the cabin, looking for bees.

"They're going to be more determined than ever to search for P.J.," he continued. "Now they probably suspect something is going on besides just a kidnapping.

"We can only hope that Wilson took care of the kid and, when you killed him, you didn't leave any clues that will tie us to him."

Kendall thought about telling the truth. Stallings' niece was alive. Wilson had refused to kill the girl, just as he had suspected. But this definitely was not a time to hit the Colonel with an "I told you so."

Besides, he wanted the girl for himself, and Stallings didn't seem to like that idea.

The Colonel turned off his flashlight. He looked down at the creek that glistened in the moonlight. Its soothing babble made him wish that he was trout fishing in Montana instead of dealing with his problem here. He had a man—once a good man—who was becoming more a liability than an asset.

Scratching and then thoughts of that girl had kept Kendall from listening to what the Colonel had to say. But when Stallings paused, Kendall looked up to see fire in the Colonel's blue eyes. He no longer was concerned with skin discomfort.

"I tried to make it look like an accident," the former master sergeant said softly. "I could have shot them, but I didn't think that would be a good idea."

Kendall looked away. Stallings was the only man whom he respected—and feared. Sure, he talked back sometimes. But he knew not to push too far. Also, he knew that the Colonel carried something besides a bottle of whiskey in his suit pockets.

Stallings gave a cold smile. "Well, you still think once in a while.

"That's good to hear. And you're right. Shooting them wasn't a good idea. But at least if you'd shot them, we wouldn't have them nosing around right now. We've got another truck coming in soon, you know. And this should be the biggest haul yet. Lots of money for a few minutes of work."

The Colonel stepped toward Kendall and took back his bottle.

"All right, you listen to me, Crater Kendall. Take care of Jackie and Ryan Conners, but make it look like an accident. A house fire, maybe, or a car wreck.

"Along with that truck coming in soon, I've got something big planned for you to do on the Fourth. You're going to make history, and I won't have anyone getting in the way before that. When you've settled down, I'll tell you about it."

Gravel crunched under his well-polished shoes as Stallings walked back to his white Cadillac.

"Until then, call your brother. You're going to need a good boat driver. And stay away from town."

Stallings climbed into the car, shut the door, and turned on the ignition. The headlights once again put Kendall's misery on display. He shielded his eyes from the glare.

"A couple of other things," the Colonel yelled through the open window. "Get those damn bees out of the cabin. Smoke them out or something. And clean out the sewer pipe once and for all. That's what I came about in the first place.

"The men say the toilet works for a while but then stops up again. I was going to get one of the guys on guard duty to strip down and check out the pipe where it drains into the creek. But, Hell, you're already wet."

In the pre-dawn dark, Kendall couldn't tell if his old commanding officer was smiling. But he was certain that he was.

Stallings spun the car around in the gravel. As he drove away, Kendall yelled curses at him.

But then he stopped suddenly and grinned. Not only did he have permission now to eliminate Ryan Conners and his girlfriend, but he knew something that Stallings didn't. He was even more pleased now that he hadn't revealed what he had learned in that bathroom on the interstate.

"Too bad, Colonel," he grinned.

The kid was still alive. Wilson had told him so, and men who are begging for their lives don't lie.

Plus, he had a pretty good idea where the brat was hiding. He had been tracking P.J. Conners when he stumbled upon the deputy and the girl's father. Yes, indeed, he would have plenty to keep him busy before whatever Stallings had planned for him on the Fourth of July."

"Ahhhh!" Kendall screamed again, as once more his physical pain demanded attention. He scraped dirty fingernails across his left arm, and blood poured from swollen lumps, brightening the red of the tattoo.

He hadn't experienced this much agony since he was a boy. After his brother Dawson awakened him with a snowball in the face, he chased the little turd out the door of the mobile home and into the woods. There Kendall stumbled and plunged his nearly naked body into an icy briar patch.

"Ahhhhh!" he yelled again and flung a rock at the cabin. It shattered a window.

"Damn! That's all I need!"

Fists clenched to keep from scratching, he headed for his van. He was going to get his gun and head up to the arches. Shooting something — anything — would make him feel better. If he were really, really lucky, maybe it would be the girl. If not, he would settle for whatever walked, crawled, or flew in those woods.

PART FIVE

LOVE SONG

CHAPTER NINETEEN

The pups didn't want her to go. They whined and started to follow, then bolted back to the den. P.J. felt badly about leaving, even if only for a little while. Moe, Larry, and Curly were her buddies. They napped with her on the bed that she had made of cedar branches. They bathed with her in the creek. Well, actually, they just thrashed around and made it nearly impossible for her to bathe. But she loved it. She loved them.

But she had to find some real food. Her stomach insisted. Two meals of minnows in three days simply were not enough to keep up her strength. And with the second meal, the smell of oily fish almost made her hurl. This was not a weight-loss diet that she would recommend to her friends.

"Sorry, guys," P.J. said as she looked back. "But I've got to find some people food. I'd kill for a mango smoothie or a turkey sub."

At her words, the pups perked their ears. They had grown accustomed to the sound of her voice.

"Heck, I'd even break someone's leg for some broccoli."

She smiled sadly as she turned and headed into the woods.

"I'll be back," she said over her shoulder. "Don't worry."

But P.J. was worried. She didn't know where she would get food. Maybe she could find some berries. She wished that she had paid better attention during that class on edible plants at summer camp last year.

She couldn't just knock on someone's door. Her uncle, the most powerful man in Parkland, wanted her dead. The sheriff was on his side—and that meant the deputies probably were too. Others also might be involved in whatever was going on at that cabin. If she talked to the wrong person, she might be captured and marched off again to be shot. Once was enough, thank you very much.

She wouldn't knock on any doors. She might not even find any doors or houses or food. She might not even find her way back to the den.

As she walked, P.J.'s heart raced with fear at the thought of being lost in the woods. She looked quickly about her, seeing only oak trees and cedars and rays of sunlight filtering through the leaves.

She stopped, fists clenched. She wanted to go back to the den. But if she did that, she'd have to eat puked-up mystery meat—or starve. She wouldn't do either. She couldn't do either.

She was going to find food, real human food.

And then what? Could she find her way back to the den? She couldn't just walk to a road and hitch a ride into town. That was asking for trouble.

Tears welled up in her eyes at what seemed a hopeless situation. As she wiped them away with the sleeve of the oversized shirt, P.J. saw that she was not alone. Bert and Ernie, the two gray adult wolves, were riding shotgun on this trip. They stood just a few yards away in the shade of a large oak. They would protect her. They would lead her back to the family.

"Thanks, guys," she said softly and set off again.

She might come back hungry. But with their help, at least she would come back.

*　*　*　*　*

As P.J. bit into the tomato, juice ran down her chin and dripped onto her shirt. Absolutely, positively, nothing had ever tasted better.

"Mmmmmm," she said, as her eyes rolled in pleasure.

Nearly two hours of walking had taken her to a small farm on the other side of the creek. She wasn't sure how she found it. Maybe she not only had a wolf family. Maybe she had some wolf traits, like a keen sense of smell. Maybe she just followed her nose to this house with its large backyard garden.

Finished with the first, she grabbed another tomato.

"Whatchya doin'?"

P.J. should have been frightened by the voice. But she was so focused on her food that it did little more than cause her to look up.

She saw a cute little blond-haired boy in overalls standing there, watching her eat.

As the reality of her discovery hit home, she fought the urge to run.

This is just a little boy, she told herself. *No need to worry. I'm okay.*

The tomato vines were little more than waist-high. By crouching down below them at the end of the row, P.J. thought that she would have plenty of time to see anyone coming toward her. That would give her the opportunity to escape.

But she had been thinking in terms of an adult coming toward her, she realized, not a child.

"Uh, I'm eating tomatoes. Want one?" P.J. replied.

"No, thanks," the little boy said. "Maters are yucky. I'm havin' smashed cheese samiches for lunch."

P.J.'s mouth watered at the thought of a grilled cheese sandwich. She could hear the buttered bread sizzling and smell the melting cheese.

"You want a smashed cheese samich?" the boy asked.

"That's very nice of you. But no, thanks," P.J. heard herself say.

She couldn't believe the words came from her mouth. Of course, she wanted a grilled cheese sandwich. And she wanted a dill pickle spear to go with it.

"Okay, bye," the boy said and disappeared back into the vines.

"Time to move," P.J. whispered.

She grabbed four more tomatoes and put them in the pockets of her shorts. She was glad that she had put on cargo shorts instead of athletic shorts with no pockets that morning she had left to shoot hoops.

Duck walking down the rows, she eyed lettuce, onions, squash, and eggplant. She decided to stop at the banana peppers. She loved peppers, especially the hotter ones. Banana peppers weren't hot, or even warm. But they were crispy and would keep well in the summer heat. She munched one as she put others in a pocket.

"Whatchya doin'?"

P.J. looked up to see a little blond-headed boy in overalls.

She grinned. "I thought that you'd be eating a smashed cheese sandwich right now," she said.

The little boy looked puzzled. "How did you know what I'm havin' for lunch?" he said.

Oh, boy, P.J. thought. *What am I dealing with here?*

"Just a lucky guess," she said. "Want a pepper?"

"Peppers are yucky," he replied. "Bye."

I'd better get out of here right now, P.J. thought. *The next time, he might have someone with him.*

But as the girl prepared to disappear back into the woods, she spied the strawberry patch. Her eyes locked on the full, ripe, luscious fruit.

"Oh… My… Gosh!" P.J. whispered despite herself.

Strawberries and cantaloupe were her absolute favorite breakfast. And strawberries were the most important ingredient in that combination. When she was younger, she once had eaten so many strawberries that she broke out in a rash. Fortunately, that didn't happen anymore.

But it might this time. She intended to pig out. Quickly she began picking the berries and dropping them into her last empty pocket.

"Whatchya doin?"

Greed made P.J. a little irritable.

What's with this kid? she thought. *Does he have short-term memory loss at age five?*

She wanted to be left alone to pluck the berries.

But she resisted the urge to show anger.

"Oh, just picking strawberries," she said. "Want some?"

"Don't like 'em," the boy said. "Bye."

"Goodbye and good riddance," P.J. mumbled to herself.

When one pocket was filled, she took peppers out of another and put in strawberries. She thought of holding the bottom of her oversized shirt and making a basket so that she could take even more. But she had a two-hour walk back to the den. That could be tiresome and awkward.

Of course, as she walked, she could eat the berries that she carried in the shirt. That way, she'd be carrying them in her stomach for most of the way. P.J. giggled at the thought.

She piled as many berries into the shirt as she dared. She eased around, putting her back to the garden, and stepped toward the woods.

"Where you goin'?"

"Uh, I have to go home now," P.J. said without looking back. "It was nice talking to you."

"Wait," a little boy's voice said. "This is for you."

P.J. turned around to see three little boys that appeared to be exact copies of one another. All had shaggy blond hair. All wore overalls. One of them carried a brown paper bag.

"Our Daddy says this is for you," he said.

Her mouth dropped in astonishment.

"It's a smashed cheese samich," he added as he handed it to her.

P.J. suddenly found a big lump in her throat. She swallowed hard to get rid of it. When she did, her eyes sprung a leak.

"Thank you," she told the trio. "Thank you very much."

"Bye," they said and vanished into the tomato plants.

CHAPTER TWENTY

"You know, considering what happened to us yesterday, I think that it's time we took a look at the big picture," Jackie said as she and Ryan walked along the trail at Pickle Springs.

They had returned to search the area for P.J. and for clues as to who might have tried to kill them. They talked as they walked. Jackie saw Ryan's frustration building as they searched.

Hands on her hips, she gazed at the route that they believed their attacker had taken in his escape. He had stayed on the sandstone, so he left no prints, only a crushed leaf or broken twig here and there.

Ryan kicked at the ground.

"The big picture for me is that P.J. is missing, and we have to find her," he said. "What are you talking about?"

Jackie shook her head.

"If we consider what else is going on, it might help us figure out what happened to P.J. and where she is," she said. "That's what I'm talking about.

"We've spent too much time working hard instead of working smart. We might be missing some really important connections that could tell us what happened to your daughter."

Ryan sat down on a boulder the size and shape of a Volkswagen Beetle. He rubbed his unshaven chin with his left hand.

"Okay," he said. "I'm listening."

Jackie walked over and sat down beside him. She was wearing shorts today, and, despite himself, Ryan looked first to her legs as she started to share her thoughts with him. Seeing this, she took his face firmly in her right hand and pulled it up level with hers.

"Ouch! Okay, okay. A man can look, can't he? I was paying attention. I've always been good at multi-tasking."

Jackie smiled. "I'm sure you are. Just call it insecurity on my part. I like the person who's listening to what I have to say to look at my face, not my legs."

They stared into each other's eyes for a long moment. Despite all that was happening, both knew that they soon would give in to the need to be together as lovers.

Ryan finally broke the long pause. "You were saying?"

Jackie clapped her hands.

"Okay," she said. "Here's the big picture:

"P.J. is missing. Whoever took her first tried to kidnap a little girl. The girl said that he had red writing on his arm."

The deputy's mind seemed to drift off down the valley with her voice.

"Jackie? Jackie? Are you all right?"

Ryan put his hand on her shoulder, and she jumped as if from an electrical shock.

"Sorry," he said. "You all right? You seemed to go away there for a minute."

"Yeah, I'm fine," the deputy said. "Soon after P.J. was kidnapped, Wilson disappeared. He just packed up and left. No one knows where he went or why."

Jackie brushed dirt off her shorts.

"So now we've got two people missing, two people who, in an odd sort of way, were tied together. Wilson found P.J.'s shirt by the side of the road. Or that's what he said, anyway."

Ryan crossed his arms and stretched his legs. "So, what's your theory?"

"I don't have one yet," Jackie said. "If I had to bet money, though, I'd bet it on Wilson as the one who could tell us the most about what's going on. He wasn't a leader, though. That's the puzzle. He had no business being sheriff in the first place."

Ryan asked the obvious. "So why was he sheriff?"

"He was elected sheriff for the same reason I was hired as a deputy," she said. "The Colonel wanted it."

Ryan stood. "Let's go see Stallings then."

"And ask him what?" Jackie said. "And besides, the Colonel didn't have anything to do with P.J. disappearing. I know that he didn't."

Ryan paced off up the path, heading for Jackie's car.

"Then Wilson, a man who wasn't a leader, tried to kill us on his own? Stallings seems the logical one to talk to about this."

"No, Ryan, wait," Jackie yelled.

She ran after him.

"We can't do that."

He turned and waited.

"Why not? I'm just trying to work smart here, following your lead. Besides, I've never liked the guy, even when Carrie was alive, and we'd see them occasionally. He always seemed too slick for me."

Jackie took one of Ryan's hands in hers. "The Colonel is a good man, Ryan. I know that he is. He tried his best to find the man who killed my sister. He got me this job. John Stallings has nothing to do with whatever is going on around here, believe me."

Ryan raised his arms in exasperation. "So that puts us right back where we were before we wasted time having this stupid conversation."

He strode past the sandstone arches, heading for the creek in the bottom of the valley. Jackie hurried to catch up.

"Ryan, I'm sorry," she said. "It's just that I owe him so much."

She grabbed his arm from behind, and he turned.

"You're right, though. He's the logical one to suspect. I'll talk to him," she said.

Ryan looked into her eyes. "You promise?"

"I promise," she said, putting her head against his chest and her arms around his waist.

Ryan hesitated but then wrapped his arms about her shoulders. They stood quietly together. Each was nurtured by the other's growing love and devotion.

"Thanks," he said finally and kissed her forehead.

Jackie squeezed fiercely, and Ryan responded in kind. They stood for a while longer.

They worked slowly and deliberately for the rest of the day, saying little. Fatigue slowed Ryan, but he remained determined. They reached the creek at the bottom of the valley just at sunset.

"I didn't think that smoke I smelled yesterday could have come all the way across from the other side," he said as whippoorwills began to call. "I thought sure that we'd find remains of a campfire around here somewhere.

"Come on. We've still got enough daylight to take a quick look on the other side."

"Not a chance, Ryan," Jackie said, pulling a flashlight from her pack. "You were sleep-deprived when you got here, and you still haven't caught up.

"Heck, why am I talking about you? I'm tired. We'll go over there tomorrow."

Ryan looked at Jackie then and saw the pain of exhaustion in her face. His heart melted. He had been a stubborn bastard all day. He pulled her into his arms and held her.

"I'm so sorry," he whispered. "You're right. Let's skip supper. As soon as we get to your house, I'll get in my car and go to the motel. You get a good night's sleep. We'll start early in the morning."

* * * * *

But he didn't go to the motel. Sharing of painful memories and a growing need to be together changed their plans.

"If P.J. were my daughter, I'd be just as determined to find her," Jackie said as they rolled down the gravel road on their way to the highway.

"Now that I know you better, though, I can't help but feel that the pain you are carrying is about more than what is happening now."

Keeping her left hand on the wheel, she gently stroked the back of his head. In the green glow of the dashboard, she saw him bite his lower lip.

"Back in the hospital, you said that you would tell me more later," she said softly. "Well, now is later."

Ryan nodded and smiled sadly.

"I've never told anyone this story," he said. "I always thought that Carrie was the only one who would understand because she believed herself to be a sister to the wolf. I guess the best way to begin is by telling you a little about her.

"The first time I heard Carrie call herself 'sister to the wolf,' I laughed and laughed—until she boxed me in the ear in front of about a thousand people in the lounge at the Student Union. That clinched it for me. I was hopelessly in love.

"After she received her master's degree in wildlife biology and I finished graduate work in photojournalism, we were married in a chapel at the University of Missouri. We traveled to Alaska for our honeymoon.

"Carrie served as my model most of the time on the trip, including the day that I placed her in a stream with a fly rod for a scenic shot…"

* * * * *

From his spot on the mountain above, Ryan peered down at Carrie through the lens and composed the photo. Just as he was about to snap it, however, a raven landed in a branch only a few feet from Carrie. Watching through the camera's telephoto lens, Ryan saw his wife turn her head to the large, black bird. She leaned toward it.

"What did he say?" he called out jokingly as the raven flew away.

"He says there's a better spot for a photo around the bend," Carrie yelled back.

And there was.

Carrie also talked to animals in her dreams. Deep, deep down, Ryan envied her nighttime adventures as he listened to her talk in her sleep, although he never told her or even admitted it to himself.

Not surprisingly, wolves were frequent characters in Carrie's dreams. They were her guides, she said. They also were the reason that the couple had gone to Minnesota after P.J. was born. Carrie wanted to earn her doctorate degree there, studying and writing about wolves in the wild. Ryan could pay the bills by selling photos of them.

But then a log truck had slid into the car on an icy stretch, killing Carrie outright. Three-year-old P.J. disappeared into a fierce Minnesota winter for three days.

*　*　*　*　*

"Wolves saved P.J.'s life," Ryan said, keeping his eyes fixed on the dark road ahead.

"I have no doubt of that. Just like Carrie was their sister, P.J. is a member of the wolf family too. Maybe a sister of the wolf, just like her mother was.

"And you can bet those wolves are better parents than I've been."

The green interior lights turned tears to emeralds on Ryan's anguished face. He fought back a sob.

"Why don't I stop for a moment?" Jackie said.

"No, no, I'm fine," Ryan said, wiping his face with his right hand. "And I'll be even better when I've told you the rest.

"Two weeks after the accident, P.J. started to talk again, asking for her mother and Buster, a stuffed toy wolf that Carrie had given her for her second birthday. She didn't remember anything about the wreck or how she had survived.

"As P.J. learned of her mother's death, she grieved and moved on with her life. I wasn't so fortunate. I knew that I would survive Carrie's death, even though it would leave a lifelong scar on my heart. But something else was wrong, something in my relationship with P.J."

Ryan paused and swallowed hard. "This is the tough part, admitting that I stopped loving my daughter."

Jackie squeezed his arm.

"For three days, P.J. had been dead—or at least that's what I believed. Then, suddenly, she was alive again.

"That should have made me the happiest man in the world, and, for a few weeks, I was. But as life returned to normal, I realized that I had become a man without feelings.

"In my head, I could say with certainty that I loved my daughter and would give my life for her. But my heart was empty.

"I continued to be the good father that I always had been. I read bedtime stories to P.J. I played 'Hungry, Hungry Hippo' with her. I rocked her to sleep. But I was a man just going through the motions.

"Two years of being a model father brought no change.

"Slowly, I realized that I was afraid to love. I was afraid that P.J. would be taken from me again if I dared to really feel love for her. I couldn't take that pain again.

"Of course, I realized that I was being selfish. I realized that I probably needed a counselor to help me through this. But I was too stubborn to seek help. *It will pass in time*, I told myself, *and everything will be all right.*

"When P.J. was five years old, I enrolled her in a boarding school in Bucks County, Pennsylvania. Then I accepted every international photo assignment I could get.

"That's why I was in Africa, trying to shoot photos of leopards just a couple of weeks ago. I was still running away."

Jackie stopped and looked over at Ryan to support him with her eyes as well as her words. "But you came back," she said.

"And you never stopped loving P.J. You just had to find the courage to confront your fear, and you did it. Some people never do."

Ryan started to protest, but Jackie covered his lips with her fingers.

"Shhh! P.J. is fine, and we're going to find her. I've never been more sure of anything in my life.

"Now, let's go to my house."

* * * * *

Twenty minutes later, they were barefoot, gobbling down Chinese takeout at Jackie's coffee table. They sat on a Persian rug of soft purples, golds, and greens.

"Now I want to tell you about my sister," Jackie said, putting down a white box and chopsticks. "I know that you've been wondering about her. It's time that I shared too."

Knowing that she would cry, Jackie reached for a napkin. Ryan put his hand over hers. "You don't have to do this," he said.

"Yeah, I do," she replied. "It's time.

"We don't know what happened to her. She disappeared four years ago at Fort Gordon, Georgia, where we both were military policemen. Her body was never found."

As she spoke, Jackie remembered those terrible days as if they had just happened. She relived the agony that had so consumed her.

Jill hadn't come back one night after going to a club in Augusta with friends. Since they lived in separate barracks, Jackie didn't discover that she was missing until the next day.

"I was frantic," she told Ryan as she pulled her hand back with the napkin and blew her nose. "You see, there had been this guy terrorizing the town and the base for about a year.

"He had raped and killed five women that we knew of.

"About a week before Jill disappeared, the military police finally arrested someone who tried to pull a woman into his car on base. I had duty in town at the time and wasn't there when they brought him in.

"But Jill and I had dinner with a friend from HQ the next night. She told us that the guy had a red tattoo on his left arm. That was all she knew. She didn't know if they had matched his prints to any on the victims, but she really thought he was the one."

Jackie crossed her arms across her body and slowly rocked back and forth.

"Oh, Ryan," she cried. "He was the one. He killed Jill, and we never found her body. We searched and searched and searched."

Ryan scooted the coffee table from between them, took Jackie by the elbows, and lifted her up. He folded her into his arms and pushed her head gently onto his shoulder.

"Why do you think he is the one who did it?" he asked, tenderly stroking her hair.

"Because… ," Jackie sobbed. "Because he was gone from jail the next day, and then Jill died.

"No one knew what happened to him or his prints or even who he was."

Her crying slowed, and she took a deep breath. She squeezed Ryan tightly, seeking comfort in the shelter of his hard, warm body.

"Yeah, a few people said that they could identify him if they ever saw him again," she said through sniffles. "But no one ever did.

"The Colonel conducted a full investigation, but we never learned anything. It was like the guy never existed. But Jill died, and another girl after her. We just never found their bodies."

Ryan handed Jackie another napkin, and she blew her nose. Then she looked into his eyes.

"But he was the one, Ryan. I know that he was."

"I believe you," he said. "And now I know why you acted the way you did today when you said that little girl saw red writing on the arm of the man who tried to kidnap her. That's one heck of a lousy coincidence."

He held her closely until she pushed away slightly, and once more, their gazes met. Lost in those green eyes, he kissed her deeply.

"Ryan, please stay here with me tonight. I don't want to be alone," Jackie said.

Embarrassed by what she said, she looked away.

He gazed at her lovingly for a long moment. He stroked her cheek with the back of his hand and lightly lifted her chin.

"I don't want to be alone either," he said. "The last few nights have been Hell for me. I love you, Jackie."

Regaining her composure and cheered by his words, Jackie smiled.

"Oh, admit it. You just love a woman in uniform," she said.

"I admit it," Ryan grinned. "I love *this* woman in uniform. And I'd love her even better out of it. Especially those legs."

"Chauvinist pig," she said playfully and wrapped her arms around his neck. "But I love you anyway, Porky."

He scooped her up and threw her over his shoulder. "Which way to the bedroom?" he grunted.

"Down the hall to the left," Jackie squealed.

"Can't make it that far," Ryan panted, heading toward the kitchen table, which was only six feet away. "Heck, woman, you weigh almost as much as I do."

"You brute," she screamed in pretended dismay and pounded on his back. "How dare you make such an ungallant accusation."

"All aboard for the Ryan Conners Kitchen Express," he replied. He bent at the knees and sat her on the edge of the table.

"Can I look at those sexy legs now?" he asked as he stared up into twinkling green eyes.

"You show me yours, and I'll show you mine," Jackie said, unbuckling her belt and unzipping her khaki shorts. "But why stop with legs?"

Ryan stood and pulled off his blue tee shirt. "Hey, you're right," he said and struck a bodybuilder's pose."

Now it was Jackie's turn to stare.

"Not bad muscle definition for a photographer," she said as she kicked her shorts at him. "What else you got?"

Ryan dropped his jeans, revealing dark green jockey shorts.

Jackie clapped. "All right. A man of color. I like that. Not bad legs either."

He stepped out of his pants and moved closer. "Your turn," he said softly as he reached for the buttons on her short-sleeve blouse. "Mind if I help?"

Slowly, Ryan followed each loosened button with a kiss to the skin he exposed. She gasped when he lingered at her navel and twirled his tongue. Then he kissed his way back up and reached behind Jackie to unsnap her bra.

She nibbled on his ear as he did so.

"If you expect a man to do his job, you're going to have to stop distracting him," he said in a husky half-whisper. "I'll give you thirty minutes to stop that."

Jackie giggled and ran her fingernails up his bare back.

"Maybe I can find something that you like better than that," she said. "I've always been good at investigations. Especially when they are undercover."

"I'll like whatever you do, believe me," Ryan said as he pushed his way on top.

He ripped off her bra and kissed Jackie deeply and passionately. She embraced him, wrapped her legs around his, and kissed him back.

Suddenly, he stopped, raised his head, and sniffed the air.

"What is it?" Jackie asked, flushed and gasping. "Is something wrong?"

Ryan grinned. "Just checking for smoke. Wouldn't want to burn the house down."

Jackie grabbed him by the hair and brought him back to her.

"I'll chance it," she said in a throaty whisper. "Now, do your manly duty."

"My pleasure," he said. "Hope you don't mind if I take the scenic route."

* * * * *

Crater Kendall smirked as he watched passion being served on Jackie Novak's kitchen table. The small opening between the bottom of the blinds and the windowsill allowed him just enough space to see what was going on inside.

As he stared, he furiously scratched the backs of his hands, totally unaware that he was doing so. Less than twenty-four hours after he was attacked by the bees, his entire body seemed to have become one large, oozing lump.

"Enjoy yourselves while you can," he hissed. "This is your last night in heaven. Tomorrow morning, I'm sending you to Hell."

Building a small car bomb had been child's play for Kendall. Mostly he had used black-market military supplies that the Colonel had purchased. The most difficult part was being interrupted by itches in the damnedest places.

Crouching behind evergreen shrubs, he was reminded of those places as he watched Jackie and Ryan make love. He wanted to scratch the itch. But he had learned his lesson about angering up the stings on his private parts.

He slinked back to Jackie's carport and took a final look at his creation.

I hope they are together when this goes off, he thought. *Of course, it might be more fun if they aren't, especially if Novak is the one who survives. Then I can take care of her up close and personal.*

Seeing Jackie sexually excited had reminded Kendall of another redhead, one that he had raped four years ago at Fort Gordon. Jackie looked enough like that woman to be her sister. In fact, the deputy just might turn him on as much as some of the children that he now found so satisfying. Seeing her beg for her life before he slit her throat could be particularly gratifying.

CHAPTER TWENTY-ONE

"I know that you are out there, you sons of bitches."

Wearing a burgundy golf shirt and creased cotton khakis, John Stallings stood at the edge of his in-ground pool. He stared into the strip of woods that ran along the back of his property and that of his mother-in-law next door. A Cuban cigar smoldered in his left hand as he sipped on a gin and tonic.

"And I'm not afraid of you. You hear? You're not going to spoil this for me."

Stallings suddenly hurled his drink against the pool shed. It exploded upon impact. The Colonel watched tiny fragments of glass sink into the water, glittering brightly in the pool lights.

"Damn!"

He kicked the largest piece of glass with his deck shoe, and it skidded into Cathy's herb garden.

"It's the alcohol talking, that's all. Just the alcohol," Stallings said, even as he grabbed another tumbler from the portable bar.

Pouring himself a straight gin, he took a long swallow, hoping liquor would stop his hands from trembling.

"I'm not afraid of those wolves, and there's not a damn thing that they can do to interfere with me. They're just animals, for Chrissakes."

He glanced down at the nine-millimeter pistol on the patio table. Then he looked back to the woods, searching for the big one, the one with the dark gold eye.

"I hope you come back here," he said. "I really hope you do."

Deep down, Stallings never wanted to see any of the wolves again. He wished that he had never seen them in the first place. His life would be a whole lot simpler if that were the case.

They were here, though, no doubt about it. With them, they brought too many potential complications, the worst of them being Ryan Conners. It was almost like those damn wolves had brought him here.

Jackie Novak was a problem, too, now that she had fallen head over heels for the photographer. And Crater, once a good man despite his questionable sexual appetite, had become more trouble than he was worth.

Stallings allowed himself a small smile. He sat down in a canvas director's chair, crossed his legs, and puffed on his cigar. Crater Kendall would stop causing problems almost immediately upon completion of his mission. And so would his brother.

The smile broadened as he remembered why he had poured that gin and tonic. Evans had called from Texas. He confirmed that shipment was coming in tomorrow after midnight. It was a large shipment, too, and that meant lots of money.

But the wolves. . . What could he do about them? He would love to hunt them down and kill them. They were a protected species, though, and he couldn't risk being caught. He needed to appear to be America's hero. Not only was he becoming a rich man very quickly, but he might soon hold national office if Crater didn't screw up on his final job.

His mother-in-law, that crazy old bat, knew the wolves were here too. She kept the pot stirred with her ranting and raving from her hospital bed. At least, though, she thought they had somehow figured in her husband's death. She believed they had caused him to have a second heart attack.

John Stallings knew otherwise.

The old man had been too nosy for his own good. He puttered around in his backyard at all hours, including late one night when the Colonel was conducting some business by phone at the pool.

* * * * *

"That's right, Murdock. I need two crates of 'goods.' No hurry on delivery. No place to put them yet. I'll call you when I have a spot."

'Goods' was the code word that Stallings had been given by Kendall for ordering black-market assault weapons from a dealer in Illinois.

Unfortunately, Frank Jennings had overheard next door. Stallings knew it when he looked up from the phone. His eyes locked with those of the old man over a row of shrub roses. And that was why his father-in-law had to die.

The Colonel tried to talk himself out of the murder at first. What had the old man heard, after all? Just that he was ordering two crates of 'goods.'

Yet after tossing and turning for two nights, Stallings knew what he had to do. Too much was at stake to risk letting Jennings live. Stallings intended to get rich while making the United States a better and safer place. He didn't care about laws anymore.

Why should he care if no one else did? Failure to enforce immigration laws and protect the borders was causing the collapse of a once great nation. Soon, if something weren't done, we would be no better than Mexico. Hell, we would *be* Mexico.

The summer night was rich with the scent of lilacs when he put on leather gloves and carried an old pillow into the backyard to wait. His wife Cathy had gone to bed at ten o'clock, as was her custom. Frank Jennings rocked peacefully in that old wooden chair of his. Mary was inside, watching television.

At a little before eleven, Colonel John Stallings put the pillow under his arm and walked silently into the yard next door. He stopped a few feet behind Frank's back and took a deep breath.

"I've been expecting you, John," his father-in-law said.

Stallings' heart raced. He had been found out! He looked nervously from side to side. Sweat poured down his sides. But he said nothing.

"You know what Indians used to say, John? They'd say, 'Today is a good day to die.'

"It's a good night for me to die, I think. I've had a good life. It's my time, the wolves say, and they tell me that they will take me to Carrie. I will like that.

"Do you know what else the wolves say, John? They say that you will fail in whatever evil you are planning. You will fail because they will not allow you to succeed.

"I can die peacefully knowing that.

"Goodbye, John."

Stallings stepped forward then and pressed the pillow over the old man's face. He looked up at the stars as he pushed and counted slowly backward from one hundred. Frank Jennings did not struggle, and, at number twenty-two, Stallings felt the old man's body go limp.

"Crazy, old bastard," the Colonel whispered as he looked down at the top of the Jennings' head. "You expect me to believe that crap?"

A rustling in the woods startled Stallings, and he reached for the pistol in his back pocket. He stared into the trees but saw nothing except fireflies.

As he turned toward the left to go back home, he heard a second sound. It was so subtle it would not have been noticed by most people. Stallings, however, was a career soldier and combat veteran. He knew when he was being shadowed.

Pillow under his arm and weapon at the ready, he whirled. Again, all he saw was fireflies.

Now the shuffling sound was behind, between him and his own house.

"Damn!" Stallings whispered. "I'm getting the Hell out of here."

At a dead run, he entered the back door of his garage and bolted it.

What have I gotten myself into? he wondered as he willed his racing pulse to slow.

He peeked out the small window in the door, and his knees nearly crumpled in relief. Dogs! That was what he had heard. They were over there in the yard around Jennings' body.

They were big dogs, too, Stallings noticed as he watched two of them sit beside the dead man.

Strange, the Colonel thought. *It's almost as if they know he's dead as if they are keeping vigil.*

Then the largest of the dogs looked at Stallings, and a shiver of earthquake proportions ran down his back. Its eyes were light amber and dark gold. They stared with an intensity that he had never seen in a man, much less a domestic animal.

"Oh, my God," Stallings whispered.

* * * * *

Now, three days before the Fourth of July, Stallings took another swallow of gin as he sat alone by the pool. He remembered how those golden eyes had turned the blood in his veins to ice. He wanted payback. He wanted to see those eyes again. He wanted to extinguish the life from them with one well-placed shot.

Yet, deep down, he also knew that he was afraid of them. Stallings suspected that no mortal—not even he—could defeat this animal.

He hoped that the alcohol would give him the courage to turn his back on those black woods and go inside the house, where it was bright and safe. With shaking hands, Colonel John

Stallings, war hero and leader of men, poured more gin into the glass. He gulped it down and waited.

He prayed that inner strength would come to him before those damn eyes looked out from the darkness and into his soul.

CHAPTER TWENTY-TWO

"Oouuhh! Ooouuuhhh! Oooooouuuuuhhhh!"

Night music erupted from the direction of the sandstone arches. It spread out across the surrounding forest and filled the valley below.

The small hairs on the back of P.J.'s neck stiffened as she sat just outside the den under a moonless sky and listened. Stars shed enough light for tonight's babysitter to see five ears prick. The pups, too, heard the howls. Moe's left ear had healed from the bear attack, but probably would remain forever floppy.

The black pup was sprawled across P.J.'s legs when the singing began. But now he scrambled to his feet and joined in the chorus.

"Oh! Watch it," the girl said.

Her scraped knee had scabbed over nicely but remained tender to the touch. Other than that, she felt the best that she had since her abduction more than three days ago. A full stomach had much to do with that. She especially relished the "smashed cheese samich" that the boys had given her.

Yet, she continued to worry. Were the sandwich, the strawberries, and the rest worth the risk that she had taken? Did the father of the boys tell anyone about her?

Even worse, did he follow her to the den? She didn't think so. She looked back often as she returned. Plus, Bert and Ernie gave no signs that danger was near.

"Ouh. Ouh. Oouuhh," Moe cried in answer to the five adult wolves scattered about the Pickle Springs area.

P.J. covered her ears with her hands and laughed at the off-key attempt. She stroked the black pup's back. "Who taught you to sing?" she said.

Moe, however, would not give up. "Ouh. Ouh. Oouuhh!"

Suddenly the pup's howls turned from mono to stereo. Larry and Curly had joined in.

"Ouh. Ouh. Oouuhh! Oouuhh! Ooouuuhhh!"

In an instant, the three began to harmonize.

P.J.'s mouth fell open in disbelief at how quickly her wolf brothers had learned.

"Hey, you guys are good," she said.

Moe glanced briefly toward the babysitter with an I-told-you-so expression as the trio continued to howl.

"Ooouuuhhh! Ooouuuhhh! Ooouuuhhh!"

Now the three sang on-key with the adults across the valley. At the exact moment their voices meshed, a chill of iceberg proportions slid down P.J.'s back. Once more, she remembered the dream in which the wolves had saved her life and claimed her as a member of their family.

She recalled how — in real life — they had given her reason to live.

"I really do belong here," she whispered. "I really do."

*   *   *   *   *

She hadn't been so certain earlier that day when Arthur had pushed and bullied her to the den entrance, and Guinevere had literally dragged her inside. The white she-wolf had used her body to block off the opening while Arthur, Bert, and Ernie remained somewhere outside.

Packed in tightly against Auntie Em, P.J. started to get angry. A pup squirmed under each arm, and Moe licked the back of her neck. She could handle the musty dog smell and the close, hot air. And she even could accept the cracking of prey bones underneath her as she tried to shift to a more comfortable position.

But, darn it! she thought. *I don't like being forced in here.*

Sweat dripped off her forehead and ran down her nose while the wolves panted quietly in the sardine-like silence. One of the gray pups — Larry, or was it Curly? — slurped at the salty perspiration on P.J.'s face, and she pushed the animal away. Seeing the shove as an invitation to play, the young wolf grabbed an ear and tugged.

"Cut that out!" the girl whispered, again pushing the pup away. This time she covered the side of her head with a protective hand.

Seconds seemed like hours, and P.J. thought she would burst if she couldn't get back outside. Still, instincts told her to stay quiet. Hands covering her eyes, she told herself to breathe slowly and relax.

Just like I do when I go to the dentist, she told herself. *Only there it's a lot cooler and more comfortable.*

Arthur and Guinevere had locked her in here to protect her from danger. And she was in danger. She briefly had forgotten about that. Both her own uncle and the man with the red tattoo wanted her dead. Did they know she wasn't dead? Were they searching for her?

Fortunately, the big, black wolf and his mate loved her just as they did their own pups. That's why they had pushed her in here. She was family.

Just across the creek, they had smelled — and then they had seen — the worst of the evil ones. He searched among the rocks and boulders.

* * * * *

Hours later, back out in the fresh air, no threats were near. P.J. wanted to sing with her family. If the pups could do it, so could she.

"Aoouuhh! Aoouuhh!" she cried.

But her howls were a pale imitation of the real thing.

From the diaphragm, not the throat, she told herself, remembering voice lessons from boarding school.

The three pups and the five adults continued their song, only they seemed to be two or three times as many. Their voices came together and then slid up and down the scale with soul-stirring majesty.

"Ooouuuhhh!   Ooouuuhhh!   Oooouuuuhhhh! Oooooouuuuuuhhhhhh!"

P.J. tried again, this time in the way she had been taught to sing.

"Aoouuhh! Aoouuhh!

"Darn it," she hissed. "Why can't I get it right?"

Then she remembered what her father once had told her during one of their Christmas vacations together. P.J. had wanted to learn to ski but just couldn't seem to get it right. She spent more time on her bottom than she did on her feet.

"If you really want to do this, you have to put your heart into it," Ryan had said.

He helped the girl back up and brushed snow off her back.

"Skill is important, but heart is everything, especially when you are learning something new.

"Failure is only a temporary condition—unless you give up."

He then patted the left side of his chest with his right hand. "When you really, really want something, this is what will get you there. Okay?"

P.J. nodded. Then she steeled herself with grim determination and pushed off—only to stumble once more.

All that day and the next, she continued to fall down the slopes. But always she got back up, more determined than ever. By the end of the trip, she had mastered the intermediate slopes.

"If I could learn to ski, I can sing," the girl whispered as she listened to the continuing chorus. "I really, really want this."

For an instant, she also knew that she wanted her father back. She loved her father as she loved the wolves. Did he know that? She wanted him to know it.

She wanted him to come for her. She wanted them to be a family again.

For now, though, the song was of most importance.

"I really, really want this," she said again.

This time P.J.'s howl came not from the throat, not from the diaphragm, but from deep in the core of her very being.

"Aooouuuhhh! Aooouuuhhh! Aoooouuuuhhhh!"

Without missing a note, her four-legged brothers looked up.

Gold eyes met brown, and they blended their voices into hers.

"Ooouuuhhh! Oooouuuuhhhh! Ooooouuuuuhhhhh!"

What P.J. had not been able to find in books or on the computer in the library, she now knew from first-hand experience. She knew why wolves howl. She knew because she realized why he was howling.

It was the most joyous, life-affirming experience of her life. She had read that wolves call to one another when they are sad, have found food, or want to warn of danger. But this exhilaration, this celebration of life under a starry sky, is at the heart of the matter.

* * * * *

So focused on the music they made, P.J. and the pups didn't see a man standing under a cedar tree, just uphill of the den. Nor did the pups catch his downwind scent.

He was a tall, heavy man with a beard. He wore blue jeans and a white tee shirt, as well as a red velvet cape that draped nearly to his knees. A large floppy hat with a feather sat atop his head. He carried a sturdy walking stick.

"Surely you are an angel, my fair maiden, for your voice is so sweet."

Frightened, P.J. looked up and saw the huge hulk of a man striding toward her.

"Who are you?" she asked, backing toward the den.

Larry, Moe, and Curly whined and tucked their tails between their legs.

"Fear not!" the man said, as he stopped and held up his free hand.

P.J. stood, with fists clenched. She was afraid her heart would hammer out of her chest. She couldn't, she wouldn't allow anyone to hurt the pups.

"Who are you, and what do you want?" the girl demanded.

P.J. felt amazement that she could be so forceful. Then again, she nearly had been killed. And now she had family, a family that she would sacrifice her life for. She was no longer the person that she had been a few days before. She was better, stronger.

The stranger knelt and bowed his head. "I am the protector of this domain and your humble servant."

The gesture startled P.J. Despite herself, she giggled. The stranger looked like one of those guys in a Three Musketeers movie.

"Come on," she said. "Who are you really?"

"My name is unimportant," he said, rising to his feet. "But my mission is vital. I am Mother Nature's defender. I fight back because she cannot."

P.J. smiled.

"Hey, you're the one who cut down all of those billboards," she said.

The man swept off his feathered hat and bowed. "Guilty, as charged."

The pups continued to whine as they paced behind P.J.

"May I sit and converse?" he asked.

The girl nodded. "Okay, but no funny stuff. I'm still not sure that I trust you. And I've got to call you something. What's your name?"

The man sat on a rock to the left of the den.

"I'll tell you mine if you'll tell me yours," he said.

"I'm P.J. Conners," she said. "And you are… "

"In another life, I was known as Theodore Wehling, a teacher of language. People called me 'Ted' or 'Mister Wehling.' Sometimes, behind my back, I'm certain that my students called me other things as well."

P.J. knelt and stroked the pups to calm them. "So that's why you talk funny."

He laughed. "Yes, I suppose that's correct, although I didn't talk this way when I was a scholar. It is only now, as I roam these woods, that I truly can be myself. And now I call myself 'Sir Tedrick,' Defender of the Natural Realm. But you can call me 'Sir Ted.'"

P.J. sat and wrapped her arms around her knees. The pups wiggled under her legs, lifting her feet off the ground. Both she and Sir Ted laughed.

"Why are you here?" he said.

"This is my family," P.J. answered simply. "This is my home — at least for now. The wolves protect me, and I protect them."

The man's jaw dropped in astonishment. "You live with wolves? Why, bless my soul, that's wonderful."

As he spoke, P.J. saw Arthur, Guinevere, and the other adult wolves standing in the shadows.

"Yes, it is wonderful," she said. "Without them, I wouldn't be alive.

"Now, would you like to meet the rest of the family?"

As if on cue, the adult wolves edged into the clearing. They carried their heads low, their ears back. Hair bristled on their backs.

Startled, Sir Ted began to stand up.

"I wouldn't do that if I were you," P.J. said. "The wolves haven't made their minds up about you yet. You don't want to go making any threatening moves."

P.J. didn't tell him that he already had been approved. If he hadn't been, the wolves never would have allowed him this close. Still cautious, they now wanted a closer look.

The big man eased back down.

"Perish the thought. Will you be so kind as to make the introductions? And please emphasize to them that I am a friend."

P.J. stood up, and the pups bolted for their parents. They jumped and squealed and squirmed—until Arthur gave a low growl.

"I named the big black one Arthur," the girl said.

"Don't tell me. His mate is Guinevere," Sir Ted added.

"That's right," P.J. smiled. "And two of the grays are Bert and Ernie, and the third is Auntie Em. She's usually the babysitter. But I took over tonight."

Arthur and Guinevere vomited up chunks of steaming flesh. The pups eagerly devoured them.

"Ah, yes, that takes care of my appetite for a while," the man said.

"You get used to it," P.J. laughed.

Sir Ted's eyes grew wide as saucers. "You don't mean…"

"Eeew! Of course not," the girl said. "That's not what I eat."

Ted smiled.

"I thought not," he said with a twinkle in his eye.

Just then, distant popping noises broke the peaceful silence of a summer night. The wolves instantly shifted from relaxed to alert. Their ears perked. Their powerful noses sniffed the air. Guinevere whined softly and nosed the pups toward the den.

"Someone must be celebrating the Fourth of July a little early," P.J. said.

"That's probably what it is," Sir Ted said softly. "But that came from the direction of the cabin. Could be those ruffians are drunk and shooting up the place again. They like to take target practice at beer cans. One night, they shot a bear."

"I saw the dead bear — at the cabin," the girl said. "You've been to the cabin too?"

"Yes, I have," he said.

"And you stay away from there. It's an evil place. Not a place for fair maidens such as yourself. I've been stopping up their plumbing, trying to make life as miserable for them as I can. Last night, I put a little 'sting' into my efforts. I enlisted the aid of some bees.

"They are doing something highly illegal down there. I'm sure of it. But I haven't yet been able to discover what."

Tell me about it, P.J. thought to herself. *They must be doing something illegal, or Uncle John wouldn't have told the sheriff to kill me.*

"Aren't you afraid?" she asked.

"Of course I am," Sir Ted said. "But evil must be vanquished wherever it is found. Now, I must bid you adieu."

The man stood, pushed his hat down on his head, and twirled his walking stick as expertly as if he were a drum major.

"And you stay away from that cabin," he said as he vanished into the trees.

CHAPTER TWENTY-THREE

"Just call me 'Dumb Dora,'" P.J. mumbled as she weaved slowly through the summer woods.

Water dripped from her ponytail onto her shoulders. It was still damp from her early morning bath in the small stream that ran near the den. The cool drops felt good in the already hot air of an Ozarks summer.

On her left wrist, she wore a good-luck bracelet. She had woven it out of wolf hair that she found in the den.

Bert and Ernie shadowed her, as silent as smoke.

Back at school, P.J. and her friends liked to watch scary movies. In most of them, they noticed a plot similarity. Early on, one of the characters—usually female—would do something incredibly stupid. She would stick her head into a dark attic to find out what was crawling around up there. She would go into the basement by herself to check the breaker box after the power went out. She would take a shower without closing the bedroom window. Or she would open the front door without asking who was there.

And usually, she would die in a particularly gruesome way.

All the girls—P.J. included—swore they would never be so stupid if put into a similar situation in real life. They would never be a "Dumb Dora."

Now P.J. was heading toward the cabin. It was the place where the man in black had been taking her to rape and probably murder her. It was the place where she had been betrayed by her uncle. It was the place where the sheriff had tied her hands and led her off to kill her.

It was the place that Sir Ted had just warned her was "evil." It was the place where the "fireworks" last night might have been gunshots.

Yes, she was a "Dumb Dora."

Bert and Ernie didn't want her going there either. The closer they came to the cabin, the more nervous they grew. They paced and whined every time P.J. paused to figure out her best route.

"But I might find a phone at the cabin—if it's empty," she said softly to the shadows that flanked her. Her phone had been in the backpack she left near the Civic Center.

"My Dad probably won't answer his cell. He's in Africa. But I can leave a message. I can tell him about Uncle John."

There was a reason that P.J. didn't share with the wolves. But she felt it deep in her heart. Like Sir Ted, she believed in vanquishing evil.

The cabin was an evil place. But before she could defeat the wickedness that was there, she had to learn exactly what was going on in that isolated place. Why did her own uncle want her dead? And why did he know that creepy guy with the red tattoo?

P.J. wasn't exactly sure where the cabin was in relation to the den.

"And even if you guys could talk, you wouldn't tell me, would you?" the girl said.

Their continued discomfort, however, told her that she was heading in the right direction.

Standing at the top of a hill, she stared down at the brush and boulders on its steep side. P.J. wanted to avoid poison ivy and snakes. She was extremely allergic to the three-leaf plant but had learned to identify it as a little girl at summer camp in Maine. Unfortunately, it grew abundantly in these woods.

"And no calamine lotion for miles," she said as she shook her head.

And snakes? Well, snakes didn't bother P.J. so much—if she saw them coming. She had held garter snakes and king snakes, and even a boa constrictor of two. She just didn't want any surprises. She had read that copperheads and timber rattlesnakes, both venomous, lived in the Ozarks.

She figured out the clearest route down the steep slope and worked her way down it. She grabbed the trunks of small trees for balance as she slid along, sending gravel tumbling in front of her.

At the bottom, P.J. paused to catch her breath. She sensed the ghostlike steps of her guardians on the leafy floor of the forest. She also noted the "rat-a-tat" of a woodpecker and the shrill cry of a hawk in the distance.

As she looked about, she also heard other sounds—boots crunching and men laughing! P.J. crouched behind an oak, watched, and waited. As soon as she could tell where the men were, she would make a wide arc around them. Like the man in black, they probably worked for her uncle as well.

They approached from the right. P.J. worked her way to the left, trying to be as quiet as possible. But her breathing seemed loud and labored to her. Her sneakers squeaked. And each crunch of leaves sounded like thunder.

She did not know that she moved nearly as silently as the wolves. She did not realize that her movements seemed loud only to her. Her hearing, too, had become wolf-like.

When she no longer could hear the men, P.J. stopped. A long, flat area lay ahead, and then another hill.

Her instincts told her that speed was important across the level land. She could be seen from a greater distance while crossing it, and the faster she went, the better. Arms pumping, she dashed toward the far hill.

When she reached its base, she moved behind a tree that hid her from the area where she had heard the men. As her heart rate slowed, P.J. breathed deeply, hands on her knees. Sweat ran down her sides. The scab on her leg itched intensely. And her breasts hurt from the bouncing that they had taken.

The pain reminded her of that morning on the basketball court when she had vowed to wear a sports bra the next time she shot hoops. Would there ever be a next time? Would she ever see her friends again—or her father? Why did life have to be this way?

P.J. just wanted to walk to the basketball court, pick up her ball and backpack, and go back to Mam Ma's. She wanted to climb into that soft, comfy bed and then wake up from this nightmare.

"Why can't I do that?" she wept. "Why can't I?"

P.J. listened as if hoping for a reply. No one answered. No spirit guide was here to help and encourage her.

She wiped her eyes with the tail of her shirt. She blew her nose into some oak leaves.

"I can't do it because this is real, not a dream," she said. "My uncle wants me dead."

Suddenly, a fierce light grew in P.J.'s brown eyes. "But that ain't gonna happen," she said fiercely. "He's going to pay for that, and so are his buddies!"

She ran up the hill, easily dodging boulders and poison ivy. At the top, she looked down on a cabin. It sat on a small rise overlooking a wide creek. At some point upriver, she suspected, her bathing stream probably fed into this larger water. Likely, she could get to the cabin by following the stream down to the creek and the creek down to the cabin.

But that didn't matter now. The cabin was below, just a few hundred yards away. P.J. looked for people around the building, in the woods around it, and along the creek. She saw no one.

Warily, she edged down the hill. Bert and Ernie whined softly. They would go no closer.

"That's okay," she whispered. "I can handle it."

P.J. darted from tree to tree until she reached the clearing. She crouched behind a large cedar. She watched. She listened. She saw no one. She heard nothing but the gurgling of the creek and crows arguing in the trees across the water.

Now that I'm here, what do I do? P.J. asked herself. *Oh, yeah, look for a phone. See what I can see.*

But what if the door is locked? What if someone is inside?

The girl rubbed her bracelet for luck and raced to the back-side of the cabin. She edged along the wall until she came to a window.

Slowly, P.J. raised her head and looked. No one seemed to be inside, but she couldn't tell much else. She saw wooden boxes and furniture. No sign of a phone.

Feeling more confident that she was alone, P.J. worked her way around the cabin to the front porch. The door was closed.

But it wasn't locked. P.J. pushed it open—and nearly puked. The odor was far worse than it had been her first time in the wolf's den. Her nostrils flared at the stale smell of sweat, the sour smell of beer, and the disgusting smell of an unflushed toilet.

She remembered what Sir Ted had said about blocking the plumbing. As she pinched her nose, she couldn't help but laugh.

P.J. looked around. Still no phone. She saw a desk, chairs, beds, and boxes, lots of boxes. She inspected the closest.

Its lid had been pried open. P.J. lifted it. Inside she saw black rifles, like those she had seen in war movies. Soldiers used them to kill people. Several other boxes were the same size. Some were smaller. They contained ammunition, she guessed.

One box was much larger, and P.J. was starting toward it when she heard the crows squawk in alarm. She heard their wings beat as they flew away.

Someone was coming! Frantically, she looked all around. Only one door. She was going to be caught!

Now she heard boots on the steps.

"Hey, someone left the door open," a man said.

"Good idea," said another. "The place smells like a sewer."

P.J. thought of hiding behind the desk or the big box. But then she would be trapped. She looked some more.

A tall, dark figure blocked light in the doorway.

"Hey! Who are you?"

The crows' warning had provided precious seconds for P.J. to find an escape. Just as the two men entered, she dived out the window that Kendall had broken. Hitting the hard ground with her shoulder, she rolled and was up in an instant. She raced for the trees.

"Hey, you! Stop!"

Guns fired behind her. Dirt kicked up on both sides, just inches from her feet.

She was in the woods now. More shots. Bullets sliced through leaves and slammed into trunks.

"Come on! Let's get her! She's just a girl. How fast can she run?"

As she darted and dodged, P.J. heard the men crunching across the gravel around the cabin. She actually felt vibrations in the ground from their bulky bodies as they rumbled into the trees.

More gunfire. One bullet ricocheted off a rock with an ear-splitting whine.

Going up the hill was tougher than going down. P.J.'s feet felt as if they were made of lead. Her breathing seemed loud and ragged. She was certain that a bullet would strike her dead at any moment. Or, if not that, then the men would run her down. As one of them said, she was only a girl.

When she reached the top of the hill, P.J. no longer could hear the grunts of the men as they strained to catch her. They weren't shooting at her anymore, either. She just might make it.

She picked up speed going downhill. But she still was afraid she wasn't fast enough. The men would have more endurance than she had. They would keep coming until she fell from exhaustion.

Fear pushed her to run faster. P.J. didn't realize it as she flashed through the trees, but Bert and Ernie were forced to run hard just to keep up.

CHAPTER TWENTY-FOUR

Ryan awoke to find himself handcuffed to the bed. He smiled.

"Jackie," he called and waited.

His smile broadened into a grin as he recalled last night and earlier today. For a moment, he relived the lovemaking.

Then he remembered P.J., somewhere out there in those woods. Someone had kidnapped her, maybe even—God forbid—raped her. And someone didn't want Jackie and him looking for her.

"Jackie!" he yelled again, louder this time. "Come on, woman. Let me out of these. No more sex until tonight!"

He shook his right arm and rattled the cuffs against the bedpost. "Jackie! Enough is enough. Get me out of these."

Suddenly frustrated, Ryan pulled hard, pinching a nerve in his bicep. He yelped and cursed, grabbing for his right arm with the left.

"Jackie!" he cried, his unshaven face now crimson.

Holding on to his right wrist with his left hand, he yanked again. Neither the cuffs nor the post would give.

"Dammit! Jackie! Where are you?"

Ryan lay his left arm across his bare chest and paused for a breath. He listened, hearing only the steady hum of the air conditioner and the low "swish" of a ceiling fan over the bed.

He looked around. The window shades still were bright. But the sun no longer tried to penetrate.

"It's high now," he said. "Must be close to noon."

"Jackie!" he called once more, not really expecting a response.

Willing himself to calm down, Ryan noted pressure in his bladder.

"Oh, that's just great!" he said. "That's just terrific! Jackie! How could you do this to me?"

Gazing around again, he saw a full water glass on the nightstand to his right.

"Just what I need," he said.

Ryan turned his head to the left, hoping to find something that would help him escape. If he didn't get free of these cuffs in another minute or two, he was going to pee all over Jackie's rose-design sheets.

That's when he remembered that he had seen folded paper under the water glass.

Lunging for the note, he knocked over the glass. Fortunately, it was plastic. It thudded harmlessly to the floor. But not before it dumped half of its contents in Ryan's hiking boot. Ignoring the spill, he opened the paper and watched a small key fall to the floor.

"The Colonel called this morning. He wants to see me. Maybe he as a lead on P.J.," Jackie had written.

"Be back soon. Thought it was better if you didn't go along. Wait for me. Okay? I'll make it worth your while."

Ryan's pulse quickened. He hadn't argued with her about Stallings because she had been so defensive of him. But both logic and instinct told him that the Colonel was a bad guy. He was involved in P.J.'s disappearance, as well as the attempt on their lives.

And now, because of Jackie's blind loyalty, Stallings had been able to lure her alone and unprepared into a dangerous situation.

"How long has she been gone?" he said, no longer feeling a need to heed nature's call. "I've got to go after her."

But first, he had to unlock the damn cuffs.

"Arrrgghhh!" he grunted, as he reached with his left hand for the key.

His fingers stopped inches short. With his right hand locked to the post, he couldn't turn his body enough to touch the floor with his left.

"Now what?" he asked himself.

Ryan dropped his right foot to the floor – and into the spilled water. The wetness reminded him of his full bladder, and he grimaced.

He inched his foot toward the key. Closer and closer and closer. But not close enough. With clenched teeth, he willed it to reach just a little farther.

It did. He watched his little toe touch the key. Closing his eyes and straining with all his might, he lifted the toe. He extended it a quarter-inch and brought it down on the key. Quickly he pulled it closer.

Now what? He still couldn't reach it with his left hand.

He had to get free. Jackie was in danger. And his bladder was about to burst!

Bladder. Water. Wet. Sticky. Ryan pushed his foot back into the water and then stepped on the key. He pushed down hard, closed his eyes, and mentally crossed his fingers. Then, quickly, but carefully, he lifted his foot back onto the bed.

The key dropped out from under his toes and onto the sheets. He grabbed it with his left hand and unlocked the cuffs.

In less than five minutes, he had relieved himself and was dressed. Then he cursed himself for not being able to find his car keys.

"Dummy!" he said finally, as he thumped himself in the forehead with his right hand and raced out the door. "You must have left them in the Blazer."

Outside in the carport, he saw that wherever he had left them now was unimportant. Jackie had taken his sports utility vehicle and left her white cruiser.

"Damn!"

Ryan ran back inside to look for her keys.

* * * * *

Jackie smiled as she walked around Stallings' house toward the patio and pool. She figured that's where he and Cathy must be. No one answered the door, and his Cadillac was in the driveway.

She looked forward to having a good conversation with the Colonel. It had been too long since just the two of them had talked.

Her mood also was lightened by a mental picture of Ryan waking up handcuffed. She giggled.

Jackie did regret, though, that she had taken his car. After sneaking quietly outside, she discovered that she had grabbed Ryan's keys instead of her own. She didn't want to go back inside, for fear of awakening him.

Oh, well, he could always drive her car if he was too impatient to wait for her to help with the search. She hoped that he would wait.

Stepping into shade at the back of the house, Jackie took off her sunglasses and tucked them into the collar of her green tee shirt. She ran her hand down the ponytail that hung out the back of her baseball cap. And she looked up to see the Colonel smiling at her. He was dressed in loose khakis and a teal polo, looking as spit-and-polish as ever. His skin was bronzed to a perfect summer gold. Not a single white hair was out of place.

"Jackie, how good to see you," he said, extending his hand. "Would you like a drink? Cathy is visiting her mother next door and I'm just sitting out here, trying to unwind from a stressful week of newspaper publishing."

"Just water, please," the deputy said as she sat in a white, woven patio chair.

"I'm so glad that you could stop by," Stallings said as he handed her a glass filled with water, ice, and a slice of lemon. "How is the search going?"

He smiled as he sat across the table from Jackie. Even in the shade of the patio, his white teeth seemed to reflect sunlight. He took a sip of his gin and tonic.

"Not so good," she said. "I was hoping that you might have some information that would help us. Ryan is really stressed by the loss of his daughter. And I'm afraid that he's feeling a little paranoid."

Stallings locked his hands behind his head and stretched his legs under the table.

"Paranoid?" he said. "What do you mean?"

Jackie looked down at her drink and nervously stirred the water with her finger.

"Well, I'm really embarrassed to mention this. You've been so good to me."

Stallings waited.

"Ryan thinks you might be involved. We were talking, trying to figure out what's going on around here. P.J. isn't the only one missing, you know. Wilson is too.

"And someone tried to kill us Thursday."

With an insincere look of concern, the Colonel sat back upright.

"Tried to kill you? Ryan thinks I did that?" he said. "Are you sure it wasn't just an accident? Rocks fall on their own sometimes, you know."

Missing his smoothly delivered insincerity, Jackie shook her head. "No, it wasn't an accident. Ryan saw someone, and we found…"

Her voice trailed off as she suddenly realized what her former commanding officer had just said.

"How do you know that a rock almost fell on us?"

Stallings grinned broadly as his right hand dropped below the table. Jackie's eyes met his. She felt the stirrings of panic in the pit of her stomach. Had she misjudged the man she trusted and admired for so many years?

Then she knew, knew with blinding certainty that Stallings was the key. He knew what had happened to P.J. and Wilson. He could tell her who tried to kill them at the arches.

Also, he was pointing a weapon at her below the table. Of that, she had no doubt.

Her training as a law enforcement officer kicked in. She must stay calm, she knew. Also, she must keep the Colonel talking until she had a chance to gain the advantage.

She forced a smile.

"Of course, it might have been an accident," she said.

Stallings stopped pretending. "No, Jackie, it wasn't an accident."

He raised the pistol.

"Put both of your hands on the table, please."

She obeyed.

"I didn't want you dead, Jackie," the Colonel said. "I like you. But you and Ryan are in my way, and I can't have that."

Jackie's green eyes flared with rage, but she stayed in control. "And did P.J. get in the way too?"

Stallings nodded. "I'm afraid so, and so did Sheriff Wilson. His death was a shame, too, because I was depending on him."

Jackie wanted to grab the gun. She wanted to pin Stallings' arm behind his back and twist it until he told her everything. She wanted to kick the son-of-a-bitch in the balls and pull out a handful of his perfectly combed air.

Instead, she leaned forward slowly and said in a low, even voice, "I looked up to you. I trusted you."

The Colonel smiled.

"Your mistake," he said.

"Why have you done this?" she asked. "At least tell me that."

Maybe, just maybe, I can stall him until Ryan charges in like the cavalry, she thought.

She knew that he didn't like or trust the Colonel. And rightly so, as it turned out.

Stallings relaxed a bit but kept the nine-millimeter pistol pointed at Jackie.

"Greed and power," he said. "What else is there?"

"Lots of things," she replied. "There's love and friendship. And there's honesty and loyalty, just to name a few."

The Colonel laughed. "Yeah, right. Those will fatten your bank account. Those will get you a winter home in the Florida Keys and a summer home in Maine. Those will make you one of the most powerful men in the country."

Jackie never had noticed before. Now she did: Stallings' blue eyes seemed to be made of ice.

"Everything about you is a lie," she said. "It's all pretense."

Stallings nodded. "And it's designed to help me get what I want. Are you really that stupid?

"Every day, people die because they get in the way of those who want to be president or senator or even governor or mayor. It's the way of the world—the natural order. It's the way those who should rule attain their rightful places."

"And your rightful place is?"

The cobalt crystal of his eyes showed black fire in their centers. For the first time, Jackie truly realized that her life could end this very day. Her pulse pounded at her temples.

"Oh, enough about me. Let's talk about you," he said with pretend modesty.

She could see once again the charming, sophisticated man that Stallings appeared to all the world.

Just as quickly, the evil returned in a fierce stare and twisted lips. "See how easy it is to fool people, Jackie?

"People are blind, and they are stupid."

Jackie shook her head. "Not so much so that they won't suspect something when I disappear. Ryan especially. He tried to warn me about you. And he's probably on his way over here right now."

Stallings smiled. "Ah, yes, Ryan. I see you drove his car. That means he will be in yours.

"I'm afraid that he won't make it over here. He's going to have car problems of a rather significant nature."

Jackie's jaw dropped.

"No! You can't!" she screamed.

"I'm afraid that I can and did," the Colonel said matter-of-factly. "The bomb was placed last evening."

The deputy's resolve to be strong dissolved in tears. Her head fell to the table, and she covered it with her hands.

"No! No!" she cried. "You can't. You can't kill Ryan!"

Stallings continued to talk calmly and evenly as if he hadn't noticed Jackie's outburst.

"Of course, now I have to make up a story to explain your disappearance," he said. "Ryan died for reasons unknown. Your car had some sort of explosive mechanical defect.

"But you…"

The Colonel stroked his chin with his free hand. "I think that you ran off to be with Sheriff Wilson. Yes, I like that idea.

"Of course, it's not very believable, if you stop to analyze it. But that's okay. It's not important that it be believable. It's just important that it is a tasty, acceptable morsel of gossip.

"People are sheep, remember? They will accept anything as long as it doesn't interfere with the boring routine of their boring lives."

Standing suddenly, he gestured for the sobbing deputy to rise. "I've revealed too much already," he said. "Not that you are ever going to tell anyone.

"I think that it's time for you to take one last drive."

Jackie rose slowly, head down, eyes rimmed in red. Rage and grief combined to make her nearly immobile. But she refused to submit completely. She leaned on the table and looked up into that hateful face.

"You won't get away with this," she said softly. "You'll see."

The Colonel offered his most condescending smile.

"But you won't," he said.

He grabbed Jackie roughly by the shoulder and pushed her forward.

* * * * *

Ryan tore through the bedroom and into the kitchen. He left behind drawers overturned, clothes pulled from hangers, and purses emptied.

"Where would she keep her keys?" he yelled. "Where are they?"

He looked for hooks on the backs of doors and on the side of the refrigerator. He ran back to the bed and crawled around it, hoping that the keys might have been knocked off one of the nightstands. He found only dust balls and an old sock.

"Where's the damned key?" Ryan yelled at a teddy bear sitting on an antique record player in the corner of the bedroom.

He stormed outside to feel under the sedan's bumpers and inside the wheel wells. He hoped that she might have taped an extra key there. Then he knocked aside garden tools and wiped spider webs off his face as he searched the storage shed at the back of the carport.

Back inside, he finally found a set of keys in the back of a desk drawer.

"What if I'm too late?" he said. "What if I lose P.J. *and* Jackie?"

He dropped the keys, picked them up, and raced for the carport. His left boot squished from the water inside, but Ryan didn't notice.

He pulled open the cruiser's front door, leaped inside, and slammed it after him in one quick motion. He jammed the key into the ignition and turned it.

"I'm not going to lose you, Jackie," he said. "I'm not going to lose you."

CHAPTER TWENTY-FIVE

Crater Kendall had always been a faster runner than his younger brother. That was why Dawson had spent time in a juvenile facility, and he hadn't.

Twenty years later, Crater still was faster. Or maybe he was just more frightened.

Knees pumping and elbows swinging, he leaped the creek and didn't look back.

"Crater! Wait for me! Craaaater! Don't leave me!" Dawson cried.

Still running, the elder Kendall looked over his shoulder. His sharklike eyes scanned the woods for danger. He saw none, but, still, he couldn't will himself to stop. Dawson would have to take care of himself.

"Craaaater! Help!"

"Dammit!" Dawson huffed as he slowed. He bent at the waist, hands on his knees, trying to regain his breath.

How had such a good day gone bad so quickly?

* * * * *

First, Crater had placed the bomb that he was certain would kill Jackie Novak and Ryan Conners. That had lifted his spirits considerably. Then he had picked up his brother at the bus station. Although he pretended not to be, Crater was happy to see Dawson.

Sporting a buzzcut hairstyle, perfectly manicured nails, and two rings in each ear, his younger brother was the same pudgy, effeminate man that he had been since getting out of reform school. Such an appearance disgusted Crater. But he knew that Dawson idolized his older brother. Otherwise, the younger

Kendall wouldn't have come running when he whistled. And that was good, both for his ego and for the job coming up.

Still, Dawson couldn't resist teasing Crater about the bee stings. "You've got so many lumps on your face now that I can't tell which one is your nose," the younger brother laughed.

"You should have seen me yesterday," Crater said, and slapped his brother on the back.

He hit him harder than he should have, but Crater thought Dawson deserved it for his disrespect.

The passing of time had reduced the swelling of the stings. But Crater believed that beer was the best thing to stop the itch. When they reached the cabin, he went inside for a six-pack.

As he stepped back outside, Crater wondered why none of the other guys were around. Someone should have been keeping an eye on things. He decided not to worry about it. He and Dawson were here now.

Crater tossed his brother a cold one and the two relaxed in lawn chairs under the shade of the small front porch. Quickly they caught up on which family members still were in prison and which had been paroled. The older Kendall wasn't particularly happy to learn that their mother had earned time off her sentence for good behavior.

She had beaten both of them on a regular basis when they were kids. She had allowed a boyfriend to sexually abuse them. She deserved to be behind bars for the rest of her life. Or, better yet, she should be rotting in Hell.

Suddenly two men rounded the corner of the cabin, both heaving for breath. They wore camouflage suits and carried rifles.

"Have a beer," said Crater, feeling generous.

"Someone was snooping around here," one of the guards huffed. "Looked like a girl. We chased her. But she got away. Looked like she was headed back into the hills on the back side."

Crater Kendall smiled broadly. Even his adoring brother thought the smile looked particularly nasty.

"Come on, Dawson," Crater said. "We're going hunting."

* * * * *

Looking back toward the creek as his breathing slowed, Crater spied wisps of black and white moving among the trees on the other side.

Then he heard growls, followed by a shriek of mortal agony.

"Ah, shit," Crater said as he pulled his knife from the sheath at his ankle.

He headed back down toward the creek. He had brought his brother into this. The least he could do was save his butt. Or rather whatever was left of it. From the sound of things, he figured those wild dogs had already removed a big portion.

As he trotted back toward the sounds of the skirmish, Crater cursed his brother for losing the rifle that he had given him. In truth, though, they both had surrendered their weapons within seconds of the ambush. They had been bowled over from behind, knocked flat on their faces by what seemed like locomotives.

The elder Kendall knew immediately that the impact had caused him to drop his rifle. He rolled sideways to avoid being hit again and scrambled onto his feet, knife drawn. What he saw froze the blood in his veins.

Four large, snarling dogs stood over the rifles. Ears flat and lips curled, the beasts flashed long, sharp teeth that Crater knew could rip out a man's throat in seconds.

Never an athlete, Dawson was slower to rise. He pushed himself up off the ground and looked over his shoulder. His brown eyes grew as big as saucers.

"Crater!" he hissed. "What's going on? You never said nothin' about no wild dogs."

"I didn't know anything about any wild dogs, you idiot!" Crater hissed back. "Now, come on. We're going to have to run for it!"

Crater leaped the creek before he realized Dawson wasn't with him.

Now he was going back to rescue his sorry-excuse-for-a-brother. Knife at the ready, he prepared to leap the shallow water. Suddenly, he stopped, put the knife away, and started running back up the hill, away from the wild dogs and whatever remained of his brother.

Looking back over his shoulder, he said, "Hell, no."

That was the same thing he had yelled twenty years ago when he escaped, and his brother was sent away for burglary.

*   *   *   *   *

The wolves never had attacked humans before. They hadn't wanted to this time, but they sensed that wolfchild was in danger from these two evil men marching toward their den.

Still, they avoided a direct attack. They waited until the two crossed the creek, and then they closed in from behind. Bert and Ernie moved to the sides while Arthur and Guinevere broke into a run.

No visible signal was given. But, as if on cue, the two powerful animals slammed into the backs of the evil ones. The men dropped their black sticks as they went flying forward and fell.

Killing them would have been a simple matter of moving in and ripping out their throats. But the wolves didn't want the intruders dead, especially near their den. They just wanted them to leave.

Instead of charging, as they might have with a deer or other prey, the wolves kept their distance. Bert and Ernie rejoined their leaders, and the four of them challenged the humans with snarls and raised hackles. They hoped that the evil ones would pursue them back across the stream and away from the den.

One of the men moved into a threatening posture, but then both of them ran. One went to the left and the other to the right, around the wolves.

Surprised by this, the wolves hesitated for a moment, but then instinct took over. The pack pursued. Arthur and Guinevere chased the more threatening of the two while the grays set off after the other.

The alpha pair stopped at the creek and watched the man scrambling madly up the slope. They would go no farther. Instead of heading back to the den, however, they continued to patrol the bank, in case the evil one returned. They whined and yipped as they paced, upset by being forced to defend their family.

The grays, meanwhile, had no difficulty in running down their quarry. He stumbled more often than he ran as they growled and nipped at his heels.

Once, when the human's backside presented a target too tempting to resist, Bert dashed in and bit the man's fleshy thigh. The taste was repulsive, though. That's why he didn't hold on and twist as he would have with an animal that he intended to eat.

The man howled but in a way much more unpleasant than a wolfsong. Then he rose to his feet once again and ran for the creek. Bert and Ernie followed leisurely. This human was no longer a threat, they knew, and besides, he tasted terrible.

*　*　*　*　*

Inside the den, the two gray pups nestled quietly against P.J.'s belly, but the little black one snuggled right under her chin, wiggling about and having a grand old time.

"Ouch!" P.J. hissed. "Moe, you bit my ear!"

Auntie Em looked at them with disapproval. Moe quieted down.

That's when P.J. thought she heard someone yell. For a long moment, no one moved, not even Moe. P.J. saw the hair raise on Auntie Em's back as she stood guard at the entrance.

The girl was certain that she was the reason that they had been forced into hiding. The men were still after her. She would rather die than put her wolf family in danger. But that was just what she had done in her stupid desire to "vanquish evil."

P.J. felt her pulse quicken. She wished she were outside where she could run. No… She would not run. The pups couldn't keep up. She would fight for her family. She would throw rocks and kick and bite and scratch. Here, she and the little ones were trapped. If anything happened to Auntie Em, she would …

Just as quickly as it came, the danger passed. Auntie Em relaxed. Moe started squirming again.

P.J. wiped her face and tried to dry her hand on her damp shirt. Because of both the danger and the heat, she would have been sweating heavily even if the young female wolf hadn't been blocking the entrance. As it was, she was drenched in perspiration—and puppy slobber. She wanted a bath in the worst way. In her mind, she smelled orange blossoms and saw mountains of soap bubbles all around her in a giant tub.

Moe licked her chin, bringing her back to reality.

Lying on her right side, P.J. slowly squeezed her left arm up to her face. Then she pushed her hand between her chin and the black pup. Unable to resist temptation, Moe clamped down on her fingers. P.J. closed her eyes and gritted her teeth to keep from cursing or crying. She wasn't sure which. She feared to look, certain that her hand had become a bloody stub. Sometimes being the only human in a wolf family was a real pain!

When she finally opened his eyes, though, she gratefully saw all five fingers by the light streaming in from the entrance. Auntie Em has moved outside. P.J. inhaled deeply of the sweet, fresh air. It was as if she had died and gone to Heaven.

Head cocked, Moe looked innocently at her. The girl pushed the pup over on its back and roughly rubbed its belly. It kicked back in delight. P.J. was so glad that she had not brought death to her family.

She then scrambled out of the den, followed by the young wolves.

CHAPTER TWENTY-SIX

"Aaaaaahhhhhhh! Stop iiiiitt!"

Eyes closed, hands clasped over her ears, P.J. cried for the insanity to cease.

"No, no, no," she told Sir Ted. "That's not the way you howl. Let me show you again."

Sitting on a lichen-covered rock in the moonlight, the teacher bowed his large, shaggy head.

"My apologies, dear lady," he said. "I must confess this wolf language remains a mystery to me. Please, show me again."

Moe, Larry, and Curly peeked around the trunk of a fallen cedar, grateful that the awful noise had ceased. If wolves smiled, that's what the gray female, Auntie Em, was doing as she lay above the den's entrance. Now that danger had passed, the rest of the pack was off in pursuit of supper.

P.J. hadn't told Sir Ted what she had done to cause that danger. She knew that he wouldn't approve.

Once more, she lifted her head and demonstrated. "Aooouuuhhh! Aooouuuhhh!"

Moe trotted over, sat beside the girl, and quickly joined in. "Ooooouuuuhhhh! Ooooouuuuhhhh! Oooooouuuuhhhh!"

Larry and Curly hastened to complete the quartet, and they made beautiful music together.

"Ooooouuuuhhhh! Ooooouuuuhhhh! Aooooouuuuhhhh! Ooooouuuuhhhh! Oooooouuuuhhhh!"

Despite the hot, humid air, Sir Ted shivered at the sound and felt the fine hairs rise on the back of his neck.

"My word, that's moving," he said when the four paused. "And If I hadn't seen you, I would have sworn by the sword

Excalibur that there were ten or twelve of you howling. It was a veritable lupine symphonic orchestra and choir.

"The way you harmonize and then change chords so smoothly is magic without equal."

"Yeah, I like it too," P.J. said. "It makes me happy."

"Now, remember. Don't howl from your throat. Start down farther in your chest and bring it up like… like…"

Sir Ted grinned. "Like I'm gonna puke?"

P.J. laughed. "Why, Sir Ted, that's so unlike you. I didn't realize that you knew such words."

The big man winked. "That one and a few others, dear lady."

Then he stood, took a deep breath, and, once more, aimed for the stars.

"Aaoueoahh! Aaoouuhh! Aoouuhh! Aoooouuuhhh! Aoooouuuuuhhhh!"

With the last cry, Sir Ted looked sideways down into the girl's face and beamed. Smiling, P.J. grabbed the big man's hand and squeezed it. Then she, too, joined in the wolfsong of happiness, as did the pups and their babysitter.

Their voices rolled down the mountain and up the other side, where they filled the air around the sandstone arches.

"Aooouuuhhh! Ooouuuhhh! Aoooouuuuhhhh! Ooouuuhhh! Oooouuuuuhhhh!"

* * * * *

Nearly consumed by grief, Ryan was slumped on one of those arches at Pickle Springs when the first howl came. It was short, and it was solitary. But it was enough. He fought back tears and smiled. Following what had happened on this day, he was startled that he remembered how to smile.

But wolfsong always could do that to him. Maybe because it reminded him of Carrie.

Also, the howl was the first real proof he had that wolves really were here. Now he had even more reason to hope that P.J. was alive. He should howl back. He should run toward the wolves yelling his daughter's name. He should be jubilant.

"I should jump off this rock, crush my skull, and end my misery," he said.

Now Jackie was missing too, and no wolf howl could make him feel better about that. She was the first woman whom he had loved since Carrie. She had provided the emotional support that he so desperately needed. Now she had disappeared without a trace.

"That son-of-a-bitch Stallings had something to do with it," Ryan said as he looked at the black valley below. "There's not a doubt in my mind. But how do I prove it?

"And if only I had gotten there sooner, I could have saved her."

As he threw a stone that clattered on a rock below, Ryan cursed his bad luck.

*   *   *   *   *

None of the three keys that he found in the desk drawer would start Jackie's cruiser. He had rattled each one back and forth in the slot. He had turned and twisted it, hoping against hope that he could disable the lock and turn over the engine. Finally, sweat running off him in rivers, he had given up. He was afraid that he would break off one of the keys in the ignition.

Ryan figured he wasted a half hour trying to start the car. He didn't know the area well, but he estimated Stallings lived at least five miles away. He tried to call him, but no one answered. He phoned for a taxi and learned Parkland had only one. It couldn't pick him up for at least an hour.

Ryan put on a dry shirt and shorts and downed a quart of water from the refrigerator. Then he alternately jogged and ran the five miles.

By the time he reached the Colonel's house, another shirt was plastered to his back. Blisters were breaking on his feet. He paused to catch his breath and look around before walking up the driveway.

Stallings' white Cadillac was there, parked in the shade of large oak trees. But his own sports utility vehicle was nowhere to be seen. Jackie had said she was coming here. So where was his car?

As Ryan trudged up the walk, the man he believed to be responsible for P.J.'s disappearance opened the front door.

"You look like you could use a cold drink and a dip in the pool," the Colonel said, a broad grin on his face. "Come on around to the back and sit in the shade while I fix you something."

Ryan followed but did not sit. The pool called him to jump in and cool off, but he ignored it.

"Where's Jackie," he said.

Stallings looked up from the portable bar. "She's not here," he said. "She stopped by earlier, and we had a nice chat. Then she left."

Ryan leaned on the back of a white, woven patio chair, the same one that Jackie had sat in a few hours before. "Where was she going?"

The Colonel handed his second visitor of the day a glass of water. "Didn't say. I would have guessed she was going back to you. You two have turned into quite an item in our little town."

Stallings sat down. He crossed his legs at the knee and folded his arms across his chest. He displayed that blinding smile that was his trademark.

"I don't believe you," Ryan said, stepping from behind the chair. "Where is she?"

Stallings suddenly turned solemn. He stood and stepped inches away from his guest's face. He directed his best icy stare into Ryan's dark blue eyes. The Colonel never had met a man who wouldn't flinch and back down when he used this tactic.

"I never did like you Conners, and the feeling is even more so today. You can leave now."

Ryan caught the glare and returned his own with the same intensity. He moved closer. "The feeling is mutual, believe me. Now, where is Jackie?"

"Get out, and don't come back," Stallings said.

Ryan nodded.

"All right, I'll go," he said. "But I'll be back. You can count on it."

Ryan walked across the backyard to see about borrowing Mam Ma Jennings' car. As he stepped between the shrub roses, he heard a glass shatter behind him. He didn't know if the breakage was caused by an accident or an angry outburst.

He hoped it was the latter. He hoped that Stallings was upset. It had been his experience that anger makes men careless and easier to outsmart. He just hoped that he would have the time to save P.J. and Jackie as he engaged the Colonel in a battle of wits.

Ryan told nothing about what had just happened to Cathy or Mam Ma. He said that he had taken his car to a garage for service. His former mother-in-law was happy to loan her red Ford Taurus to him. He made polite conversation for about five minutes and then left.

By the time he reached Pickle Springs, the sun was setting. Its rays turned high white clouds to dusty rose. He had hoped against hope that Jackie would be there. She wasn't.

So now he sat on the arch, feeling as if he had never been so lonely and devastated in his life. The cool sandstone comforted his tired legs, but he took no consolation from it. The sweet scent of honeysuckle wafted up from the bush below but brought him no pleasure.

Bone-tired and mentally exhausted, he watched darkness creep across the sky from the east and silent bats wheel above the creek below. He heard a barred owl begin its sad song. Neither the sight nor the sound, however, registered with his senses. Nothing could stir him anymore. Nothing, that is, except despair.

It grew as a great hard lump in his chest and pushed and pushed. Finally, it escaped as soul-wrenching sobs that wracked his body. Tears erupted next, and Ryan covered his face with his hands.

"Oh, God," he cried. "Please let this be over. Please."

And then he heard the first howl, proof that wolves really were here. It was short, not enduring as wolfsongs usually are. Yet it comforted as if it had been the voice of a loved one. He smiled.

Still, the howl could not sustain. Jackie's disappearance, combined with P.J.'s, was just too much. The yowl satisfied only as would a last cigarette for a man awaiting a firing squad.

Ryan cursed himself. First, he had failed his daughter. Then, he had failed the first woman he had loved in nearly a decade.

He still wanted to die, to leap off this rock, and silence his pain. He knew that Stallings was to blame for the loss of his loved ones, but he could do nothing to prove it.

Just as he hurled a stone into the valley and wept for his misfortune, the next howl began. It was the worst that he had ever heard. Ryan paused, his arm still outstretched.

The sound so stunned him that he forgot his pain.

"If a wolf can be tone-deaf, that one is," he said and found himself chuckling.

In seconds, one wolfsong had made him smile, and another had made him laugh.

How can this be? he wondered.

Then came a true wolf chorus, and Ryan thought his heart would burst. He closed his eyes and leaned backward on the rock. His body was a dry sponge, and this joyous music filled it with life once again. It seeped into every pore and filled him with determination. He refused to surrender to grief, anger, and exhaustion.

"You're with them, P.J. I know you are," he sobbed. "And I will find you. I promise I will."

CHAPTER TWENTY-SEVEN

The truck arrived at the cabin well after midnight. The driver turned off his headlights and stepped down from the cab. He wore a baseball cap, dirty yellow tee shirt, and jeans. Three days of beard stubble covered his face.

He squinted as a flashlight suddenly shined into his face.

"Hello, Evans. How was the trip?"

The beam lowered.

The driver pushed his cap up and looked around. Under the starry sky, he saw a half dozen other beams scattered around. He couldn't see who carried them.

"Fine, Colonel. Got a big load for you. They're crammed asshole to elbow in there."

The driver turned back to the cab and grabbed a black leather pouch. "Your cut. Should be a hundred-thousand and some change in there."

Evans walked around to the back of the truck. He slipped a bolt back and opened the doors.

"Estamos aquí. Hora de salir," he said. "We are here. Time to get out."

Several men jumped down first. Then, they began to help others, including women and children.

"Vaya con estos hombres," the driver said. "Go with these men."

One of the men from the truck stepped forward. "¿Adónde vamos?" he asked. "Where are we going."

"Usted comerá y dormirá. Le llevarán mañana a donde usted vivirá y trabajará," Evans replied. "You will eat and sleep. Tomorrow, they will take you to where you will live and work."

"Yeah," said a half-whispered voice behind one of the flashlights. "Tonight, you'll get a really good night's sleep."

The Colonel turned his light in the direction of the voice. "Enough of that!" he snapped.

"Crater, take these people to their quarters."

Almost invisible in his black shirt and jeans, Kendall stepped forward.

"Venido," he said. "Come."

More than fifty men, women, and children followed him along the shore of the creek. Some stopped briefly to rinse their faces in the water. One young mother dipped a rag and gently put it on her baby's forehead.

The other men with flashlights fell in behind and along the sides. Evans and the Colonel watched as the group slowly disappeared around a bend just upstream of the cabin.

"Business is booming," Evans said. "We can expand if you want to buy another truck. Illegals love the idea of having a job and place to live waiting for them. They'll pay all that they can beg, borrow, or steal to get here."

Stallings rubbed his chin. "I'll think about it. Right now, we have to take care of these, and I've got some other important business.

"I'll be in touch."

The driver gave a half-salute. "See you, Colonel."

Evans climbed into the cab, turned the truck around in the gravel, and headed back up the dirt road.

Colonel John Stallings followed him in his white Cadillac. Kendall would take care of the rest.

* * * * *

P.J. bolted upright from her bed of cedar boughs. She wasn't sure what had awakened her. Maybe it was the whining and pacing of the wolves. Maybe it was the explosions that she now heard in the distance.

"It's okay," she told her wolf family. "The Fourth of July is coming up. Someone is setting off fireworks, just like the other night. Nothing to worry about."

"Pop, pop, pop! Pop, pop, pop!"

But as P.J. listened, she realized that the sounds came from the direction of the cabin. Those men had weapons, not fireworks. Lots of weapons. She had seen them.

Suddenly, her heart thumped heavily. Could they be shooting those guns? And if they were shooting them, what were they shooting at? Beer cans for target practice?

She knew that they'd killed a bear. Maybe they were shooting another one. Or maybe a deer. No, that was too much firing to be directed at one animal. Or even at beer cans.

Maybe the noise *was* fireworks. Maybe the men got drunk and were shooting Roman candles and skyrockets.

But P.J. didn't see any flashing lights in the sky to suggest that.

And the noises. There were too many "pops" too close together.

Maybe they were lighting firecrackers. Yes, that had to be it. They were drinking beer and lighting firecrackers. Possibly they were blowing up cans and bottles, the way that little boys do.

But P.J. could not imagine the man in black doing anything playful. He was evil. And he was there, at the cabin.

The pups were outside the den now. They scampered to her, and she held them. Auntie Em edged closer but stayed out of reach. The pups loved her tickles, kisses, and caresses. But P.J. had yet to touch one of the adults. They kept their distance, and she respected their space.

She was glad that she had the pups, though. She needed something to hold on to right now. If those weren't fireworks that they were hearing, then something terrible was happening.

P.J. wrapped her arms around all three pups. Moe licked her face, not realizing that he was washing away tears.

*   *   *   *   *

They walked in near blackness. A few beams of light showed the way to those in the front and along the sides of the group. But Maria and Pedro had been forced into the middle with their daughter, Elena. They had become separated from their son, Miguel, and Maria was frantic with worry.

Yes, he was somewhere close by. Probably he was walking with friends that he had made on the truck. But being close wasn't enough. Something was wrong. She could feel it. She wanted him by her side.

Pedro carried little Elena and whispered in her ear to keep her calm and quiet. Gravel crunched under their sandals. Sweet-smelling water ran nearby. Some tried stopping to wash their faces and to drink. Others fell to their knees, sick from travel. The men prodded them on.

They were so tired and hungry.

And Maria was afraid. Many, many hours ago, the man who had taken their money had seemed so nice and helpful as they climbed into the truck.

Then, the long trip quickly had turned into a nightmare. The air conditioner was too weak to keep them cool. The driver would not let them out when he stopped. They were forced to relieve themselves in the truck. It was so humiliating.

Now the two men who had been waiting for them here did not smile. The leader's eyes were as cold as ice. Another in a black shirt had the bloodthirsty stare of a shark. Others waited in the background with flashlights. She could not see their faces but feared what they might look like.

She was afraid especially for Elena and Miguel. She and Pedro had brought them to the United States for a better life. They had worked two jobs each for months, saving every peso. They had borrowed money from any relative who would loan it to them. They finally had raised enough to pay for the trip.

Then they had paid the fee. They had climbed on the truck. And they had been brought to the United States. But this wasn't the way it was supposed to be. They were not supposed to be led away in the dark by strange men who did not smile.

They were told that they were being taken to a place where they could rest. But they had left behind the truck that had brought them from Texas and the only building they had seen. They walked into deeper and deeper darkness.

Suddenly, they stopped. Maria heard shrieks and cries from those along the edges of the group. What was happening? What could they do? Where could they run?

Most importantly, for Maria, where was Miguel? She could not stand the thought of her son being hurt or frightened.

"Miguel!" she called. "Miguel! ¿Dónde estás? Where are you?"

Then the night erupted. Thunderous explosions deafened them. As those who had been around Maria's family fell away, short, bright flashes of light blinded her.

Maria felt Pedro's hand squeeze hers. Then he, too, was falling, pulling her arm. Elena screamed. Maria lunged for the baby to shield her from harm.

But she could not reach the child. Dozens of fiery blows pushed her away, causing her body to jump and jerk as if she were a puppet on strings.

Maria fell silently among the many others who lay dead or dying in the black night.

PART SIX

ESCAPE

CHAPTER TWENTY-EIGHT

P.J. awoke to more puppy kisses. She hadn't thought that she would sleep anymore. Those noises were too troubling. Over and over, her mind had replayed the awful possibility: People might have died at the cabin last night. They might have been shot with those black rifles that she saw in the box.

At some point, though, she escaped into sleep. Now, the sun was high, the morning air was cool, and the wolf pups wanted to play.

P.J. didn't feel like it. Once again, her thoughts tracked onto endless replay. People had been murdered. She was certain of it.

She wished that she knew how to contact Sir Ted. Maybe he could help. But he was almost as ghostlike as the wolves. He was here one second and gone the next.

Also, P.J. really didn't know that much about him—just as he didn't know what happened to her at the cabin. As if by unspoken agreement, they didn't ask personal questions. Could she trust him?

Probably she could. The wolves had allowed him near her and their den. But it didn't matter since she didn't know how to find him.

So, on her own, P.J. had to do something, anything. She couldn't just stay up here, eat strawberries, play with the puppies, and pretend nothing had happened.

It had. She was certain of it.

The pups demanded attention. Curly pulled at her shirt. Moe and Larry prodded her with their noses.

"Not now, guys," she said, pulling her hair out of her eyes. "I'm sorry. I have to do something."

She pushed them away.

The pups didn't know human words, but her tone of voice startled them. They looked at her with cocked heads and questioning eyes.

"Ahhh," P.J. said. "I'm sorry. I didn't mean to do that. Come here."

Quick to forgive, they ran to her. She gave them furious belly rubs. Then she stood. "Okay, that's all for now. We'll play later."

I sure hope that we play later, P.J. thought. *I was almost killed down there yesterday. Now they know I'm out here, and they're going to be looking for me.*

P.J. washed her face and arms in the stream. She put her hair back into a ponytail and pulled up her shorts. They were looser than they had been a few days ago. No doubt about it, she had lost a few pounds on her diet of tomatoes, banana peppers, strawberries, and roasted minnows. Ewww! Now she wondered how she could have eaten those oily, smelly fish.

The weight loss made her happy, though. Her growling stomach did not.

Fourth of July is coming up, she thought. *Maybe today or tomorrow. I've lost track of time.*

That means hamburgers, hot dogs, baked beans, potato salad, watermelon…

P.J. shook her head to get rid of those mouth-watering visions.

As she ate her breakfast strawberries, she looked up the hill. On the other side, the pups were either wrestling with one another or harassing their parents.

"I hope that you don't get hurt because of me," she said softly. "I hope that I'm not putting you at risk by being here. But you're the only family I have."

She looked downstream. Bert and Ernie stood there with sunlight on their shoulders. Their eyes met hers. They were waiting for her.

The wolves knew. Somehow, they knew not only where she was going but how she planned to get there.

P.J. smiled.

"Thanks, guys," she said. "I'm glad you're with me. But please be careful. Those are bad people down there."

Bert and Ernie turned and vanished into the shadows. P.J. followed. She was confident that this stream emptied into the creek that ran by the cabin. Once she reached the junction of the two, she would turn left and head downstream. Eventually, the cabin would be on her left.

The girl didn't know how or why she knew this. But she knew. "Maybe it's my wolf intuition," she said softly. "Maybe I know the same way that Bert and Ernie know."

What P.J. didn't know was whether this route would be longer or shorter than the one she had taken yesterday. That didn't matter. It would be safer. Those men had seen her running up the hill behind the cabin. Almost certainly they would be watching for her there.

As P.J. followed the water, she thought again of Fourth of July foods—and Fourth of Julys in general. She and her father weren't always together on that holiday, as they were at Thanksgiving and Christmas. But she remembered some happy ones with him.

One Fourth, her father took her to Cape Cod. Even in July, the water was cold there. It took her breath away when she dived in. They watched the fireworks at Provincetown. They fished for stripers. They built sand castles. They rode a bicycle built for two. They wore funny bibs and ate lobsters. They ate boiled clams—"quahogs," they called them—with potatoes, corn, sausage, and onions.

P.J.'s stomach gurgled. "Oops, tummy, sorry about that," she said. "You and me both. I sure would like some French fries.

"But no more thoughts about food. I promise."

The stream was widening now, as well as growing deeper. P.J. edged into knee-deep water to avoid a patch of poison ivy. The chill of the water sent goosebumps up her legs, onto her body, and down her arms.

As she trudged along, tiny bits of gravel worked their way into her shoes.

"Great," she said. "I'm hungry. I'm cold. I have rocks in my shoes. Now all I need is for my period to come a little early and I'll be all set."

P.J. couldn't help herself. She laughed. "My period." It sounded funny. It sounded as if she were so grown up now that she had started menstruating two months ago.

"Well, I'm not grown up," she said. "I'm a twelve-year-old girl. I still sleep with stuffed animals. I have kittens on my pajamas. I have no business being out here by myself. I want to go home!"

Tears poured down her cheeks as P.J. sloshed toward shore. She climbed up on land and plopped down on a fallen tree. Huge sobs wracked her body. She dropped her arms to her knees and lay her head on her forearms.

"I don't know what I feel anymore," she cried. "Why am I going where someone wants to kill me? I'm so tired and confused. And I'm so hungry. I want to go hommmme!"

Slowly, the tears ran dry, and her body stopped shaking. Once more, P.J. heard the rush of the water nearby and felt the warmth of the sun on her back. But she couldn't move. She couldn't speak. She was exhausted, both mentally and physically.

That's when she felt a wet nose pushing under her left arm. She resisted.

It insisted.

Finally, P.J. raised her head. When she did, she looked into golden eyes. A huge tongue gently flicked a tear from her cheek.

"Bert!"

She leaned to embrace the wolf, and then quickly stopped herself as the animal backed up. P.J. reached her hand toward him and stroked the thick fur on his neck. He moved closer and licked her arm.

Ernie came shyly to her other side and sat down. P.J. extended her right arm to him. He sniffed and then licked it. She scratched around his ears.

The three sat there quietly for several minutes, side by side by side.

P.J. didn't want to feel better. She wanted to give up. But despite herself, she found strength returning to her body and, more importantly, her spirit. All that stuff that she had said was unimportant. What was most important was that she was not alone.

She had a family. She loved these wolves and they loved her. In fact, they loved her so much that they overcame their own fears and allowed her to touch them. They shared her sorrow. And, by sharing it, made it lighter and easier for her to carry.

P.J. still didn't understand why she had to go on to the cabin. It was dangerous. The man in black might be there with his hateful smile and his deadly knife. But it was the right thing to do. She was sure of it. Once again, she thought of Sir Ted's insistence that "evil must be vanquished."

* * * * *

P.J.'s instincts had been correct. The small stream did flow into the larger creek. As the girl turned left, she noticed dark clouds building.

Probably going to rain today or tomorrow, she thought. *I'm lucky that it hasn't rained while I've been with the wolves. That den would not be my favorite place to get out of the weather. Wet wolves would be as bad as wet dogs. Yuck!*

Instantly the air seemed cooler. The trees taller. The day darker. P.J. didn't mind.

It will be easier for me to sneak around and not be seen.

P.J. wondered where Bert and Ernie had gotten to. They had been staying within a few yards of her. Now they were nowhere to be seen. Nor did she hear any movement among the shadowy sycamore trees along her left side. In fact, she heard no sounds at all except for the rush of water. No birds sang. No squirrels chattered.

Must be getting close to the cabin. Animals are afraid to be too near to it. Look what happened to that poor bear.

As she rounded a bend, P.J. stepped over a fallen tree lying across her path. That's when she heard the roar. Looking up, she saw crows and vultures fly from left to right across the creek. Whatever had made that sound frightened them. The crows squawked in anger at being disturbed.

The girl cocked her head and listened.

No, that roar is not coming from an animal, she decided. *It's a car or truck. No, something bigger than that.*

P.J. slowed her pace now. She must be careful. She suspected that she was fairly close to the cabin. That meant the men making those sounds probably were the same ones who had tried to shoot her the day before.

Up ahead, she saw live, green trees give way to dead ones. Their broken branches lay on the ground around them like fallen corpses. Her heart quickened.

I haven't been here before, she told herself. *Or have I?*

Beyond the gray trees, she saw an open area. It followed the creek around a bend. Steep rock walls lined the opposite shore.

The creek was like this where that man chased me, she thought. *That's it. Has to be. No big deal.*

P.J. stepped carefully among the fallen branches. One wrong move, and she could trip. Possibly she would fall on one of the many sharp ends that pointed skyward. She shuddered at the thought.

As she cleared the biggest cluster of trees, the roar sounded much closer. But she couldn't see anyone or anything like a truck or a tractor.

Have to be careful now. Can't let them see me. Might not get away a second time.

Just ahead, P.J. saw something large and dark near the water.

Is it alive? Doesn't seem to be.

Cautiously she crept from trunk to trunk. The dim light didn't help her vision. She edged a little closer. Up the hill, the roar wasn't growing any louder. She moved closer.

The bear! It was the remains of the bear. That's what the vultures and grows had been feeding on when the roar scared them away.

As P.J. studied the bear's body, she suddenly realized that this was much more than the creek where she had been chased.

"This is the creek of my dreams," she whispered. "This is where I saw the bones."

Icy fingers of fright walked down her spine.

P.J. didn't want to go forward. But she refused to go back.

"I have to find out what's going on," she said through clenched teeth.

She held her nose as she scampered by the bear's body. She refused to look at the remains, but P.J. could hear flies buzzing all about the rotting flesh. The roar remained steady at the top of the hill.

As she stepped over one more fallen branch, she looked back at the bear. That's when the skeleton grabbed her foot—just like in the dream.

P.J. Conners knew that men nearby wanted to kill her. She knew that the slightest sound could give her away. She knew that she must remain as quiet as possible if she were to find out what awful things her uncle was doing.

But she could not help herself. When the skeleton grabbed her, P.J. Conners screamed.

And screamed again as she fought to free herself. Away from the icy grasp, she almost ran back toward the dead trees without looking back. She didn't want to see what awful thing had grabbed her. She didn't want to have nightmares about it for the rest of her life.

Yet she had to know. She squeezed her eyes shut. Then she turned, expecting to confront a horror that she could not imagine.

She didn't see a grinning skeleton, however, when she finally opened her eyes. She saw flesh. It belonged to a boy, maybe her age or a little older, lying on the other side of the branch. He had brown skin, black hair, and dark eyes. He wore blue jeans and a New York Yankees tee shirt. Dried blood coated a large, ugly bump just below his hairline.

His face showed no expression. His voice said no words. His eyes showed no life. But he reached for her.

P.J. ran back and, with all her might, pulled him to his feet. "Come on," she said. "We've got to get out of here."

She headed for the nearest deep cover, just at the edge of the clearing. The boy stumbled at first, nearly pulling P.J. to the ground. But then he regained his balance, and they plunged into the trees. P.J. pulled him down behind an oak.

"Okay, let's stop a minute," P.J. whispered.

The steady roar continued.

"Maybe they didn't hear me," she said. "Maybe we're safe."

She nibbled on her lower lip. "Listen, I've come this far. I have to see what's going on here. As soon as I find out, I'll get you out of here. I promise."

P.J. tugged the boy to his feet. She led him up the wooded slope, alongside the clearing. The roar grew louder.

As they neared the top, the boy realized where they were going. He pulled away from P.J. and shook his head violently. Then he grabbed her arm and tried to take her with him into the woods.

P.J. shook herself free. "No!" she said, "I have to see."

She crept from tree to tree. Looking back, she saw that the boy had not run away. But he was staying well back from her and deeper in the trees. The roar was noticeably louder now.

"That's fine," she whispered. "You stay out of sight. I'll see what's going on, and then we're out of here."

At the top of the hill, P.J. crawled among the low branches of a large cedar and looked out into the clearing. The roaring stopped. A bulldozer had pushed a large pile of sand and dirt to one side. Now it sat quietly to the side.

As the girl watched, two uniformed men carried over a large bundle and threw it into the depression that the bulldozer had made. The object appeared to be blue and red. Two more carried another of similar size but different colors. A fifth dropped in a smaller bundle.

They went back for more.

"¡Mi familia! ¡Mi familia!" the boy cried softly. "My family! My family!"

More bundles went into the pit. The men talked and laughed as they dumped them in.

And suddenly, P.J. knew the terrible secret of the cabin by the creek. Her eyes finally registered the horror of what she was witnessing. Those weren't bundles. They were people. She could see the arms, legs, and, yes, even the faces of the dead. She also saw wounds. And blood.

One man tossed the body of a baby as casually as if it were a bag of garbage.

P.J. lost her breath. Her arms and legs went numb. The humid air had turned into a solid mass pressing her into earth.

Her uncle and his men were killing people — lots of people.

She fought to regain her strength. If they didn't move quickly, they, too, would be killed and buried in the landfill.

"I'm so sorry," P.J. told the boy.

As she wiggled to free herself from the cedar, P.J. heard one of the men behind her yell.

"Someone's over there! Along the edge of the trees!"

"Come on," P.J. whispered as she grabbed the boy's hand. "We have to get out of here. Fast."

As they ran, P.J. realized that she couldn't move as fast with the boy as she could alone. Would those men catch them because of that?

"No, they won't!" she said determinedly.

Dodging a low limb, she wondered if Bert and Ernie were close by.

Of course, they were. They were her guardians.

She hoped that they wouldn't get hurt. But she could sure use their help.

P.J. and the boy reached the top of a hill and plunged down it. The boy tripped over a rock. As he fell, he took P.J. with him. They rolled and bounced to the bottom.

As the two regained their feet, P.J. heard someone crashing through brush at the top of the hill on the other side. Their pursuers were getting closer. Soon, they would be close enough to see P.J. and the boy. That meant they could shoot at them.

P.J. had no doubt that they would shoot. They were protecting a terrible secret, one that could send them to prison for the rest of their lives.

"This way!" she said. She pulled the boy to the right, where the ground was more level. If they went up another hill, they would be bigger targets.

*   *   *   *   *

From the top of the hill, Billy Newland saw the children. He was younger and faster than the other men. The girl had escaped once from those fat, old guys. She would not get away from him.

They still were too far away for a clear shot. But in a couple of minutes, he would be close enough. He licked his lips and ran down the hill. At the bottom, he raised his rifle and looked down the barrel. He put his sights in the middle of P.J.'s back—just before she dodged behind a tree.

"Too many trees," he hissed. "But it won't be long."

Holding his weapon across his chest, he resumed the chase.

Now his targets were climbing a hill. Few trees were on it.

He stopped next to a rocky bluff

"Perfect!"

Newland raised his rifle. Carefully he aimed at his target. He licked his lips. Nothing to block his line of fire this time. This would really get him in good with the Colonel.

A second before he squeezed, he heard a rustling above him. He looked up just in time to see what appeared to be an enormous, red bird plunging straight toward him.

"What the…?" he managed, just before the lights went out.

CHAPTER TWENTY-NINE

Ryan paced the gravel parking lot behind the fireworks stand. The man who had promised to meet him was late.

He realized the danger that he was in. But he was twice as desperate as he had been yesterday. Now two people whom he loved were missing. Plus, he had no evidence with which to prove that John Stallings, the most powerful man in Parkland, was somehow responsible. The anonymous caller had suggested that he could provide information "confirming your suspicions."

Of course, the caller also could be someone hired by Stallings to kill me here behind this giant tent alongside the highway, Ryan thought. *Right now, someone could be leveling a rifle at me from those woods.*

The wildlife photographer paused to put on his sunglasses. He peered at the trees that bordered this small lot used by employees of the fireworks stand. He closed his eyes then and took a deep breath. His whole body ached from the pounding that he had given it during the past few days as he and Jackie searched the mountainous area around Pickle Springs.

His head throbbed, too, probably because of lost sleep. With Jackie to keep him company, he hadn't minded so much. But now someone seemed to be firing up a jackhammer in his gray matter.

Ryan had napped for an hour or so at Pickle Springs, drifting off as he listened to the wolfsong. Then he had dragged himself back to Jackie's house, where he waited for the dawn. About five o'clock, a ringing phone jolted him from fitful sleep. The caller told him to be behind Benny's Wholesale Fireworks at ten.

He was there at nine, and now it was ten-thirty. Ryan backed into the narrow rim of shade provided by the edge of the tent and waited. The hot, thick air smelled of auto exhaust and coconuts.

Coconuts? Ryan wondered if his sense of smell could be short-circuiting because of exhaustion.

"Heck, everything else is," he said. "No reason for my nose not to fail me as well."

The only other time that he'd ever felt this weird combination of distress and goofiness was after a night of drinking tequila shooters in Mazatlan with some charter boat captains.

"No one can drink like sailors," he said, "especially me."

Still, he wished that he had a bottle of the gold liquor right now. He would drink away the pain and the sadness and...

Get a grip, man. You're losing it.

Once more, Ryan sniffed the air. "But I really do smell coconuts."

* * * * *

Out front, the customer parking lot quickly was filling up on this last day before the Fourth of July. Most came to buy fireworks, of course, since Benny had the best prices in the county. Others, usually guys alone or with their drinking buddies, came to see Benny's girlfriend, Tiffany.

Benny had built a little tanning platform for his well-endowed girlfriend, right next to the side entrance of the tent. He accessorized it with plenty of cold drinks, fluffy towels, and coconut-scented tanning oils. Sometimes, Tiff was joined by a bikini-clad girlfriend or two.

Parkland's religious community, especially the female portion, was enraged by this sales tactic. But Benny had been smart enough to open his business outside the city limits. No one in town could interfere.

Frustrated that the town could do nothing, some occasionally talked of putting a match to the business and closing it in a most explosive way. Being a regular churchgoer himself, Benny was well aware of these threats. In response, he kept plain-clothes security guards patrolling the aisles and parking lot at all times. From inside the tent, one of those guards kept an eye on Ryan.

About eleven, the exhausted photographer realized that he was going to pass out if he didn't sit down. He staggered back toward the car that he had borrowed from Mary Jennings.

Ryan no longer smelled the coconuts. He didn't notice that Tiffany wore an especially skimpy pink and green bikini today. He didn't care that Benny's intent was to use his luscious girlfriend to help him clear out inventory before he started reducing prices.

"Watch where you're going, you drunk!"

A blaring horn brought Ryan back to reality. His heart raced as he realized that he had nodded off as he walked. In his clumsiness, he nearly had been run over by an extended cab pickup with a front seat full of tattooed teenagers. As Ryan stepped aside on wobbly legs, one of them flashed the universal hand sign of disrespect.

Willing his pulse to slow, he opened the unlocked door on the driver's side of his borrowed car and plopped down. The sun-warmed fabric burned his bare legs, and he was grateful for the stimulation. He knew that he needed coffee, strong coffee, and a lot of it.

Fighting to clear his brain, Ryan closed his eyes and breathed deeply. Once. Twice. Three times. Then he rolled his palms around in his eye sockets. Finally, he stared into the rear-view mirror. He saw messy hair, bloodshot eyes, and an unshaven face.

How he looked, however, was not important.

What did concern him, though, was a stick leaning against the seat from the floor in back. He didn't remember it being there before. Of course, he could have missed it. Then again, he was a photographer. He saw details.

"No, that schtick was not there," he said.

As he spoke, Ryan realized that he was slurring his words. He not only was walking like a drunk but speaking like one as well. The teens were right.

"What was I thinking about?" he asked as he rolled down the window.

"Oh, yeah, the schtick."

Ryan turned and looked in the back. The floor was filled with fireworks, including a large rocket attached to the stick that he had seen.

"Hey, I didn't buy those," he said. "Did I?"

Ryan turned back around and rubbed his chin. He feared that his mind rapidly was turning to mush.

"Proly not even safe for me to drive," he said, thinking absently that he smelled smoke.

Still, Ryan Conners was a survivor. He had proved that by beating a leopard senseless with a digital camera.

"Hell, no, I didn't buy those fireworks!" he screamed.

Pushing on the door that he hadn't yet fully closed, he dived into the gravel lot and rolled away. Just as he did, he heard a "pop!"

Seconds later, Mam Ma Jennings' red Ford Taurus erupted. First, a thousand tiny explosions filled the interior with smoke. Then the trunk burst into flames, and the windshield blew out. Blazing balls of blue, green, and red "thumped" out of the blaze. Strings of firecrackers peppered the air with one "pop-pop-pop" after another.

Sizzling fountains spewed rainbows of sparks, and rockets raced for the heavens. There they painted the pale mid-day sky with Technicolor stars.

People in the parking lot ducked behind cars or fell to the ground. Those inside the tent stepped to the doorways to see what was going on. Gawkers quickly became sprinters when they saw the explosions.

Tiffany was among the first to scream as a small rocket exploded inches above her midriff. It spoiled her tan with second-degree burns.

"Holy shit!" Ryan said, feeling the adrenaline rush restore his sobriety. "That's the fat lady singing."

He bounced to his feet and ran, hoping to safely distance himself from what he was certain to come.

Impact from the car's exploding gas tank picked him up and threw him into the tall grass beside the gravel lot. Rolling onto his back, Ryan watched a large rocket rise up out of the blazing rubble of the car. Instead of climbing, though, it zigzagged twice before deciding on a final destination—the interior of Benny's Wholesale Fireworks.

A second fireworks show began. Smoking rockets streaked out the doors, where they struck parked vehicles or exploded in the woods. A few sliced across the highway. One hit a windshield and shattered it, prompting the driver to slam on his brakes. A car following too closely behind plowed into him.

Ryan heard screeching breaks, followed by the sounds of breaking glass and crunching metal.

Other cars pulled off along the road, and their occupants climbed out to watch.

Inside the tent, cones and sparklers sprayed burning brilliance, and the canvas walls caught fire. Rockets and radiant balls billowed out of the top. Concussions shook the ground. Then, for a blessed moment, all was quiet.

A scream broke the silence, and Ryan uncovered his head. He saw a little girl of perhaps three or four years old stumbling for the tent. Blood dripped from her cut lip, and black smudges stained her yellow romper.

"Mommy!" she cried. "Mommy! Where are you?"

His own suffering forgotten, Ryan regained his feet and raced for the child. He scooped her up just in front of the tent's main entrance and darted away.

"It should be just about time for the grand finale, sweetheart," he told the girl as he pulled her down with him into the weeds at the edge of the parking lot.

"Thump! Thump! Thump!"

What remained of the tent suddenly fell in on itself, and a mortar barrage of Roman candles began.

"Thump! Thump! Thump!"

Dozens of red, white, and blue balls arched skyward.

Finally, a fleet of screaming rockets zoomed skyward.

"Bam! Bam! Bam!"

As they exploded, flames flowed down the sky in strands of purple, blue, orange, and yellow.

"Bam! Bam! Bam!"

The ribbons blazed and then curled into blackened ashes that floated softly to earth.

As explosions slowed, Ryan uncovered his head for a second time. He saw a thick layer of smoke spread across the parking lot and the remains of the fireworks stand. He heard more children crying and parents trying to comfort them. In the distance, sirens wailed.

An overweight woman with singed hair and wild eyes materialized out of the haze and picked up the little girl. She didn't bother to say thank you.

Ryan looked up to watch a small army of parachutists descend from the final aerial display. Another round of firecrackers gave them covering fire.

He suspected that he now had enough adrenaline racing through his veins to keep him going another week.

"The Colonel is going to give me some answers this time," he said as he regained his feet. "One way or the other, he is going to give me some answers."

CHAPTER THIRTY

P.J. decided that the boy was strong, stronger than she might be if she had just seen her family killed. She had held his hand at first and pulled him along as they fled. But then he had pulled free and ran beside her.

One guard almost had caught them, but then he seemed to vanish. Maybe he couldn't keep up. Maybe he was sneaking up on them now. Or maybe the wolves had scared him away.

But more than one man would be looking for them now. And they wouldn't give up. Her uncle—that creep!—would see to it. She had seen the awful things that his men were doing behind that cabin. She had seen the bodies of those murdered.

And she had rescued a survivor.

"Come on," she huffed. "This way."

The dark-haired boy followed her down a hill toward the small stream that separated the den from the arches. P.J. wanted to keep danger away from the wolves. She believed that the best way to do that was to not go near the den.

Sure, the wolves would fight to protect her, but those men had guns. The wolves would lose. She and the boy would die.

And the puppies. P.J. couldn't bear the thought of anything happening to Larry, Moe, and Curly. Those men had killed children and babies. They likely would enjoy torturing poor, helpless animals.

No, she would stay away from the den. They would find another place to hide.

She thought about the farm where the little boys had given her a "smashed cheese samich." But she still didn't know if she could trust the adults. Besides, the farm was across the main creek and too far away. At the pace they had been running, she and the boy would crumble from exhaustion before getting there.

P.J. knelt and washed her face in the cool water of the stream. The boy did the same. Then he drank from cupped hands.

With the afternoon sun below the hills to the west, the stream was in deep, cool shade. The sweat that soaked P.J.'s shirt suddenly turned icy. She shivered a bit and wrapped her arms around herself.

"I'm P.J.," she said. "What's your name?"

The boy continued to drink.

She lightly touched his arm and he jumped back, falling on his bottom in the gravel. His eyes grew wild. He looked around frantically as if searching for a place to run.

P.J. held up her hands.

"No, no, stay," she said. "I'm sorry. I didn't mean to scare you."

Maybe he doesn't speak English, she thought. *After all, he's probably from Mexico. And I did hear him cry for his family in Spanish.*

Or maybe he can't hear. Maybe he's deaf.

He might be in shock.

The thought frightened her. In school, she had learned that going into shock could be harmful, if not fatal. But he ran. And he drank water. If he was in shock, he probably would pull out of it.

P.J. smiled at him. She stood and held out her hand. The boy took it, and she helped him to his feet.

"Come on. Let's follow the stream. We'll walk for a while instead of run. I think that we're far enough away to do that."

And Bert and Ernie haven't shown themselves. They probably would warn me if those guys were getting close.

As they sloshed along, P.J. tried to think of a place that they could go to rest and hide.

Not the den. Not the arches. Good view from up there, but no place to hide.

Even with no destination in mind, even with awful men chasing them, P.J. began to feel better as they waded along. That creek at the cabin had been poisoned with evil. Dead trees, vultures, bodies…

But this little stream was different. Minnows skittered in the deeper pools. Cicadas chirped a summer song. Dozens of black and yellow butterflies flitted about orange flowers along the banks. This little stream was alive and, with its many blessings, made P.J. happy to be alive as well.

Up through the dark, green leaves that shaded them, she saw deep blue sky. That, too, made her stronger.

But where do we go? Not the den. Not the arches.

Just then, P.J. saw a dark, blurry spot in the woods. Slowly, it took a more defined shape. Rounded ears. Big shoulders. Long legs. Big feet. Long, white teeth. It was a wolf!

She paused. The boy bumped into her and she looked back at him. His body was alive. He drank water. He ran. But his brown eyes were lifeless.

When P.J. turned forward again, the outline of a wolf had become Arthur. He looked at her with those gold and amber eyes.

And then he smiled.

No, not Arthur! Arthur didn't smile. Wolves didn't smile. But Grandfather did. That was in dreams, though. This was broad daylight.

Am I dreaming in broad daylight? No, then it wouldn't be a dream. It would be a… What? Oh, yeah, it would be a hallucination.

Am I hallucinating?

"¡Mirada! ¡Un lobo!" the boy said.

"No, not a hallucination, I guess," P.J. said. She didn't know much Spanish, but she did know that "lobo" means wolf.

As they watched, the black wolf ran upstream. Then, it stopped and looked back. It smiled again. Despite the shade, the gold and amber eyes sparkled.

"¡Madre del dios!" the boy said in a low voice.

P.J. couldn't help herself. She chuckled. "I'm not sure what that means," she said. "But I probably agree with it.

"Come on. Let's go. So, you can talk? Can you speak English? My Spanish is terrible."

The boy said no more. P.J. noticed, however, that his eyes showed a flicker of life.

The wolf weaved slowly among the trees. He paused often. Possibly he realized that the two were nearing exhaustion. Possibly he wanted to give P.J. time to think.

As she walked, that's just what she did. Her mind labored on the puzzle. Why did Arthur want them to follow him? Of course! He had to be taking them to a safe place.

And it had to be Arthur. Grandfather wouldn't appear during the day and in front of another person. Heck, he *couldn't* appear during the day and in front of another person. He wasn't real.

On the other hand, Arthur never had smiled before. What was *that* about?

The arches, P.J. thought. *Why does my mind keep going back to the arches? They're not a good place to hide.*

Suddenly she knew.

That's the last place Grandfather talked to me in a dream. What did he say? It might be important.

P.J.'s friends often marveled at her memory. She remembered song lyrics, movies, and all kinds of trivia. Even more impressive for them, she often remembered what was taught in class.

He said that many love me and many are nearby and one is coming, she thought. *He said I have a family and I have a home.*

All true. The wolves had been nearby. Their den had become her home.

No, no it didn't become my home. They are my family, but that den wasn't my home. I slept outside. I hated going in the den. What did he say exactly?

"You do have a family. And you do have a home not far from here."

Could he have been talking about someplace besides the den? Someplace not far from the arches? They had passed the den on the left not too long before. Right now, they were parallel with the arches. They were at the top of the hill on the right side. The wolf was leading them farther up the stream to…

Yes, yes, that's it. Arthur — or Grandfather — is taking us to a place where we will be safe. He's taking us to my home.

Forgetting her fatigue, P.J. started to run again.

"Mother of God," a voice said.

P.J. whirled around. "What did you say?"

"That's what 'Madre del Dios' means in English," he said.

"You speak English then," she said.

"Yes. My mother learned in school. She taught me and my father. Her dream was for us to live in Los Estados Unidos — the United States."

He shook his head then and started crying.

P.J. touched his arm. "I'm so sorry," she said. "Those men are going to pay for what they did to your family and all the others. You and I are going to see to it.

"But right now, we need to hide and rest."

The boy sniffed and nodded.

"By the way, my name is P.J.," the girl said. She held out her hand.

The boy smiled. Brown hand gripped white.

"En su servicio. My name is Miguel."

P.J. pointed toward the black wolf that sat watching them with gold eyes and a half-smile. "That's Arthur or maybe Grandfather. I'm not sure which.

"Those men want to kill me too. The wolves are my family. They protect me. Now they'll protect you too.

"Come on and I'll tell you about it."

The black wolf headed upstream once more. P.J. and Miguel followed.

CHAPTER THIRTY-ONE

For the second time, Colonel John Stallings pounded his fist against the desktop, and, for the second time, windows in the cabin rattled. His blue eyes bulged with anger, and his cheeks flushed through his carefully cultivated tan. The room reeked of sweat and gunpowder, as well as singed hair and burnt clothing.

"You were a murderer and rapist while you were under my command," he said.

He stalked back and forth in a small open area between the fireplace and chairs where Crater Kendall sat with his brother. A pillow cushioned Dawson's bottom.

Crater stared at the floor. Dawson quivered like a Chihuahua plucked from a deep freeze.

"But you didn't let it interfere with your work. You were a good soldier."

Stallings kicked over Dawson's Big Gulp cup and stomped it. A Coca-Cola geyser stained Crater's sneakers and what remained of his jeans. Dawson's eyes grew wide, and he mewed in despair. He was certain that this insult would push his older brother over the edge. One of these two men was going to kill the other. He hoped that he didn't die as well.

Crater didn't move.

"Now you're a child molester. I can accept that. A man should have hobbies," Stallings ranted.

"What I don't understand, though, is how someone so completely evil also can be so damn incompetent! You couldn't kill Ryan Conners with a car bomb, so you try to blow him up with firecrackers?"

Stallings stopped and looked down at the brothers. Their heads, chests, and arms were stained with ash and black soot.

They looked as if they had been retrieved prematurely from a barbeque grill. Their pants were shredded. Dawson was missing a shoe. Crater had lost most of his right eyebrow.

The elder Kendall kept his eyes locked on the soda-soaked floor. Dawson looked nervously from one man to the other. He remained terrified that the end of the world was just one more insult away. He had seen his brother tear apart men for far less than he now accepted with quiet indifference.

"It was my fault," the younger brother said timidly.

As he spoke, he played with a nail file that no longer would stay in the tattered front pocket of his cargo jeans.

"Crater was just gonna shoot the guy's gas tank. He thought Benny's would be a good place to do it because of all the fireworks. That way, nobody would ever know what happened.

"But the guy got there before we did. He wasn't in his car, so we had to wait for him to come back. We waited and waited and…"

Dawson's voice trailed off.

"And?" Stallings commanded.

"Well, Crater went over to look at a girl in a bikini, and that's when I got the idea to put fireworks in the guy's car. I figured it would make a much bigger explosion when Crater shot the gas tank, you know?"

Dawson looked up at the Colonel with terrified brown eyes.

"I just got them in there when Conners came around the side of the tent and got in the car. I didn't have time to call Crater. And I was afraid that Conners would get away.

So I lit a firecracker and threw it in the back window. I figured a backseat full of fireworks would blow up a gas tank just as good as a bullet. But…"

Dawson dropped the file and flinched at the memory.

*　*　*　*　*

He hadn't expected the explosions to begin so quickly. Even Ryan was farther away from the car than Dawson when the barrage began.

As the younger Kendall turned to run, a rocket drilled him in the back and exploded. It knocked him to the ground and set his shirt ablaze. He rolled in the gravel, smothering the fire and causing excruciating pain to his wolf-bitten buttocks.

Before he could regain his feet, a string of crackling firecrackers flew out the passenger window. It landed on his chest.

"Pop! Pop! Pop!"

They burned away what remained of his shirt and peppered his skin with hundreds of tiny burns.

Beating out the flames on his chest, Dawson staggered upright and then realized that he couldn't see where he was going because of the smoke.

"Crater! Crater!" he called frantically as he ran.

He bounced off people and rubble as if he were a ball bearing caroming about in a giant pinball machine. Finally, someone grabbed him by the belt and pulled him below the hovering layer of smoke.

"What the Hell happened?" yelled Crater, straining to be heard above the booms, pops, whines, whistles, and shrieks.

Even with tearing eyes, Dawson could see that his brother was no better off than he. Crater's black tee shirt was reduced to a collar and two tattered sleeves that continued to smolder. Holes in his jeans still smoked around the edges.

Suddenly Crater's eyebrow went up in flames.

"Dammit!" he cursed as he beat out the fire with his hand.

"What happened, Dawson?"

"I, I don't know," his brother yelled. "Everything just blew up."

"Where's Conners?" Crater demanded. "Did you see him?"

Just then, both watched a man dash toward the collapsing tent and grab a little girl who was about to go inside. Clutching her to his chest, he vanished back into the smoke that surrounded what remained of Benny's.

"Damn! That's him," Crater growled.

He reached for the knife strapped to his ankle.

But his hand never made it, as both men were jerked to their feet. Tumbling about, they bumped into the chest of a man the size of a small skyscraper. Crater gulped, and Dawson whimpered as they gazed upward and into the bloodshot eyes of one angry security guard.

"You two, come with me," he said.

He started to drag them toward the highway.

"Hell, no!" Crater yelled as he stomped on the man's foot.

Then he whirled and delivered a crippling knee shot to the groin. For the second time, he started to draw his knife.

"Crater, no, we don't have time," Dawson pleaded. "This place is gonna be crawling with cops in a second."

"All right. All right," Crater said. "Get going. I'm going to say goodbye."

As Dawson fled into the slowly vanishing smoke, Crater kicked the guard repeatedly in the ribs and back. He ended the attack with a skull-splitting blow to the side of the head.

*   *   *   *   *

Back in the cabin, Stallings shook his fist.

"So you crippled some poor jerk just trying to make a few extra dollars while Ryan Conners still is alive and well," he said.

"Now both of you listen to me, and listen to me well. I am not going to let that bastard spoil our plans. Since you can't put him away, I will. He won't be the first I've had to eliminate. And he probably won't be the last."

He looked pointedly at both Crater and Dawson, as if his eyes were delivering a message. "Screw this next job up," they seemed to say, "and you will be next."

Dawson whimpered. Crater turned his head.

The Colonel walked to the cabin door and opened it. Afternoon sun beamed through, conveying a false sense of warmth to the icy conversation.

"Just so you know, Crater, I'm also going to take care of Jackie," Stallings said.

Kendall glanced hatefully toward the Colonel. Then he looked toward the prize that he could not have. Tied and gagged, deputy Jackie Novak sat just to the right of the door. Her eyes were closed and her head was down. If she heard what was being said, she didn't reveal it.

"Yeah, I know that it's a disappointment, especially since you already killed her sister," Stallings said. "But that's the way it is. I want to make sure it's done right. And I want to make sure there's no trace of her or Conners when I finish with them. I'll put them in the landfill myself."

"And the girl. What about her?" Kendall said. "She's still alive. We've seen her twice. She wouldn't be if you had let me have her."

The Colonel turned back around. "You're right, Crater. My mistake.

"I have everyone else out there searching for her right now. They'll find her. They're looking along the roads, as well as back in the hills. She won't get away.

"We might have found her sooner if you hadn't kept that information to yourself."

Stallings walked to Jackie, grabbed her hair, and jerked her head. "Ah, ah, can't fool me. I know you're listening to every word. But it won't do you any good.

"I'll keep you around a bit longer. You might make good bait for lover boy. But this will be your last Fourth of July. I guarantee it."

He looked back toward the brothers. He smiled broadly.

"Besides, boys, I have a much bigger job for you. Lots of fireworks this time too."

Then Stallings was serious again. He started at Dawson, who turned his head.

"What I want to know right now is whether you two are up to it?"

Glancing once more at Jackie, Crater mumbled a response.

"I didn't hear you, sergeant," Stallings said. "Look at me when I address you. Can you do it or not?"

"Yes, sir!" said the older Kendall, his flat, black eyes glaring at Stallings.

"All right," the Colonel said.

"I want you two to load your van and then drive to a motel up near St. Louis to spend the night. Don't talk to anyone about anything. Don't go to any bars or strip joints. Stay in that motel room until morning.

"Then go to that spot on the Illinois side of the river that we talked about. The boat will be waiting for you, gassed up and ready to go.

"Times for all of the events are in that newspaper article on the desk. Remember, this has to be done precisely to the minute."

A long moment of stillness passed. The Colonel watched Dawson's eyes move slowly from his brother's face to the large, gray safe in the far corner of the room. Stallings flashed a wicked smile.

"As promised, you will get your one-hundred-thousand dollars when the job is done, even though you have screwed things up royally with your incompetence.

"You wouldn't be so stupid as to try to help yourself, would you, sergeant? Surely you know that I've taken precautions."

"Yeah, I know," the elder Kendall said softly.

Stallings chose to be direct this time in issuing his threat.

"And don't mess this up, Crater. Or I will kill you. I will kill both of you."

Stallings looked once more at Jackie.

"And don't touch her!" he said as he stomped out of the cabin. The door slammed behind him.

Crater stood, grabbed his brother's ear, and jerked hard. Dawson yelped.

"We are going to do this job, and we are going to do it right because you are going to do exactly as I tell you. Aren't you?"

The younger brother nodded and rubbed his sore lobe. "Yeah, Crater, I'm going to do what you tell me. Geez, you didn't have to hurt me."

Crater shook his head in disgust.

"You are one sorry excuse for a human being," he said. "I don't know why I put up with you."

They heard the Cadillac's big engine start and the tires spin gravel.

Dawson rose. "Hey, man, we're brothers, right?

"Right"?

"Yeah, right," Crater said as he walked slowly toward Jackie. He pulled his knife from the sheath on his ankle. He stuck the point under her chin and raised her head with the blade.

"Don't bet on not seeing me again," he said. "And don't bet on the Colonel stopping me. I'm going to give you a taste of what I gave your sister. And you are going to squeal just like she did.

"I'm going to get that girl too. I owe her big time for what she did to me.

"Those idiots out there never will find her. But I will."

Dawson didn't like it when his brother was this way. "Hey, Kendall, come on. We've got work to do."

Crater turned. "Yeah, you're right. Let's load the van. I'm ready to raise a little Hell, and downtown St. Louis is as good a place as any.

"Then, after I tie up some loose ends back here, I'm taking that money and heading for Mexico."

Dawson followed slowly, walking with stiff legs to avoid putting any more stress on the stitches in his backside. During his panic at the fireworks stand, he'd almost torn them out.

"I'm going too, right?" he said. "We're going together. We're brothers."

"Yeah, right," Crater said. "We're brothers. But it's not by choice, I assure you. Now stop whining and help me load up.

"You don't screw things up anymore, and I might let you go with me."

Dawson nodded eagerly and moved up alongside his brother, who was lifting a long, wooden box.

"I promise, Crater. I promise I'll do things right," the younger brother said. "Here, let me carry that."

He attempted to take the box from his brother, who resisted.

"I'll carry this. You get the smaller one," Crater said, pulling back.

But Dawson insisted. He had messed up things royally so far. He wanted to make amends. He would carry this box for his brother. With all of his strength, he yanked.

The younger brother wasn't strong enough, however, to handle the sudden shift of weight. The crate fell—landing squarely on Crater Kendall's left foot.

CHAPTER THIRTY-TWO

P.J. and Miguel paused, staring at a huge bend in the stream.

Arthur — or Grandfather — was nowhere to be seen. P.J. knew that they were close to wherever the wolf had been leading them. Otherwise, he wouldn't have disappeared.

"Look at the size of those cliffs and the opening in them," she said. "I'll bet someone could live under there."

Someone did live under there, a tiny voice in her head told P.J. *Someone does live under there.*

Despite the warmth of the day, she shivered.

What kind of person today lives in a cave? What kind of person am I if this is my home?

As they neared the mouth of the cave, refreshing air wafted out from inside. They saw lush, green ferns growing in the shady edges. They heard water trickling down the walls. They smelled cool wetness.

Maybe it's not so bad, she decided.

"This is it," P.J. said. "I know that it is. We'll be safe here. We can rest and plan what to do next."

Miguel nodded. Talking as they walked had helped bring his mind back from a terrible place. He was stronger now and determined.

"Yes, we will rest," he said. "But I know what I want to do next. I want revenge on los bastardos. They killed my mother and father. They killed my little sister, Elena."

P.J. chewed on her lower lip. She understood how Miguel must feel. But they were just a couple of kids. They must be careful or they would die as his mother, father, and sister had died. Men would toss their bodies into a hole. Vultures would feed on their remains. A bulldozer would bury them.

"There are lots of them, and they have lots of guns," she said. "We can't fight them."

She smiled. "But, hey, there are two of us. We'll figure out something. Okay? Now, let's get inside."

P.J. led the way into the black entrance.

Inside, P.J. heard children laugh and dogs bark. A woman spoke words that she did not understand. She smelled meat cooking.

Drumbeats began, and someone joined in with a flute.

P.J. stopped and closed her eyes. She could see them! She was with them. All around her, Indians went about their day-to-day routines. One, an old man who looked like Grandfather, put down the flute and smiled.

That's when P.J.'s knees turned to mush, and she crumbled. Fortunately, Miguel was there to catch her. "Pobrecita! Ella es va cansada. She is so tired.

"Yes, we will rest," he said. "Para ahora. For now."

*　*　*　*　*

A young woman wearing a buckskin dress roasted meat over an open fire. She hummed as she worked, smiling at children who laughed and played nearby. The air was rich with scent as fat dripped and crackled in the fire. An old man approached.

"Sit, Grandfather," the woman said. "Soon, I will have meat for you to eat."

The man shook his head.

"I have not come to eat," he said. "I have come to tell you that Kara is on her way.

"She will not be long. And she is bringing a friend."

The woman's dark eyes grew bright with anticipation. "And her father? Will he come too?"

The old man pulled a flute from the waist of his leather trousers and began to play. The children danced around him, made even happier by the melody.

"What about her father?" the woman asked again. "Will he come as well?"

The old man stopped playing. "I don't know. Once, I thought so. Now I am not sure. But Kara and her friend are coming. Be happy for that."

The women bent to turn the meat. When she looked up, the old man was gone. Standing in his place was a young girl with brown hair and brown eyes. The woman grinned and hugged the girl, who returned the embrace.

"Welcome home," the woman said.

"This is home?" the girl asked. "This is where I live?

The woman stroked the girl's cheek.

"It is where you used to live," she said. "And it is where you are always welcome. You are safe here. As are you, so are we all. We are the wolf clan."

Kara looked around. "But where's my father? I can feel him close by. Isn't he here? I want to be with him."

The woman shook her head sadly.

"He is not here," she said. "And Grandfather could not tell me if he is coming. He said that once he thought so. But now he is not sure.

"I worry for your father. He might be in danger. If you feel him, he might be close by. But now, you must rest. You have come a long way. And you are tired."

The woman stroked Kara's face once more. "Rest, little one. Rest."

* * * * *

"P.J.! P.J.!"

In the darkness, P.J. felt a cold hand clasp her arm. She jerked upright, her brown eyes wide. She just managed to keep herself from screaming.

"Todo correcto," she heard a voice say. "It's all right."

The girl remembered where she was. She was sleeping in a cave with Miguel. Her breathing slowed, and she sighed.

"What happened?" she said. "Wow, I was really gone there."

She wiped her face with her hands.

"You were dreaming, I think," Miguel said. "You said, 'No! No! I won't rest. I have to go. I have to save him.'

"Who is he?" the boy asked.

P.J. looked toward his voice. She could just barely see his outline in the darkness.

"I think…," she began. "I think that my father is somewhere close by. He can help us. But first, we have to help him."

PART SEVEN

FIREWORKS

CHAPTER THIRTY-THREE

The Kendall brothers stashed Crater's van at the get-away site south of St. Louis. Then they stole a car to drive to the motel on the Illinois side of the river.

While Dawson showered, Crater grabbed a bucket and headed for the ice machine. It sat in an alcove near the swimming pool, where two adults and several children splashed about. As Crater rounded the corner, a boy of maybe seven or eight years of age pulled a grape soda from the vending machine.

The elder Kendall stopped quietly and stared at the youngster who hadn't yet noticed him. Still dripping with water, the boy popped the top on the can and took a long drink. His wet, orange trunks clung to smooth, slender legs.

Crater licked his lips. He glanced quickly around him to be certain no one else was close by. He could have some fun here, and the Colonel would be none the wiser.

"Hey, kid," he said. "You lose a puppy?"

Startled by the voice, the boy looked up with wide brown eyes.

"Did you lose a puppy?" Crater asked again. "I found one over on the other side of the motel. It's a cute little thing, all black and fuzzy."

"No, sir," the boy said.

"Would you like to see him anyway? He's a real good-looking dog. Maybe you could even take him home with you."

"My Dad…" the child began.

But Crater didn't let him finish. He was next to him now, hand on the boy's shoulder. The soft, wet flesh against his rough fingers aroused the man, and he fought to maintain control.

Just be patient, he told himself. *He's almost yours.*

"Oh, come on," Crater insisted. "He won't care if you just look at him, will he?"

"No, I don't guess so," the boy said.

Kendall gently escorted him away from the pool. Then he paused and extended his hand.

"My name is John Stallings," he said, enjoying the private joke. "What's yours?"

"I'm Brent," the boy said.

"Glad to meet you, Brent," Kendall said.

He carefully cupped the child's elbow in his hand and urged him forward. The boy was his now. He had taken the bait and Kendall had reeled him in.

He didn't know where he would take the kid, but he'd find a place. Crater swallowed hard and willed his hands not to close on the boy's tender neck—not yet, anyway.

Plenty of time for that later. Enjoy the moment. The kid's mine!

They were on the back side of the motel now, but there was no privacy. A fast-food restaurant lay just across the parking lot, and the drive-up window was doing a brisk business. A boy in a yellow and white uniform pushed bags of trash into a dumpster.

"Come on," Crater said. "The pup's by my car. I'll take you to him."

Fortunately, he still had the keys in his pocket. He would get the kid to the car, knock him out, and then take him somewhere nice and private.

The boy hesitated.

"Uh, I don't think so," he said. "I'd better get back to the pool. My Mom will be worried."

Crater frowned. But he wasn't worried. This was according to the script that he used so many times before.

"Ah, come on," he said. "She won't mind. The pup is really cute.

"Tell you what: You can take it back and show it to her. I know that she will like it. Maybe she can convince your Dad to let you keep it."

The boy beamed.

"Sure!" he said. "She's good at stuff like that. And we've got a big backyard. I'll feed it and take care of it. They won't have to do a thing."

The walk past a dozen or so rooms seemed to take forever for Crater. But finally, they were there. They stopped beside a blue Ford Mustang that the brothers had found at a mall parking lot — with the keys inside — little more than an hour before.

Kendall wiped the sweat from his forehead and took a deep breath. He flashed a wide smile at the boy.

"I put him in the trunk to keep him safe," he said.

He stepped to the back of the car and stuck the key in the lock. "Come on over here and see him."

The lid popped as Brent hurried to see his prize. He leaned into the trunk, and Crater raised a metal flashlight over the boy's head.

"There's no puppy in…" the boy said.

"Hey, good news. I found the dog's owner."

Clenching his teeth in anger, Crater lowered the weapon. He wheeled around, knowing full well who was standing behind him.

His hair still wet from the shower, Dawson grinned as he held a cardboard tray full of hamburgers, fries, and soft drinks.

"I found the puppy's owner, and then I went to get us some supper," he said.

Dawson looked at the boy, who now had a sad expression on his face.

"Sorry, son," he said. "Maybe you should go on back to your family now."

Brent stared at Dawson for a moment.

"Ah, rats!" the boy said. "I wanted a puppy."

Then he took another drink of his grape soda and hurried back toward the pool. His wet feet slapped on the sun-warmed concrete.

Dawson's smile disappeared. He avoided eye contact with Crater.

"Come on, bro," the younger brother said as he stepped inside. "Supper's on."

Crater stood awhile longer by the Mustang, his fists clenched in rage. He loved his brother. And he hated him, especially when Dawson reminded him who was the better man.

*   *   *   *   *

One afternoon when he was twelve, Crater Kendall opened the front door of their mobile home to find Jake with his hand down his dirty boxer shorts. The man grinned at him. He wiped his hand on the sofa and motioned for the boy to come in.

"Hey, Crater, want to have some fun?" he said.

Crater had been finishing the fifth grade for the second time when their mother brought home the ex-con. The guy stood at least six feet, six inches and weighed nearly three hundred pounds. While their mother waited tables at the diner, Jake lay on the couch. He drank beer, smoked cigarettes, and watched game shows on television. His favorite was "The Gong Show."

He wasn't the best of the men that his mother had brought home. But he didn't seem like the worst either — at least, not at first. Some of them had beaten Crater and Dawson.

Jake just shoved them around a bit. He told them to not talk back to their mother and to take out the trash. But he didn't hit them.

Instead, he looked at the Kendall brothers with eyes that Crater knew hid some deep, dark secret. And then he started to wrestle with them. He put them in headlocks and patted their bottoms. Or he pulled them onto his lap, where Crater felt something that he knew he had no business feeling.

Their mother never had defended them when other men hit her sons, and she didn't defend them now. Instead, she piled their dirty dishes in the sink. She poured herself another glass of cheap whiskey. Then she passed out in front of the television.

Crater avoided going home as much as he could after school. He knew that the longer he stayed away, the more likely it would be that Jake had passed out. He would sleep until Crater's mother came home with leftovers from the diner for supper.

Dawson was four years younger and, even then, a real wimp. Crater didn't like being seen with him. But he didn't want Jake getting his dirty hands on his brother either. So Dawson tagged along with his older brother. They played bottle-cap baseball, broke bottles over at the dump, and stole bicycles from the other side of the tracks.

But one afternoon, Dawson complained of an upset stomach.

"I got to go home, Crater," he said. "I'm about to get the runs."

He reached out to touch his brother's arm, but Crater pushed it away.

"Go in the woods, you wuss," the older Kendall said.

Dawson shook his head. He gazed with pitiful eyes at his brother.

"Okay, let's go," Crater said finally.

Crater had been the first into their trailer. That is why he, not Dawson, saw Jake masturbating.

Crater paused for a moment as Jake pulled his hand out of his shorts. Then he stepped aside to let his brother enter. Dawson sprinted for the bathroom.

"He's got the runs," Crater said, starting to back out the door. He avoided looking in those hungry eyes.

Jake picked up a beer can from the orange shag carpet, took a long swallow, and belched.

"Ah, come on, kid," he said. "Let's have some fun."

Crater edged back out onto the top step. But before he could pull the door closed behind him, the big man had lunged across the narrow room and grabbed his arm. He might be a slob and a drunk, but he still was faster than a twelve-year-old.

"You come with me, Crater," he said. "I'm gonna show you something they do in prison. You might as well learn it now, 'cause that's where you're going. You and that candy-ass brother of yours."

Jake plopped back onto the torn and musty brown sofa and pulled Crater with him.

"No! I don't want to," Crater yelled, pounding at the man with his free fist.

He didn't know what Jake would do to him. He didn't know what the man *could* do to him. They were both boys, after all. But he knew that he wouldn't like it.

A blow to the collarbone stunned Jake for an instant, and he loosened his grip. Crater kicked him in the shins and ran. The ex-con yanked the boy back by the collar and backhanded him onto the sofa.

Refusing to give in, Crater kicked and pounded his fists into the man's chest — until Jake slapped him a second time.

"Now you listen to me, you little asshole. You're going to do what I tell you, or I will kill you right here and then party with your little brother.

"Now, be still. I've got a big surprise coming your way."

Breathing hard now, Jake unbuckled Crater's belt and pulled his jeans down to his knees.

"Roll over," he commanded.

When Crater refused, the man put his hand around the boy's neck and squeezed.

"Roll over," he said again.

"Uncle Jake…"

The ex-con loosened his grip, and Crater looked up to see his brother standing in the hallway. He was naked from the waist down.

"I was sick, Uncle Jake," he said. "But I'm feeling better now. "I'll do what you want if you'll let Crater go. Okay, Uncle Jake?"

Jake stood up, grinned, and beckoned for the boy. Crater ran out the door.

The brothers never talked about what happened that day, but Crater never forgot.

*　*　*　*　*

"You're a piece of work, you know that?" Crater said. "How in the Hell did I ever get such an incompetent brother? It's a good thing I allowed us some extra time."

While carrying a foam ice chest to the bass boat, Dawson had stepped into knee-deep muck. It had sucked off his shoes, and he had fallen face-first into the mud. A disgusted Crater had to pull him out and clean him off before they could do the job for Stallings.

Now Dawson sat on a rock as Crater dumped water onto his head from the ice chest. The younger Kendall sputtered and wiped off his eyes with the palms of his hands. An awful sewer smell hung heavy in the humid air around him.

Still limping because of the crate injury to his foot, the older Kendall filled the cooler again. He hurled more water at his brother. Finally, the blackish-gray goo was turning from a solid coat to muddy streaks. A third rinse cleaned off Dawson's face.

"I'm sorry, Crater," the younger brother said. "I couldn't see where I was going. Shit happens."

Crater shook his head in disgust.

"Only when you're around," he said. "You've always got a truckload with you. I don't know why I put up with you. Let's go."

Dawson nodded meekly. He hopped off the rock and trudged toward the boat.

"You sure you know how to drive this thing? I sure as Hell can't kill a senator and drive a boat at the same time," Crater said as he pulled his brother aboard. "You are one sorry sack of cow manure. You know that?"

Dawson grinned. He loved his brother. And he knew that he often said things he didn't mean.

"Yeah, I know," he said. "And, yeah, I can drive the boat. Let's go."

They climbed aboard. Brown water drained down their legs and puddled on the floor of the boat. Dawson had no shoes. They still were buried in the stinky muck.

As Crater sat down beside him, Dawson turned on the ignition. He shifted the throttle and backed off the mud bank. Then, with surprising ability, he pushed the throttle forward and turned the boat in a smooth half-circle. He headed for the Missouri side, where the first Hispanic senator for Missouri, the Show-Me state, was about to address his supporters. Many of them likely would die with him if Crater's aim was true.

"Not bad, little brother," Crater said above the roar of the outboard.

His watch showed five minutes to twelve. They would be right on time.

Dawson smiled at him, and Crater felt a twinge of something that made him uncomfortable. He punched his younger brother in the shoulder.

"Won't be long now," Crater said. "Mexican beer and Mexican women."

"And I can go with you, can't I?" Dawson yelled above the roar of the outboard.

Now, despite himself, Crater did smile back.

"Yeah," he said. "You can go."

The elder Kendall picked up a pair of binoculars and looked toward the St. Louis Riverfront and its famous Gateway Arch.

On shore, hundreds of thousands of people defied the midday sun to participate in what is generally considered to be the nation's grandest Fourth of July celebration. He saw teens gathered around a stage, clapping their hands and dancing to a rock and roll band. He watched a father share a hot dog with his son. He spied an elderly couple sitting at the bottom of the Arch steps, dangling their feet in the river and giggling like children.

Above the dull buzz of the crowd, Kendall thought that he could hear electric guitars playing "Kokomo," a Beach Boys hit. Humming a bit of the melody, he smiled.

And then he noticed a path being cleared through the people as a black-haired man and his assistants headed for a podium at the base of the Arch.

"Our target is right on time," he said grimly. "One shot from this rocket launcher is going to give these folks a Fourth of July that they'll never forget."

Dawson looked at his brother. "Why we doing this anyway?" he asked. "Besides, for the money, I mean."

Crater grinned.

"Colonel Stallings hates bean-eaters, even ones who were born in this country. And he thinks that he can get elected senator with Lopez out of the way."

Just a couple of hundred yards out from the Missouri side, Crater put down the glasses. He crawled to the back of the boat. He lifted the dull black weapon to his shoulder.

"I might be able to hit him from here," he said, looking through the sight. "But let's get a few yards closer, just to be certain."

Suddenly the motor sputtered, caught again, sputtered, and died.

"Damn, Dawson. What did you do now?" Crater said. "Get that engine started, man. We need to get closer."

"I didn't do nothing to it," Dawson said. "It just died."

He tried the ignition again. And again. And again. The outboard coughed each time but refused to start.

"Sure we got gas?" Crater asked, putting down the rocket launcher. "That was your job, you know."

"We got gas," Dawson said. "I don't know what's wrong."

Dead in the big water, they moved swiftly downriver with the current sweeping below the Arch. Waves rocked the small boat as Dawson looked upstream. He saw a commercial barge moving toward them. It might have been as much as a half-mile away, but it was closing fast.

"What are we gonna do?" he cried. "We're stuck out here. We're gonna be run over!"

Ignoring his brother's panic, Crater gazed coolly at the looming barge and then looked at his watch. It was noon, time for a killing. The Colonel had emphasized that the job must be done precisely at that moment. But so what if they were minutes late? Lopez was a politician. He was supposed to talk for only five minutes, but he probably would be up there for fifteen.

They would restart the engine, get out of the way of the barge, and motor back up. Then he would send the Mexican to Hell, along with a few dozen of his supporters. He might even try a second shot and see what kind of damage that he could do to the Arch.

Crater scooted to the engine.

"Keep the bow pointed downriver so we don't get swamped," he told Dawson as he removed the cover.

He peered at the engine's insides.

"Hell, I don't know what I'm looking for," he said. "Dawson, come back here and see what you can do. I'll hold the wheel."

Crater set the engine cover down and started to crawl forward. As he did, he noticed something stuck to the underside of the top. He looked closer. It was a timer attached to a small package.

"Jump!" he yelled.

Crater dove into the river just as the stern exploded and flames gobbled up the rest of the boat.

The concussion carried across the water to the Arch, where Senator Lopez spoke about the blessings of liberty and diversity. Many in the crowd exclaimed and pointed at the bright ball of fire. The senator paused and smiled.

"Looks as if we are being treated to an early fireworks display," he said. "I wonder who we have to thank for that?"

CHAPTER THIRTY-FOUR

The gray female whined as she paced in front of the den. The pups had been safely stowed inside. As babysitter for the family, she knew that she should be in with them, blocking the entrance, but her worry demanded that she move.

Three steps to the left she went, and then three steps to the right. Her eyes bright with fear, her ears erect, she moved as predictably as a wind-up toy. She watched the woods with a mixture of hope and dread. The rest of the pack was out there, but so was danger.

Evil ones had roamed the wolves' territory for days now. Some days they came closer to the den than on others. Today one of them—more foul smelling than the others—passed particularly near. He was just across the stream and up the hill, near the sandstone arches.

Every few minutes, the black pup attempted to run out into the bright light of midday, and she shooed it back. It didn't want to play. It wanted to search for its sister, wolfchild. She understood its desire. She missed the one with two legs also. But she also knew that evil was near. She shoved the pup back inside with her muzzle, gently biting its bottom to provide added incentive.

Occasionally, it challenged her authority with a snarl and flattened ears. But bared teeth and a stern look were enough to put the pup on its back in a submissive posture. She then would take its snout in her mouth and gently but firmly clamp down to show who was in charge. Afterward, she would lick it lovingly and push it back onto its feet.

Chased back into the den's depths, the black one would join its siblings in a chorus of soft cries. Then it would charge out once more, as stubborn as its father.

The black alpha, his mate, and the two gray males, meanwhile, patrolled the creek from below the den to the home of the Old Ones. Wolfchild and her friend had spent the night in the cave.

This morning, the two young humans had followed the stream for a while and then climbed the steep hills. Hidden by foliage and as silent as shadows, the alpha pair ran on either side of them. The two gray males protected the rear.

As the stench of evil grew stronger, the wolves slowed. They studied the children, surprised that the two took no notice of the scented warning. Instead of raising their noses to sniff the wind, the boy and wolfchild walked with heads down. Instead of listening, they talked. Instead of watching the woods, they looked at each other.

Mindful that danger grew with each step, the alphas pressed on as guardians for the boy and girl. The gray males, though, fell farther and farther back. Finally, they turned and retreated to the creek.

Loping on long, strong legs, the alpha female whined softly, looking to her left. The humans did not hear her, she knew, but her mate did. He answered, and she, too, ended the journey.

The alpha male continued to run just a few yards away from wolfchild. He was reluctant to leave a member of his family. But he had the welfare of others to consider as well. He was their food bringer and defender.

He was brave and not afraid to face this evil that grew ever closer. But if anything happened to him, the rest would go hungry and unprotected.

He gave a sharp yip, and wolfchild looked his way. The young human slowed and then stopped. Their eyes met. The black wolf stepped closer, lowered his head, and whined a goodbye. Then he melted back into the deep woods.

Now, he, the white female, and the two grays stood guard along the stream, mindful of the danger that was passing so close to them. The departure of wolfchild had made them all sorrowful. But they were determined to protect home and family against the black-hearted one who came so close on his way to the place of evil.

CHAPTER THIRTY-FIVE

Colonel John Stallings marched briskly from his white Cadillac toward the cabin. His polished wing-tip shoes reflected a brief flash of afternoon sun. Dark clouds were rolling in and in more ways than one.

He had been angry when he saw no one protecting the front gate. His men had been ordered to be on patrol 24 hours a day. They were supposed to be especially careful since the girl had been seen at least twice.

Now he was glad that no one was at the gate — and no one appeared to be at the cabin. That meant fewer people whom he would have to kill.

Stallings stepped onto the porch. He looked up at the threatening sky. "Thunderstorms are coming. I'd better hurry."

He didn't want a wet gravel road to dirty his car.

Crater — that fool — had failed to kill Lopez. But he had seen the explosion out on the river played and replayed on television news. It had been spectacular. At least he didn't have the Kendall brothers to worry about anymore.

Still, there were too many loose ends. The girl was out there somewhere. And so was her father.

Stallings wasn't going to wait for it all to come tumbling down. He was going to get the money from the safe — not just his share, but *all* the money. Then he would blow up the place and Jackie Novak with it.

Next stop would be some island in the Caribbean. He didn't know where yet, but he had plenty of options. He could live comfortably on the money that they had collected from those stupid illegals. Comfortably, Hell. He could live great.

But he might grow bored. If he did, plenty of people out there would be willing to pay for his military expertise. Maybe he would have to learn a little Arabic.

He had long ago stopped thinking of himself as a patriotic American. His loyalty was to John Stallings, and only John Stallings. His services, his military expertise, both were for sale to the highest bidder.

The Colonel chuckled as he opened the cabin door and walked inside.

*   *   *   *   *

As Stallings stepped into the cabin, Ryan Conners lifted the trunk of the Cadillac and carefully crawled out.

He looked around as he stretched his cramped muscles. He guessed that he had been inside the trunk for at least eight hours. He wasn't wearing a watch, and the thickening gray sky kept him from figuring out the general time of day by the position of the sun.

Ryan saw a cabin. It sat on a small rise near a creek.

Stallings must have gone in there, he thought.

He crouched behind the Cadillac and carefully scanned the area. He saw no one else, but he did notice his SUV parked behind some trees, off to the right. After Jackie had driven it to Stallings' house, he must have brought it here to hide it.

Is Jackie here too?

A sudden gust of cool wind blew Ryan's sweaty hair out of his face. He breathed deeply. He remembered the stale, heavy air in the trunk and how he had struggled against feelings of claustrophobia. Despite shade provided by the large oak trees that lined Stallings' driveway, the heat had been almost unbearable.

But Ryan had been desperate to find out what happened to P.J. and Jackie, and he was certain that Stallings had the answers.

He couldn't follow him in Jackie's patrol car. With so little traffic on these rural roads, the Colonel would notice instantly if someone was tailing him.

So, in the pre-dawn hours of morning, he had opened the door of the Cadillac. He had pressed the release button for the trunk lid. Then he had crawled inside and looped a rope through the lock bracket on the lid. He pulled the lid down, just short of locking, and tied it in place. That had allowed just enough space between car and trunk lid for fresh air to enter.

As the car bounced down a gravel road, Ryan had been fearful that a jolt might slam the lid just enough to lock it. Then he would be trapped. He would die of suffocation or heat stroke. But he had been lucky.

Once more he checked to make certain that the thirty-eight caliber revolver was fully loaded. He had found the gun at Jackie's house when he went back to look once more for her keys.

Ryan searched everywhere, but couldn't find them. He even had looked under her car. He kept a spare key taped to the underside of his vehicle and thought she might as well. She didn't. But he did find a bomb that Stallings or one of his men had placed there.

You're going to pay for that, Ryan thought as he crept toward the cabin. *And you're going to pay for whatever you've done to my daughter and to Jackie.*

The shutters were closed on a window just to the left of the door. But a narrow gap between them allowed Ryan to look inside. He saw chairs, a desk, and lots of boxes. He saw Stallings kneeling in front of a safe.

The son of a bitch is getting ready to run.

He did not see Jackie.

Maybe she's back in the left corner, where I can't see her. Okay, here goes.

Gripping the knob on the door and pushing hard, Ryan roared into the cabin. "All right, Stallings…"

Before he could finish, a blow to the head sent him tumbling to the floor.

Crater Kendall kicked at the body. Then he pointed his pistol once more toward Stallings and smiled.

"All right, Colonel, get on with it," he said. "I've places to go and women and children to rape."

Kendall grinned toward Jackie.

"You're lucky that I have such self-control or you wouldn't be alive right now," he said. "But I didn't want to be in the middle of something and have the Colonel walk in on us. We'll have plenty of time later."

Stallings set the money on the desk, and Kendall raked it into a canvas bag. "Who knew that killing illegals could be so profitable?" he said.

"Must be a couple of hundred thousand here,"

Stallings shook his head. "More like five hundred."

Kendall whistled. "Man, with this and the hundred thou that I have stashed, I can buy a bunch of beer — and a bunch of sweet little kids."

He used his pistol's barrel to rub furiously above his right eye.

"I'd say that I've earned it. Bees attacked me. A wolf nearly chewed my ass, and then the fireworks burned off my eyebrow. Damn rocket launcher probably broke my big toe."

Kendall looked hatefully at Stallings. "You killed my little brother. And worst of all, you tried to kill me. Almost did it too."

He tossed a rope to the Colonel and pointed at Ryan. "You do the honors."

Stallings knotted Ryan's legs together and his hands behind his back.

The man with the flat black eyes then tied Stallings to a chair.

"I could just kill both of you before I leave," he said. "But, gee, you have all these incendiary devices here. And this nice timer.

"I'll just set it for an hour so that you will have lots of time to meditate on your sins.

"Meanwhile, I'll go enjoy some more of mine."

He set the explosives under Stallings' chair and attached the timer.

"Oh, yes, I like the looks of that," Kendall said. "Happy landings."

Then he untied Jackie's body and legs and pulled her from her chair. He shoved her toward the door.

"Come on, bitch," he said. "Fun awaits."

Just before he stepped outside, Kendall stopped and turned around.

"Oops! Almost forgot your keys, Colonel. I'm going to drive your nice, white Cadillac over to my van. I parked it at the Pickle Springs parking lot and came cross country. That's why you didn't know I was here, waiting for you.

"Then I'll piss in it and torch it. A van, with all that room in back, is a much better choice for me. Don't you think?

"You have a good day now."

Kendall closed the door and shoved Jackie down the stairs.

Her hands cuffed in front of her, she nearly stumbled. She squinted, but not nearly as much as she would have if the sun had not been buried by building thunderclouds. After spending most of two days tied to a chair, her muscles were numb and unresponsive.

But her mind remained sharp. She looked around, eager to figure out a way to escape from this madman—and to get back to Ryan. She had to make sure that he was all right. And she had to get him out of that cabin before it exploded. With all of that ammunition in there, nothing would be left but a few cinders.

As they neared the Cadillac, Kendall stopped and jerked Jackie to a halt. "Shit!"

She followed his gaze and saw that the tires on the car had been flattened. She fought back a smile. Someone else was out here, someone who didn't want Kendall to escape.

Suddenly a rock struck Kendall in the left temple, and he reeled back a step. Instinctively, he raised his arm to protect himself "What the…?"

Another stone hit him on the shoulder.

"You let her go, or the next one will hit you in the nose!"

Now Jackie did grin. Then she realized that the voice belonged to a child, probably a girl. Could it be P.J.? Whoever it was, she wouldn't have a chance against Kendall.

She hoped that the child would back off. She would rather take a chance with Kendall by herself than risk a child being harmed.

"Get out of here! Run! Run!" she yelled.

Another rock clipped Kendall behind the right ear. He grabbed Jackie to use as a shield.

"All right, kid," Kendall said. "You come out right now, or I'm going to kill the deputy."

Jackie lunged free. "Run! Now!" she screamed.

This time a rock nearly knocked the gun from Kendall's hand.

"All right, that's enough!" he ordered. He grabbed Jackie by the collar.

"I'm counting to three, and then I'm going to shoot her if you don't come out. One! Two! Th…"

P.J. stepped from the brush, her face flush with anger. "You do, and you'll be sorry."

Kendall laughed. "This just gets better and better," he said. "What do you know? My two favorite gals here together."

An exaggerated frown darkened his face.

"But I can't take you both with me," he said. "One of you will have to stay behind."

He pointed his pistol at Jackie's head. She closed her eyes and bit her lip. She had no doubt that he would pull the trigger.

"You do that, and I'll run away," P.J. said. "And we already know that you can't catch me.

"Let her go, and I'll come with you."

"No!" Jackie shrieked. "No! I won't let you. Get out of here, P.J., please!"

P.J. looked at the deputy and smiled. "It's okay," she said. "I can handle him."

Jackie was so stunned by the girl's confident words that she failed to see the anger rise in Kendall's face.

Rocks still clenched in both hands, P.J. glanced at the man in black. "Okay, what's it going to be?"

Kendall pushed Jackie to the ground. "All right, you little bitch, get over here."

He took one of the cuffs from Jackie's wrists and snapped it around the trunk of a small tree. He tossed the keys into the creek.

"The blast should take care of you, too," he said.

Kendall seized the collar of P.J.'s oversized shirt and pushed. "Move it, kid. We've got a ways to go. And this weather doesn't look good."

He shoved P.J. toward the hill at the back of the cabin. She stumbled and fell. She rose and was shoved again. "Run, dammit! Now!"

P.J. ran. Gravel scrapes burned her knees, and she blinked back tears. She would not cry in front of this evil man.

She was sorry for the worry that she had caused the nice woman who tried to protect her, but she was doing the right thing. She would be all right. She had her wolf family. She had her new friend, Miguel.

Most importantly, she had her father! He had come for her. He would keep coming for her.

Her dream in the cave of the Old Ones had teased her with the possibility. That's why they had gone to the cabin. Then she and Miguel had seen him when they looked in the broken window. P.J. had nearly cried out when she saw Ryan lying on the floor. But he was tied. Dead men don't need to be tied. That meant he was alive.

Originally, they both were going in through the window. But then P.J. realized that the man in black was taking the deputy. He would do terrible things to her, just like he would have to that little girl back at the Civic Center. She couldn't let that happen.

P.J. might have lost a little weight during the past several days, but she still had her shortstop throwing arm. She wouldn't let him take the woman. And she didn't!

Miguel was untying her father right now. He would get him out of the cabin before it blew up. The two of them would free the deputy, and they would come after her.

"Where are we going?" P.J. asked as they jogged through a forest of oak and hickory.

Even without the sun, the heat combined with high humidity to make both miserable. Sweat stained their backs, and their breathing grew ragged and heavy.

"Shut up," Kendall said.

He slammed the heel of his palm into P.J.'s back and sent the girl tumbling off the path and down a rocky hillside.

"Umph!" The girl rolled into a trunk that knocked the wind from her. The pain nearly made her pass out. She drew herself into a ball and lay there, eyes shut. She waited for her breath to return.

Kendall hobbled down the bank. He kneeled and grabbed P.J.'s shoulder to roll her onto her back. He glared down into the girl's blood-stained face. It had been cut by rocks, as had her hands.

The man in black flattened P.J.'s nose with the gun barrel.

"I think that I'll kill you right here," he said. "You're not worth the trouble."

Still unable to order her abused body to move, P.J. felt her heart shift into overdrive. She thought it would burst from her shirt. The pain of the cold metal pressing into her face made her eyes water.

She feared for her life.

Was I wrong? she wondered. *Are the wolves not going to help me after all?*

As P.J. closed her eyes, she heard a click.

It's the hammer on the gun, she thought. *I'm going to die now.*

But no shot followed. And the barrel no longer was pressed into her face. P.J. opened one eye and then the other. Kendall had turned slightly away from the girl and was staring into the surrounding woods.

P.J. heard another click, just like the first. It wasn't the pistol being cocked after all. Something was crunching twigs as it moved about in the dense undergrowth.

Kendall pointed the gun at the sound. "What the Hell…

"You come any closer, and I'll shoot the kid!" he yelled. "I mean it!"

Movements ceased. The man stood and pulled P.J. with him.

"Dammit, kid, I'd like to kill you now," he said. His shark eyes left no doubt that he meant it.

"I can always find plenty of others to make me happy. But looks like I'm going to need some insurance for a while."

Kendall half-pulled, half-pushed P.J. back up the hill, and once more made her run. Rustling resumed in the trees along the path. The man didn't hear the sounds. But P.J. did.

Yes, yes, she thought. *My family is with me now.*

CHAPTER THIRTY-SIX

Ryan chewed aspirins as he charged up the hill behind the cabin. He didn't have time for a headache. The bastard who gave him the headache had his daughter.

He had her as Miguel helped Ryan up from the cabin floor and led him outside. He had her as he discovered that Jackie was alive. Alive!

Ryan nearly burst with happiness at the sight of the red-haired deputy. Then Jackie told him that Kendall had P.J. and was heading for the sandstone arches to recover money that he had hidden. From there, he would go on to his van at the Pickle Springs parking lot.

Jackie wanted to go with him. But Ryan didn't want to wait as Miguel fetched the keys for the handcuffs from the creek and freed her. Every second was important.

Instead, he tossed Stallings' cell phone to Jackie and grabbed the aspirin bottle from the glove box in the SUV.

"A spare key is under the front bumper on the right side," he said. "Drive over to Pickle Springs and come in from there."

As Ryan ran in the direction that Jackie had pointed, he wondered if the blow had given him a concussion. The bump sure was sore, and he had felt a little blood in his hair. But his memory seemed all right. He wasn't seeing double of anything. Except for the splitting headache, maybe he was all right. And he could endure the headache—and much, much more if necessary—to rescue his daughter.

Oh, no, he thought suddenly. *Maybe my memory was affected. I remembered my cell phone, but forgot the pistol!*

He was going into battle with only a bottle of aspirin and a phone in his pockets. No way was he going back to the cabin for the gun. Seconds were precious.

"Hell, I knocked out a leopard with a camera," Ryan grunted as he neared the top of a hill. "And I wasn't even mad at him."

A few stray drops of rain slapped him in the face. He welcomed the cold and wet relief. He noticed brief bursts of wind rattling leaves. What he could see of the sky looked dark purple.

"Storm's coming," Ryan said.

P.J. will slow him down, Ryan told himself as he weaved around a large rock on a downhill slope. *I have to be gaining on them.*

He noticed that some of the rocks he saw now were the same color and texture as the arches. He was getting close.

"I'm coming, P.J.," he whispered. "I'm coming."

* * * * *

Miguel found the keys to the handcuffs in the creek. He sloshed ashore and brought them to Jackie. She held out her hand.

He hesitated. "Are you a good guy or a bad guy?"

But the boy with the sad brown eyes didn't give her time to answer.

"Señor Conners said to give the keys to you. But I am not sure that I should let you go. The other man who is in the cabin… That man, he killed my mother, my father, my sister, and many other people. And you… you were with him."

Jackie swallowed hard and fought to keep from crying. During the time that she had been Stallings' prisoner, he had told her all about how he and Kendall were becoming rich men. He had laughed about it. He was proud of it.

"Nobody up here ever will report them missing," he had said. "They're illegals."

Working with a man named Evans down in Texas, they promised homes and jobs in Missouri to Mexicans in exchange for money, sometimes thousands of dollars per person. When they arrived here, they were escorted to the landfill and shot.

Somehow, Miguel had escaped.

"I'm a good guy, sweetie," she said. "One of the men who killed your family also killed my sister. He's the one who took P.J.

"I need to get free so that I can help Mr. Conners catch him and make sure that he never hurts anyone else. Okay?"

Miguel nodded. He handed the keys to her. "Sí, señorita. I will help you."

Jackie quickly freed herself from the cuffs. Fists clenched, she raised her arms and stretched. "Oh, that feels so good.

"Now, I need to get Stallings out of the cabin before it blows up," she said as she rubbed her wrists. "It's tempting to leave him there. But you and I both know that's not the right thing to do.

"While I do that, you get the spare key from under the front bumper of that car behind the trees. Ryan said that's where he keeps it."

As Jackie ran toward the cabin, she noticed a stiff wind blowing and dark clouds growing in the southwest.

"Wicked sky," she said.

When the deputy opened the door, she was jerked inside and thrown across the room. Stallings had freed himself. He stood over her, pointing a forty-five caliber pistol at her head.

He saw her look at the gun, and he smiled. "That's right, Jackie. It's military issue. Brand new, out of the box. You'd be surprised what you can buy from the Army when you know the right people.

"You know, I really hate to leave all of these M-16 rifles, rocket launchers, and other assorted goodies behind. But I need to travel light. And I won't need much on an island in the Caribbean."

He pointed toward the door.

"All right, let's go. That idiot Kendall thinks that he got all the money. He's not even close. I kept some hidden in the Cadillac for a rainy day. I guess that day's here."

A few large, fat drops splattered their faces as they marched across the gravel toward the white car.

"Humph, a real rainy day," the Colonel said.

"The money's under the seat on the passenger side. Get it," he ordered. "I left the keys to Ryan's car back at the house, but our little wetback friend should be back here in a minute with the spare. So nice of you to ask him to get it for me."

"I'm already back, Señor."

As Miguel spoke, he slammed a camera tripod from Ryan's car across the back of the Colonel's legs, sending him to his knees. Then he jumped on the man's back and rode it to the ground. He hit Stallings all about the head with his small, brown fists.

"¡Asesino! ¡Asesino! Usted mató a mi familia," he yelled. "Murderer! Murderer! You killed my family!"

Stallings reached around with his free hand and tried to pull Miguel off him. When that didn't work, he tried to hit the boy with the gun. It fired, shattering the windshield of the Cadillac.

Jackie grabbed his arm, pulled his wrist back hard, and took the weapon.

Miguel still pounded.

"Miguel, Miguel, it's okay. I have the gun," Jackie said softly. "You can stop now."

The boy looked up, his eyes red with rage and sorrow.

"Él asesinó a mi familia," he said. "He murdered my family."

"I know. I know," Jackie said. "And he will be punished for doing that. I promise you."

She gently pulled the boy to his feet. "You were great," she said. "Here, you put the cuffs on him.

"Hands behind your back, Colonel," she added, with the pistol leveled at her former commanding officer.

Miguel snapped the cuffs in place.

"Taken down by a little Mexican boy," Jackie said with a bright smile. "How about that, Colonel?"

CHAPTER THIRTY-SEVEN

"All right, kid, dig," Kendall said as he pushed P.J. forward. He looked carefully about the sandstone arches, pistol at the ready.

Over the centuries, runoff during storms had deposited soil and debris just to the left, in a wedge behind two sharply angled boulders.

As she stumbled toward the spot, P.J. managed to get both torn hands under her chest to prevent another fall on her face. With blood drying on her forehead from the previous spill, she pushed herself up and then sat on her heels. She looked up at Kendall.

Sweat irritated the angry red bald spot where fireworks burned off his eyebrow. Kendall rubbed it roughly with his free hand.

"Does that hurt?" the girl asked. "And what about that left foot? You've been favoring it. I don't think that running on it is good for you."

"Dig," said the man with shark eyes.

Both still labored for breath. They had covered the distance between the cabin and Pickle Springs in just a little more than twenty minutes. Normal walking time over the rough terrain was nearly an hour. And, yes, Kendall had to admit, his sore toes paid the price for such a pace. But he wasn't about to tell the girl.

"Why do you hate kids?" P.J. asked between deep breaths. "All I did was try to keep you from hurting that little girl. And now you want to hurt me. I don't understand."

Actually, P.J. did understand, some at least. She knew what a "pedophile" was, and this guy was all that and more. Mostly she was stalling. The longer they stayed here, the more likely that help would arrive.

"Shut up and dig," Kendall huffed. "One more word, and I won't hurt you. I'll kill you."

Although smaller, injured, and unarmed, P.J. would not be denied. Yes, with the gun shoved in her face earlier, she had been frightened. But this past week, she survived betrayal and loneliness. She had lived with wolves. She had grown to know herself as she never had before.

She had become a force to be reckoned with.

Plus, now she knew that her family was somewhere nearby, just waiting for the chance to rescue her.

"You do that, and you'll have to dig yourself for whatever you have buried here," P.J. said. "When you do that, you'll have to take your eyes off the woods. And when you take your eyes off the woods…"

The girl finished the sentence with a shake of her head instead of words. She then busied herself, removing sticks and leaves from the spot where Kendall had buried his money, money earned by murdering people.

A gust of wind and rain blew across the arches, and P.J. looked up into an angry sky of black and gray clouds.

"There's a cave down that way," she said as she pointed. "It's going to rain hard pretty soon, I'll bet. We can stay dry down there."

Kendall pointed at the ground with the pistol.

"Dig!" he said. "I'm not worried about a little rain getting us wet. I want my money. And I want you to shut up."

P.J. wasn't worried about getting wet, either. The Old Ones lived in the cave, she remembered. They were spirits, not living beings. You couldn't touch them, and they couldn't touch you. But being with them would be better than being out here alone with Kendall, at least until the wolves and her father came to help her.

"You should be worried," she said. "Lightning is coming too. This is not a good place to be when there's lightning. Did you know that lightning kills more people than snake bites?

"Of course, there are lots of snakes around here too. Copperheads and rattlesnakes. Did you know that?"

Kendall clenched his teeth. This kid was driving him crazy! Why didn't he just kill her now?

Because I do need the insurance, he told himself. *When that cabin goes up, cops are going to be all over the roads, and I just might need a hostage to get out of here.*

He gazed toward the southwest, where the clouds looked the most threatening. He wanted to once again tell her to shut up, but he said nothing.

"Excuse me," P.J. said. "Excuse me."

Despite himself, Kendall looked back toward the girl.

"Did somebody hurt you when you were a kid?" P.J. asked as she worked. "I'm sorry if they did. But that doesn't mean you should hurt someone else, you know, especially kids. Grownups aren't supposed to hurt kids."

"Yeah, well, this isn't a Disney movie where the little girl charms the villain and makes him see the error of his ways," Kendall said. "You think that I haven't killed kids before? You think that I won't kill more after I'm through with you? You're wrong.

"Now, dig you…"

Low growls cut short Kendall's command. He looked up to his right to see two gray wolves peering down. Heads lowered and ears flattened, they flashed fanglike teeth under curled lips. Their yellow eyes met his black ones, and he shuddered.

Regaining his composure, Kendall raised the pistol.

"I wouldn't do that," P.J. said. "Look."

She pointed into the front arch at a large white wolf in similar stance. It growled even more fiercely than the ones above it.

"And there."

An even larger black wolf stood regally in the back arch, closest to the man and his prisoner. Its gold and amber eyes blazed with confidence. It clearly intended to frighten with silence.

The tactic worked.

"Call them off," Kendall said. "Call them off, or I'll shoot you. Then I'll shoot them."

"Wolves don't normally hurt people," P.J. said. "But you do that, and they will tear you to pieces. They're my family."

P.J. heard a rustle uphill. She stood and looked, expecting to see Auntie Em, the fifth adult in the wolf family.

"And I'll help them," Ryan Conners said as he stepped from behind a tree, a sturdy branch in his right hand.

"You've got one way to get out of this alive, and that is to leave my daughter right there and get the Hell out of here."

Ryan hefted the stick and held it across his body, ready to use it as a weapon. The gray and white wolves growled again. The black stepped closer.

Kendall pointed the gun at Ryan and held it there.

"The wolves don't like that either," P.J. said.

"Screw you all," Kendall said. "Crater Kendall doesn't lose to a kid, a man with a stick, and some overgrown dogs. We're not finished with this. You can count on it."

Dropping the gun to his side, the man in black ran down the hill and into the trees.

P.J. raced to her father, and they embraced.

"You're hurt," Ryan said, gently touching the cuts on his daughter's face.

He wanted to say much more. He wanted to tell his daughter what a terrible father he had been. He wanted to apologize. He wanted to promise that he would do better. He wanted to say a million things.

But he knew that there would be a better time—a safer time—to say them.

"I'm okay, Dad. Really, I am," P.J. said. "I knew that you and the wolves would save me."

She looked up at her father and smiled. "I love you, Daddy," she said.

She wanted to say more. She wanted to say she was sorry for whatever she had done to drive him away. She wanted to say that she was sorry for thinking that he had abandoned her. She wanted to say she was sorry for thinking that he didn't love her.

She would have time for that later. They were going to be together now, and not just during holiday vacations and for a week or two during summer. She was sure of it. They were a family again.

"I love you too, P.J.," he said.

He held her arms. "My, you've grown."

Ryan stroked the girl's head and looked into brown eyes that always would stir fond memories.

"You're really your mother's daughter," he said and once again pressed P.J. to him.

"What now?" P.J. asked. "Should we go after him?"

Ryan smiled. "I'd like to, believe me. But he has a gun, and we don't."

P.J. put her hand in her father's. "But we have the wolves. They can help us. He's a bad man. He should be in jail. He and Uncle John both should be. They did terrible things. They killed people. They killed Miguel's family."

Pebbles tumbled from above. Father and daughter looked up and then into the arches. The wolves were gone.

"Well, we had the wolves," P.J. laughed. "And they'd be there again if we need them."

Her father shook his head. "We don't want to get them hurt either. The police should be getting to the cabin soon if they're not there already. Jackie was going to call them.

"We're going on up to a parking lot where Jackie will meet us. Even with the wolves, I don't feel safe out here."

Hand in hand, they climbed down from the rocky area surrounding the arches. Then they headed for the parking lot as thunder rumbled in the distance.

*　*　*　*　*

Crater Kendall laughed as he climbed back toward the arches. Yeah, he'd threatened the little bitch and her father. And maybe he would deal with them later.

No big deal, though, if he never saw them again. He could get his hands on plenty of other kids when his appetite demanded it. All he had to do was cruise a suburban street on a summer evening or stop by a game room, a movie theater, or a playground. He could get one by force. Or he could get one by trickery. He had done both.

But the priority now was to get the money that Stallings had paid him. It was still buried. If Conners and his daughter were foolish enough to still be around when he dug it up, so much the better.

Kendall knelt by two boulders and began to dig with his hands in the soil between them. Suddenly he heard steps on the rocks above him.

Well, this time, he was going to shoot both of them…

But when he looked up, Kendall was staring into the barrel of Jackie Novak's forty-five caliber pistol. She stood about fifteen feet above him, on the top of the arch. With her feet planted, the deputy held the handgun firmly with her right hand and steadied it with her left.

"I won't miss from here. I promise," she said. "Just give me an excuse to pull the trigger."

Kendall dropped the plastic bag of money that he had just uncovered and started to rise from his squatting position. He put his handgun on the ground beside it.

"Stay right there," Jackie said.

"I wish the sun was shining. It really accents the highlights in your hair," Kendall said with a grin.

He steadied himself with his right hand.

"Reminds me of another redhead."

"Shut up, Kendall," the deputy said. "Push that gun down the hill."

The Army veteran rubbed his salt-and-pepper beard with his left hand. Jackie saw "Death Before Dishonor" etched on his arm. Its crimson color reminded her of blood—and her sister, Jill. That was her blood staining his skin and the blood of all the others that he had killed.

"Now!" she screamed.

Kendall nudged the pistol with his boot, and it clattered away.

"Temper. Temper," he said. "You lose control, and you lose the advantage."

"Shut…" Jackie began, but then caught herself.

The son of a bitch is clever, she thought. *He knows how to push my buttons. He thinks that if he reminds me of the danger of losing control that I will be more likely to do it.*

Jackie flashed an icy smile as she deliberately made eye contact.

"You're so considerate," she said calmly. "Thanks for reminding me.

"Now, if you'll excuse me, I have to make a phone call. You make one move while I'm doing it, and I'll put a bullet between your eyes."

Sobered that his strategy had failed, Kendall said nothing.

Jackie dialed the number for Ryan's cell phone.

"Hi," she said. "Yeah, I know.

"The key to your SUV wasn't under the bumper. It must have fallen off. And I couldn't get a signal to call you from down at the cabin.

"I came cross country instead. I have Crater Kendall. We're at the arches.

"Yeah, that's right. My pistol is aimed at his head, and I'm hoping that he tries something. We'll be there in 20 minutes or so."

She paused. And listened.

"I love you too," she said. "Be there soon."

Jackie directed her attention back to Kendall. A strengthening breeze whipped her hair over her shoulders. Short blasts of rain splattered on the rocks.

"What's in the bag?" the deputy said. "Bring your lunch along on this little adventure? Open it and dump out the contents. Slowly."

Kendall poured out three stacks of bills that were secured with rubber bands.

Seeing the money made even more real the horror of what Kendall had done to get it.

The dark-haired man with one eyebrow and a face still scarred by bee stings smiled. "Hey, what can I say? I'm good at what I do. And I get paid well for doing it."

Jackie's green eyes narrowed into slits.

"You won't be doing it anymore," she said. "Now, pick up the money, and get up slowly. We're going to the parking lot, and you're going to a life behind bars."

Suddenly an explosion sounded off to the west, and Jackie glanced over her shoulder. When she looked back, Kendall was gone.

"Damn!" she hissed and quickly scanned the area all around her.

She saw Kendall's gun still lying on the rocky ground and breathed a small sigh of relief. The money was there too. But Crater Kendall, her sister's murderer, was free once again.

This position allowed her a good view in all directions, but Jackie realized that it also made her vulnerable. Maybe Kendall had another gun.

He also had access to plenty of rocks. One of them, thrown with enough force, could kill as certainly as a well-aimed bullet. She had to get down.

Pistol in her right hand, Jackie slid down the sandstone on her back. Before her feet could hit the ground, though, she was jerked sideways. She landed on her bottom with a loud thump. Impact nearly jarred the weapon from her grip, and she squeezed harder. The gun fired twice. Concussions echoed across the valley below.

Then the pistol was gone, yanked from her grasp. Still trying to regain her senses, Jackie hadn't yet seen her attacker. But she knew who he was, and she knew that she would die if he gained the upper hand.

The first thing that she saw clearly was the reflection of dim light on metal. Kendall had the weapon. She kicked hard in that direction.

And missed the hand with the gun. The blow struck flesh, however, and Kendall doubled up in pain.

"You bitch!" he bellowed.

Jackie regained her feet and fled downhill. She hoped to pick up the other pistol in full stride and then dive behind a cedar.

She slipped on loose gravel, though, and fell forward. She scraped both knees and ripped a front pocket on her shorts. Before she could get up, Kendall was on top of her. He grabbed her hair and yanked her head backward.

"So, you want to put me in jail," he said in a stage whisper.

His breath was hot against her neck and cheek. She kicked and swung her arms wildly. Kendall laughed.

Then he released her head and grabbed her arms, pinning them behind her with his large left hand.

"I have something else in mind. Something that we can do right here."

Kendall nuzzled his head under her hair and bit the lobe on Jackie's left ear. She screamed and jerked backward, hoping to slam her head against his. He saw the blow coming, however, and dodged it easily.

Kendall was sexually excited now by the fear and helplessness of his victim. He shoved the pistol into the back of his pants. He grabbed Jackie by the shoulder. As he stood, he rolled her over and fell on top of her.

To do so, though, Kendall had to let go of her arms. As he did, she pounded on his face and shoulders. One of them connected with his often broken nose. He cursed as blood ran down his face and trickled onto his shirt.

In retaliation, he slapped Jackie with a savage backhand. As she lay still, he wiped his face with the tail of his black tee shirt. Raising up slightly, he unsnapped his jeans and pulled down the zipper.

A light but steady rain began to fall. Thunder rolled ever closer.

As Kendall began to push his pants down onto his legs, Jackie's eyes opened wide. He barely managed to grab her arms before she could pound him again. She spit in his face, and he slapped her.

"You really know how to turn me on," he hissed and pressed his body against hers.

She felt his arousal and screamed.

"That's right," he said as he hit her a third time. "That's what I like."

Kendall slid up her body and pinned her arms with his knees. He pulled a dirty handkerchief from his pocket and stuffed it into her mouth. As he did, he half-noticed a metallic clatter on the rocks. Whatever it had been, it wasn't important enough to stop what he was doing and look.

"Now I think it's time to get you ready for some fun."

He took the belt from Jackie's denim shorts and looped it around one of her hands. Expertly he pulled it behind her back and tied her wrists together. "This is just the way that I did it with your sister, too," he said.

"But you're more fun."

Once more, Kendall began to lower his pants, but this time, the snap of a twig brought him up short.

"Damn! It's those wolves again. Got to be."

Kendall looked nervously around him.

"Conners wouldn't be crazy enough to come back here with his kid, especially since all he had with him was a stick," he said.

He zipped his pants and stood. He yanked Jackie to her feet. She tried to run, but he tripped her and put his foot into the small of her back.

"I'm really going to enjoy you," he said. "But we need to find a place more private. Those damned wolves have caused me enough problems. I don't need 'em around for this."

He looked quickly into the sky. "And rain's coming. From the looks of things, one Hell of a storm. You and me, we're going to make our own thunder and lightning."

He grabbed Jackie's hair and pulled her to her feet.

"Maybe I'll keep some of this as a souvenir," he said. "Hang it from my rearview mirror."

Kendall pushed her uphill, where he picked up the money. He stashed it in the plastic bag, which he stowed in a front pocket.

"Now we're going to a nice little cave down there by the creek. Two of us will go in. I'm not sure how many will come out."

Suddenly, he stopped short and yanked her hair, nearly pulling her off her feet. Pain teared Jackie's eyes, but she refused to acknowledge it. She would not show weakness, she vowed. And she would not give up.

Maybe she would get her chance on the way down the hill. Or maybe in the cave. If it was dark enough in there, she might be able to grab a rock and hit him before he knew what happened.

Kendall ran his tongue along the edge of her right ear. "This won't be as comfortable as a motel room, with a nice soft mattress. No room service. But we'll make do."

Jackie jerked and tried to pull free.

Kendall laughed at her frantic effort and pulled back hard on her hair, forcing her to her knees.

"I hope you are this wild in the cave," he said. "If you're not, well, I have ways of turning up the intensity. I can do wonders with my knife. One way or the other, slut, you are going to provide the perfect send-off for my trip south of the border."

* * * * *

Both of his small hands on the large pistol, Miguel forced Stallings up the gravel road toward the gate. He carried the Colonel's key ring. One of the keys on it would unlock the gate.

As they rounded a bend, the cabin almost was out of sight when a deep rumble shook the ground. An instant later, shards of glass rained down on them as the windows and door blew out.

Both dived to the ground. The Colonel couldn't do much to protect himself with his hands cuffed behind his back. He rolled on his side and tried to hide behind a small tree. Miguel tucked himself into a ball and covered his head with his hands. He forgot about the pistol that he had dropped.

A much more forceful explosion ripped holes in the roof and toppled the chimney. Miguel felt his teeth rattle. More small blasts followed. Then rapid gunfire erupted as boxes of ammunition ignited. Bullets ricocheted off gravel and slammed into trees. Launched like rockets, splinters of all sizes pierced trees and stabbed the ground.

One buried itself in Stallings' left leg, and he bellowed in pain.

Stray rounds continued to pepper the area. Several tore into the back of the Colonel's Cadillac, and the gas tank exploded. Stallings' secret stash of blood money went up in flames and smoke.

Both man and boy flinched at another round of loud, staccato bursts. Swirling winds from the approaching storm sent smoke their way. It burned their lungs. Miguel coughed and wiped his watering eyes.

As the boy looked up, Stallings used his good right leg to kick him in the stomach. With Miguel doubled up in pain, the Colonel kicked him in the head, knocking him unconscious. Then he bent awkwardly to search for the keys to the cuffs in the boy's pockets.

He found the car keys first and looked back toward a burning hulk of scrap metal that had been his car.

"Damn!" he said. "Money is gone too."

Flames leaped off logs that had been blown in every direction. Stallings felt the warmth on his face. Someone, somewhere, would have heard the noise and maybe even seen the explosion. At the least, they would see the smoke. The fire department would be here in 15 or 20 minutes.

State troopers likely were closing in now. Jackie had called them before going after Kendall.

Stallings knew that he had to work fast. Finally, he found the keys to the cuffs. Working carefully, he managed to free his hands. Cursing as he did so, he pulled the splinter from his left leg.

The Colonel looked at Conners' SUV, which, somehow, had been spared when the cabin and all the ammunition in it exploded. "Damn! No key for that either."

He picked up the pistol and stuck it in his belt.

"I'll just have to find a ride on the road," he said.

He never would be governor. He no longer had the money he was counting on to live in luxury on an island in the Caribbean. But he had killed one Hell of a lot of the people who were ruining this country.

And he was going to get away with it.

CHAPTER THIRTY-EIGHT

Ryan and P.J. saw only Kendall's van at the parking lot for Pickle Springs. Even during pleasant weather on weekends, few people visited this area. The scenery was spectacular, but the terrain was too rough for most to enjoy. Today, stormy weather fast approached. That ensured no one else would be there.

Ryan checked his watch.

"We've still got about 15 minutes before Jackie should be here," he said. "I'm going to check out the van. You keep watch for her and Kendall."

P.J. nodded.

"Boy, Dad, I can't wait to eat some real people food," she said. "When I was with the wolves, I saw how they feed their pups. Did you know they…"

Ryan laughed as he finished the sentence for her. "The word is 'regurgitate.' Yes, I know. That's how they feed their young. You didn't…"

P.J. screwed up her face. "Eeewwwww! No!"

Then she flashed her teeth in a wide grin. "But I did eat roasted minnows."

Now Ryan screwed up his face and laughed.

"Okay, enough of this," he said. "I want you to tell me all about it later—over real people food. For right now, keep watch."

He opened the door on the back of the van. A blast of hot air and the sour smell of human sweat combined to nearly take his breath away.

"If you see anything that doesn't look right, tell me right away," he said. "And don't stand out in the open. Come back here behind the van."

Ryan didn't want to frighten P.J. She already had enough of that for a lifetime. And, besides, Jackie had captured Kendall. They had nothing to worry about. She would come climbing up the trail with him as her prisoner any minute now.

Still, Ryan didn't want to be careless. As a wildlife photographer, he knew that could lead to tragedy. You always had to expect the unexpected. If you let up your guard for one instant… Well, if you did that, you could wind up with a leopard in the blind with you.

"Sure, Dad." P.J. didn't argue with or question her father. She didn't mind at all having someone tell her what to do for a change. She was especially happy that it was her father.

As his daughter watched the trail, Ryan sorted through the clutter in the van, most of it camping gear. He noticed red stains on the blade of a chainsaw.

Yeah, I know, the guy's a monster, he thought. *But is he capable of that? Could those stains be blood?*

Ryan didn't dwell on that possible horror. He was looking for something. He didn't know what. Maybe a weapon—although not a chainsaw. A cell phone and an aspirin bottle still were all that he was packing. He would feel a lot more comfortable holding a weapon that he could use to protect P.J. —just in case.

Ryan opened a large plastic storage box. He saw peanut butter crackers, beef jerky, and other food. He started to yell out to P.J. that he had found some "real people food" when he noticed the small box.

Ryan popped its top. He lifted out a pair of orange shorts. They were damp. And they were much too small for an adult to wear. Underneath, he found hair ribbons, a tiny sneaker, and other items of children's clothing.

Suddenly the realization of what he was seeing nearly made him pass out. He was going to vomit if he didn't get outside— and fast.

Ryan stumbled from the van. He grabbed the side for balance and breathed deeply. Light rain felt wonderful on the back of his neck.

"Dad! Dad! Are you all right?" P.J. wanted to help him, but she didn't know how.

Her father forced a smile.

"Yeah, I'm okay," he said. "Just got a little too warm in the van for me."

Just then, the black sky finally fulfilled its promise. Thunder boomed. Lightning crackled. And torrential rain began.

P.J. started to jump into the van.

"No, no, we can't do that," Ryan said. "It stinks in there too. The guy must keep a skunk for a pet."

"But, Dad, we're getting soaked!" P.J. said. "And lightning is dangerous. Don't you remember? You're usually the one who tells me that."

"Let's get into the woods," he said. "It's not the best, but all those trees will give us a little protection. Jackie should be here in another ten minutes or so."

They started back down the trail. Wind blew torrents of rain nearly sideways. The two used their arms to protect their faces from the stinging blasts.

"I have a better idea!" P.J. shouted. "There's a cave not far away. We can get in there."

Ryan nodded as they moved in among the trees and paused.

"All right, but what about Jackie? I really don't want to leave her alone with Kendall any longer than we have to," he said.

"If Jackie has been to Pickle Springs before, I'll bet that she knows about the cave," P.J. said. "She might be heading there right now."

Her father pointed down the trail.

"You've sold me," he said. "Jackie does know the area. She was the one who brought me out here the first time. Let's go!"

The farther they ran away from the van, the better Ryan felt. He hadn't been sure that the red stains on the saw were blood. But he was certain what he saw in the small box. Kendall took trophies from all the children that he killed.

* * * * *

Ryan and P.J. crouched behind a hickory tree, just upstream from the cave. For a moment, the rain had slackened. But the thunder and lightning were relentless. A sudden gust of wind rippled the girl's shirt as if it were a tattered flag.

"What are we waiting for, Dad?" P.J. yelled.

"Just being careful," Ryan replied.

She could barely hear him through the rumbles, booms, and cracks of the storm.

P.J. pointed toward the cave entrance, where two gray wolves sniffed around. She moved closer to her father and cupped her hands near his ear. If she couldn't hear him, he probably couldn't hear her either.

"Nothing to worry about," she said. "See how their tails are low, and their ears are straight? That means there's no danger close by. If their ears were back and their tails up, that would mean trouble."

Ryan nodded. He spoke into her ear. "You've learned a lot living with the wolves, I see. Where are the rest of them?"

P.J. pointed toward shadowy woods growing darker by the minute. For a wonderful moment, the thunder and lightning stopped.

"Arthur and Guinevere—they're the leaders—are out there, somewhere close by," she said in the brief silence. "You can count on it."

The girl paused and looked down at the stream. Green leaves drifted by in the increasing current. Winds had torn them from the trees.

"Along with you, I think of the wolves as my family," she said. "Is that all right?"

Even as he squeezed his daughter's leg to reassure her, Ryan continued to scan the area. He wanted to see Jackie.

What he feared seeing were those flat, black eyes. In all of his years of photographing wild and dangerous animals, he never had seen anything like them. Not in lions, leopards, or even crocodiles. Maybe they most resembled those of a mako. But a shark's gaze was lifeless without being evil. This man had been to Hell and brought back eyes given to him by the Devil.

"Sure, it's okay," he said, now looking at the cave. "But I draw the line at letting them sleep in your bed or eat at the table."

Ryan glanced quickly at P.J. and grinned. The girl smiled back.

Thunder growled just above their heads, and a zagged flash struck somewhere up the hill toward the arches. Wind tore off more leaves and whirled them around father and daughter. Rain returned with a vengeance.

"All right, your wolf friends have reassured me, and that lightning is getting way too close," Ryan said. "Let's get into that cave."

Both felt relief in the quiet away from the storm. Slowly their eyes adjusted to the dark.

P.J. started to tell her father about the Old Ones who still lived here but held back. Getting him to accept the wolves as family probably was enough for right now, she decided. Once more, though, she heard women talking as they cooked and children laughing as they played.

And, yes, that was roasting meat that she smelled. Or maybe it was just her imagination, stirred by hunger pains.

I want to eat about a million hamburgers, she thought. *And none of that soy stuff, either. Real meat.*

As Ryan moved carefully around the cave, P.J. closed her eyes. Once more, she saw Indians around her. She again saw the old man—her grandfather?—playing a flute.

The old man put down the flute and looked toward P.J. But he did not smile this time. His face was solemn.

"Be careful," he said. "Danger is…"

Outside, the charcoal sky exploded, and rain pounded down. P.J. couldn't hear the old man above the downpour.

"What?" the girl said. "I didn't get that."

Ryan looked toward his daughter with a questioning look.

"I didn't say anything," he said, raising his voice to be heard above the angry storm.

Runoff from the mountain above streamed over the top of the bluffs and across the opening. Now, they were on the backside of a waterfall.

Just enough light pierced the falls for the two to see each other. Ryan signaled P.J. to join him on the left side of the cave.

"We'll be safer if no one sees us," he said as he pulled the girl back into darkness.

They knelt and waited. The rain and runoff combined to make the outside world nearly invisible. But P.J. thought that she could just make out the shapes of Bert and Ernie as they crossed in front of the cave. She wished that they would come inside but realized that they might be reluctant because of her father. Also, they couldn't be her guardians from in here. Arthur and Guinevere, she was certain, were not too far away.

The outside roar still was loud. But being inside and so close together now, they could speak in a normal tone of voice.

"I love you, Daddy," P.J. said.

"I love you, too, P.J.," he replied.

The girl felt her chest tighten and her eyes fill with tears. She had to tell her father more about the wolves. She had to know what he would say. Now might not be a good time, but she couldn't wait.

With their knees touching, Ryan could feel her body tremble. He looked over to find her crying.

"What's wrong, P.J.?" he said as he gently wiped away the tears from her cheeks. "It's okay. Whatever it is, you can tell me."

P.J. buried her face in her father's shirt.

"You'll leave me again if I tell you," she said. "You will think that I'm strange like mother was, and you'll leave me and never come back. Look at all the trouble that I've caused already."

Ryan pulled his daughter up and squeezed her.

"I'll never leave you again. Never," he said. "And besides, your mother wasn't weird. She was wonderful. Where did you ever get that idea?"

P.J. swallowed hard and fought to calm herself. "Mam Ma said mother wasn't normal. She said that wolves talked to my mother and they are the reason she died.

"This summer, I've been having dreams and remembering things. I remember the wolves from when I was little, Dad."

The girl took a deep breath. She looked away, embarrassed to look into her father's eyes.

"And I remember that you sent me away to school and I hardly ever saw you anymore. It's because of the wolves, isn't it? You stopped wanting to be around me because I'm weird about wolves, just like Mother."

Ryan grasped P.J. by both arms and looked her in the eyes. "Now you listen to me, P.J. Conners. "What I did was wrong, and it had absolutely nothing to do with whatever special bond you have with wolves.

"I never stopped loving you. I just didn't know how to show it. Your mother's death hurt me very deeply, and I was afraid.

"The way that I acted all of those years had nothing to do with you, except you were the one who suffered because of my fear."

He folded his arms around her, and P.J. snuggled into his chest.

"My tears are getting your shirt wet," she said between sniffles.

They both laughed. The rain already had drenched them both.

"Now, as to the wolves," Ryan continued. "I owe them a debt of gratitude that I can never repay. They saved you from freezing to death, P.J. And now I just saw them save you again back at the arches.

"Mam Ma was right about one thing, though. Wolves talked to your mother. Other animals did, too, sometimes. I didn't believe Carrie at first when she told me about it, but she beat me into submission."

Now Ryan cried as he remembered those happier times. He hugged P.J. and smiled down at her.

"Your mother was one-of-a-kind," he said. "And you are her daughter. If you tell me that wolves talk to you, then I will believe you, and I won't think that you are weird."

P.J. felt so happy, so relieved. Where should she start? The dreams at Mam Ma's house? The wolf that spoke with her grandfather's voice? The Old Ones?

CHAPTER THIRTY-NINE

A sharp crack suddenly pierced the white noise of the storm. P.J. looked out through the waterfall to see one of her wolf family fall. She leaped and raced for the outside.

"P.J., wait!" Ryan yelled.

But his call went unheeded as the girl streaked through the water.

Ryan followed to find a drenched P.J. kneeling over a dead wolf. Blood poured from a hole in its chest and washed away in the rain.

"Bert!" P.J. screamed. "Someone shot Bert!"

The girl fell across the animal's side and lifted its head lovingly. "Oh, Bert, Bert, please don't be dead," she cried. "Please don't be dead!"

Rain swept away P.J's tears, too, but not her grief. She stood and tried to pull the animal with her. Its head slipped from her wet hands, and she collapsed onto her knees. She buried her head in the animal's neck. Thick fur muffled her cries.

Realizing the danger they were in, Ryan grabbed P.J. by the shoulders. He yanked her up and looked frantically about. What next? The cave was a trap. The rain was blinding. He didn't know which way to run because he didn't know from which direction the shot had come.

Less than ten feet away, two figures materialized in the liquid air. One of them was Jackie, arms behind her back. The other was the man in black, with a pistol pointed at Ryan's chest.

"I told you that this wasn't over," Kendall said. "Now, get inside."

He pushed Jackie, and they followed Ryan and P.J. through the falls and into the cave.

"My, my, isn't this cozy?" Kendall said as he wiped his face and beard with his free hand.

"Jackie, are you all right?" Ryan asked.

"Shut up and sit down," Kendall said, shoving Jackie to the ground.

Ryan obeyed and pulled P.J., still crying, with him.

"I'm okay," Jackie said.

She shook her head, trying to loosen heavy, wet hair from her neck and shoulders.

"This is working out better than I could have hoped," Kendall said.

He paced in front of the trio, weapon at his side. "We come here to get out of the rain and have a little fun.

"And we find you."

He stopped by the deputy, placed the end of the barrel under her chin, and lifted so that her eyes were forced to meet his. "I brought her back here so we could…"

"Shut up!" she yelled suddenly, jerking her head free. "Just shut up!"

Long, wracking sobs erupted from deep inside Jackie. Words of despair came with them. "Oh, Ryan, I really screwed things up. I'm so sorry."

Only halfway recognizing who was there and what was happening, P.J. crawled to Jackie and started to untie her arms.

"Leave that alone, kid," Kendall said.

P.J. ignored him. Through her sobs, she kept trying to loosen the belt around Jackie's wrists.

"I told you to leave that alone!"

Kendall slapped P.J., sending her sprawling.

Ryan roared in rage but found a gun in his face before he could get to his feet.

"I should just shoot you now and then have some fun with the two of them," the man in black said. "But you're going to do something for me first.

"I seem to have lost the keys to my van while Ms. Novak and I were having fun up at the arches. You remember the place, don't you, big man?

"You're going to find those keys and bring them to me. If you fail, I will kill them both. If you find the keys, I'll let you choose which one will live.

"Now, get up slowly and get the Hell out of here."

Ryan stood and looked at the two people whom he loved most in the world. They sat side by side in the dark cave, P.J.'s arm around Jackie's waist. He couldn't see their faces but knew the grief that must be there. He heard one of them sniffling, fighting back tears, but couldn't tell which. Maybe it was both. He wanted to go to them, to hold them close.

He also wanted to collapse onto the ground, crawl into a fetal position, and never open his eyes again. That way, he wouldn't have to deal with this worst-of-all nightmares. Ryan closed his eyes to pray for strength and guidance.

"Are you going to do what I told you, or should I shoot one of them now to show you I mean business?" Kendall said.

"I'm going," Ryan said in a carefully measured voice. "And I will be back."

"Take your time," Kendall said with a smirk. "I'm sure the three of us can find something to keep us busy."

"You hurt either one of them…"

Kendall pointed the pistol at P.J.'s head.

"I'll do what I damn well please, and there's nothing you can do about it. Now get going."

* * * * *

Fists clenched, Ryan stepped out through the waterfall and over the dead wolf. He took no notice of the rain that pelted him as he looked back toward the cave.

"You hurt either one of them…" he said again.

Based on what P.J. had told him as they walked to the cave, Ryan knew the arches were upstream and to the left. He saw that the creek had risen at least six inches during the past few minutes. The cave sat only slightly above the streambed. He wondered how safe it would be if a flash flood came rolling down the valley.

"I'd better cross it now," he said. "Might not be able to later."

Ryan forced himself to turn his back on the place where P.J. and Jackie remained in mortal danger. He sloshed through the water and up the bank.

He thought that he noticed movement on both sides of the stream. But in the continued heavy rain, he could not be certain. A chill ran down his back. For an instant, he feared that the wolves might attack him in retaliation for the death of one of their own.

No, they would not harm me, he decided. *The wolves already know about Kendall from back at the arches. They know that he's the bad one. They're my allies, if anything.*

Ryan set off at a jog, wary of the slippery ground underfoot. If he broke a leg, he could do nothing to save P.J. and Jackie—and Kendall almost certainly would put a bullet in his head.

"This is all my fault," he told himself. "We should have stayed at the van. We could have seen them coming across the parking lot and set an ambush. At least P.J. would be safe now."

The rain slowed, but still, it stung Ryan's face when he looked ahead. Mostly he watched his feet to be certain he didn't hit a slick spot.

"But if I had let them get into the van, then Kendall prob-ably would be raping Jackie right now," he said. "At least that's not happening."

Ryan took a deep breath. "And it's not going to happen either. I will see to that."

He suspected that his chances were slim and none of finding those keys.

And even if I did, so what? he thought. *I'm fooling myself if I believe for a second that Kendall intends to let any of us live.*

"There's got to be a way out of this," he said. "There has to be a way to get Kendall away from P.J. and Jackie."

During a glance up and to his left, Ryan saw clouds thin-ning at the top of a mountain. At that same moment, the rain stopped as abruptly as if someone had turned off a faucet.

Just as quickly, Ryan felt the discomfort of wet shirt, wet shorts, and wet underwear. A cold wind on the backside of the thunderstorm blew down the valley and sent shivers through Ryan's drenched and tired body. He heard his feet squishing in saturated hiking boots.

Ryan stopped, put his hands on his hips, and bowed his head.

"What am I going to do?" he said through ragged breath. "What the Hell am I going to do?"

Suddenly, he felt warmth on his face and, looking up, saw that the clouds had passed far enough to the east to free the sun. It blazed brightly. Trees on the wooded slope dripped diamonds.

A wolf howled behind him. Then another and another. He didn't know what they were saying. He suspected they were mourning the loss of the gray. The song seemed sad but haunt-ingly beautiful.

Turning toward the chorus, Ryan saw rain still falling behind him. And beyond that rain, just in front of the cave, a rainbow touched the earth. As he gazed at one of life's most wondrous miracles, he felt strength flow back into his aching limbs. He felt hope return to his troubled heart.

"They're not mourning his death," Ryan said. "They're celebrating his life. He died defending family — my family. And they are proud of him."

Ryan fought back tears as he listened to the wolfsong and marveled at the rainbow.

"I'm proud of him, too," he whispered. "And I will honor his death by defending my family.

I'll figure out something. I'll tell Kendall that I have the keys and he has to come out for them. I'll…, Ryan thought aloud as he ran toward the cave.

Suddenly, the rainbow blinked out. Looking over his shoulder, the determined father saw more black clouds coming. He ran faster.

A shot shattered the dead silence between storms. A second, a third, and even a fourth followed rapidly.

"Oh, Lord, no!" Ryan screamed as he raced along the slippery slope.

Twice his feet flew from under him. Twice he managed to save himself from crippling falls by grabbing onto trees. He sucked in great gasps of humid air to feed his oxygen-starved lungs. Regaining his balance, he kept running. His pounding heart deafened him. Or so he thought.

Two more shots proved otherwise.

"P.J.! Jackie!" he screamed. "I'm coming."

*　*　*　*　*

Click! Click! Click!

Inside the cave, Kendall kept pulling the trigger, even though the pistol was empty.

"They won't die!" he screamed. "I shot the damn things, and they won't die!"

Eyes blazing, wolves filled the cave's entrance from one side to the other. They snarled and growled as they approached. Saliva dripped from their muscular jaws and bone-white teeth.

Kendall threw the gun. It seemed to pass right through the animals, just as the bullets had.

"Get the Hell out of here!" he yelled.

Still, the wolves came.

P.J. held tightly to Jackie, and the two watched wide-eyed as the madman backed toward them.

Kendall pulled a knife from his boot. He grabbed P.J. and kicked Jackie back down when she tried to stop him. Then he pressed the flat side of the blade against the girl's throat.

"Call 'em off, kid, or I'll do you right now," he said.

"Call who off?" P.J. asked.

But she knew. She couldn't see them. But she knew.

"The wolves!" Kendall yelled, pushing harder with the blade. "Call off the wolves!"

Jackie also looked panic-stricken. Only she feared a madman with a knife, not wolves.

"Su...Sure," P.J. said, not knowing what else to say to this man who suddenly had lost control. "Sure I will. Just take the knife away so I can breathe."

Kendall lowered the knife but kept the girl positioned between himself and the cave's mouth.

"How many are there?" P.J. asked, stalling for time.

"Do it!" Kendall screamed.

P.J. realized what was happening. Just as she saw and heard the Indians, Kendall was seeing wolf spirits. They shared this place with the Old Ones and protected it from evil. But she wasn't about to tell the man with the red tattoo that the wolves weren't real.

"You have to let us go," P.J. said quietly. "You have to let us go, or they will kill you. They're angry that you killed one of their family. Let us go, and they will let you live."

Before Kendall could respond or put the knife back to P.J.'s throat, he was knocked to the ground by a blow to his knees.

"Run, P.J., run!" Jackie yelled as she scrambled to her feet.

Kendall grabbed her foot and nearly pulled her down. Sobbing in fear and desperation, she kicked free. "No! she screamed. "No!"

Jackie stumbled outside into the lull between storms She saw P.J. looking up the left slope.

"Come on," Jackie said. "Let's get out of here."

The girl pointed. "Dad!" she yelled. "Dad, we're all right!"

P.J. waved, and both saw Ryan wave back.

"Come on," Jackie said. "We'll go to him. Quick now, untie my hands."

Before P.J. could react, though, they heard a roar. They looked up to see an avalanche of water crashing down the valley toward them. The flood grabbed them up from the sand bar in front of the cave and swept them downstream.

*　*　*　*　*

Kendall forgot about the wolves. In trying to escape, the bitch was defying him. He would not allow that. He would get her back. Yes, he would get her back and much, much more.

He would kill the kid in front of her, and then he would take his time with Jackie Novak. He would rape her, and he would cut her, and he would watch life leave her eyes. That would be the best of all.

But before Kendall could regain his feet, the wolves surrounded him. As he watched, their golden eyes turned fiery. He thought that they must be the hounds of Hell come to take him back with them. Their hot breath and razor-sharp teeth added to that impression.

"Get away from me, you bastards! Get away!" he yelled.

The wolves crept closer, and now he could smell them. They reeked of death. His death. And Crater Kendall smelled of urine, for he had just peed his pants.

Still, he would not go quietly. Kendall picked up the knife and waved an invitation.

"Come and get me," he said.

Without warning, a wall of wet, cold blackness washed over him and carried him to oblivion.

CHAPTER FORTY

"Noooooo!" Ryan shrieked as he watched the flash flood sweep away his loved ones.

So focused was he that the surging water almost took him too. But he regained his senses just in time to clamber up the slope and out of reach. Rain pelted down again with a vengeance and nearly blinded him. Thunder shook the earth.

What could he do now? The flood would carry P.J. and Jackie far faster than he could run alongside. And he didn't know the area. If he tried cutting across this hilly land, he couldn't be sure that he was going in the right direction. If he guessed wrong, he would have no chance of rescuing his loved ones.

Clinging to the trunk of a small cedar, Ryan sank to his knees and once again prayed for guidance. He needed help now as he had never needed it before. Jackie and P.J. might be able to escape the flood on their own. But if they couldn't…

Lightning crackled. On its heels came a sharp bark that sliced through the near-deafening rain. Ryan looked up to see a white wolf staring at him. Guinevere barked again.

Ryan staggered to his feet and managed a small smile.

"I should have known that you would be around to answer my prayers," he said. "Lead the way."

The wolf ran uphill, and Ryan followed. The downpour and the slippery ground combined to slow his pace, but he would not be denied. He followed Guinevere to the summit. He could hear the roar of water down below, but foliage kept him from seeing it.

"P.J.! Jackie! I'm coming!" Ryan yelled as the white wolf melted into the trees and the rain ceased.

Half-running, half-sliding, he fought to stay close. Guinevere looked back and barked again. Ryan thought he detected an urgency in the wolf's voice that wasn't there before. He ran faster, closing in on his guide and the raging flood below—until a slippery rock stole away his footing.

Arms and legs flailing, Ryan swept past the wolf. Rocky outcroppings punched his kidneys. Thorns grabbed his skin. Wet saplings slipped through his frantic hands. Just as his feet plunged into the raging water, he grabbed hold of the rough bark of a cedar and managed to hold on. He kicked mightily, trying to free his legs from the still-rising water.

One hand lost its grip, and the current lifted his body. It slammed into his shoulders and head. It surged over his face.

Ryan thrashed and spit. He kicked and kicked. He reached his free arm as far as it would go—and then some. His shoulder burned with the effort. Finally, though, his fingers just barely closed around the small tree again.

It bent with his weight, and Ryan could hear its shallow roots tearing from the thin, rocky soil. He kicked again and managed to free himself from the flow. Quickly he inched his hands toward the tree's base, pushing with his hiking boots as he did so. Just as he wedged his feet securely between rocks, the tree pulled free. Its roots flipped mud into Ryan's face.

Holding onto the tree with one hand, he wiped away the muck with the other. He spit gritty dirt from his mouth. Quickly, he looked upstream. He hoped to see P.J. and Jackie coming his way. He refused to consider that they might already have swept past him.

"P.J.! Jackie! I'm here!" Ryan cried as he worked his body into a more secure position.

Just uphill, the white wolf barked again. Ryan looked to see that she had been joined by a gray. Both sat watching him.

Ryan felt a twinge of hope. They weren't urging him to follow them. They were waiting.

If they thought that this was the right spot for a rescue, then it must be. When he looked downstream, though, his heart nearly stopped. Just a hundred yards away, surging water crashed into rocky bluffs. They usually were well above the stream. Anyone still in the water at that sharp channel turn might be dashed to pieces. Or she might be pushed under the bluffs and drowned.

But Ryan wouldn't think about that. He would pull them from the water right here.

The second storm was past now. He looked up to see blue sky filling in behind it. Birds began to sing again, but their chirps and twitters barely could be heard above the roar.

Ryan watched trees torn free by the flood sweep past and slam into the towering rocks. The crushing impact nearly made him frantic. That could happen to his loved ones.

"P.J.! Jackie!" he called again.

And then he saw them, riding the water on their backs. P.J. was slightly in front.

"Dad!" the girl screamed. "Jackie's hands are still tied with that belt. I couldn't get them loose."

Ryan knew then that P.J. was holding Jackie above water. She was using a rescue position that she probably had learned at summer camp.

"Don't worry!" Ryan yelled. "I'll save you. Kick this way as hard as you can."

The girl and the deputy tried but gained little. They still were a good fifteen feet out from the bank and approaching fast in the frothy water.

If only I had a rope, Ryan thought. *That's all I need to get them out of this.*

But he had no time to waste with useless thoughts. He had no rope, and that was that. He would have to rescue them another way.

"P.J., you've got to untie her wrists," he cried. "Then both of you swim hard toward me."

They were nearly alongside him now. Ryan watched as P.J. unlocked her arm from Jackie's neck. Both went under in the middle of a huge swirl. Ryan could only guess at their position as he trotted to keep pace. The wolves followed.

Long, eternal seconds passed. Neither of his loved ones surfaced, and Ryan fought paralyzing fear. He had to keep moving. He had to keep close, to be ready to save them when they came to the top.

If they came to the top.

"P.J.! Jackie!" he bellowed, face red and eyes bulging.

He would not let them drown. He would raise them by pure force of will.

"P.J.! Jackie!"

Ryan stumbled and fell. He fought to his feet and kept going. Despair swelled inside him. But he would not let it free.

"P.J.! Jackie!"

Jackie thrashed to the surface, gasping for air, just a few feet from rescue.

"This way!" Ryan called. "Swim hard!"

P.J. bobbed to the top about ten feet downstream of Jackie.

"Swim!" Ryan hollered as he stumbled along the flooded creek. "Swim hard!"

"I'm going after P.J.," Jackie cried. "Pull us in together. Use this."

Rising up as far as she could in the water, she heaved the belt that had been around her wrists. Ryan grabbed at it and missed. Finally, he snagged it just before it splashed into the rapids.

With powerful strokes, Jackie quickly caught up with the girl. They fought to get closer to shore.

As Ryan ran toward them, he pulled out his own belt and buckled it onto Jackie's. It wasn't a rope, and it wasn't very long. Yet it might be enough.

But Jackie and P.J. couldn't get close enough for Ryan to reach them with the belts. The bluffs loomed large and deadly just a few yards ahead.

In desperation, Ryan pocketed the belts and grabbed an uprooted sapling. He thrust it toward the two as he ran. Jackie lunged for it and missed.

Ryan raced ahead, planted his feet, and shoved the tree as far out as he dared. This time Jackie managed to just grab the upper end. The sudden weight, combined with the pull of the current, nearly plunged Ryan headfirst into the creek.

He managed to withstand the surge. Then he leaned back toward shore, where he grabbed hold of a cedar with his left hand. He had stopped their descent. And he felt as if he were being torn apart.

Now what could he do? He almost certainly could pull one person to safety. Two, though, weighed too much for one man. The strength of the current made it impossible. He had succeeded only in delaying the inevitable.

Even if he could wrap the belts around the tree, it still would be a holding action. Alone, he never would be able to muster enough strength to save his family.

Still, he had to try. Fighting fiercely to keep his balance, Ryan let go of the tree and pulled out the belts. Before he could loop them around the trunk, though, the white wolf grabbed one end. She tugged sharply, nearly yanking his arm out of its socket. Ryan's right hand slipped along the trunk of the sapling, but he managed to hang on.

"Dad, let Guinevere help you!" P.J. yelled.

The wolf planted her powerful back legs and pulled again. This time Ryan was ready. He jerked too. Together they backed up two steps. They were working together, man and wolf, to save their family. Straining with all of their might, they eased Jackie and P.J. within three feet of shore. The girl, with her free left arm, stroked fiercely and gained another few inches. They were almost safe.

But even two strong backs weren't enough against the raging current. Man and wolf slid forward as the angry creek refused to surrender Jackie and P.J. Ryan felt his right hand cramping and knew that he couldn't hold the sapling much longer.

"No, dammit!" he cried as he looked toward his loved ones. The tree was sliding from his grasp, and so were they.

Calling upon all the strength remaining in his battered body, Ryan pulled. And pulled. And pulled.

Jackie and P.J. nearly were within grasp once again. Looking up, Ryan saw why. The gray wolf had joined the white, and the two labored just as hard as he.

With one final heave from the trio, Ryan dropped the tree and grabbed Jackie's hand. He dragged her and P.J. up onto the bank, and the three humans collapsed from exhaustion.

Jackie regained her breath first. She crawled to Ryan and planted a kiss on his muddy lips. P.J. joined her there. They both peered down at their savior, who had yet to open his eyes.

"Dad? Dad? Are you all right? You and the wolves saved us!" P.J. said.

He opened his eyes and smiled.

"All in a day's work," he said. "But no more nature hikes for a while. All right?"

P.J. and Jackie pulled him to his feet.

"No problem," P.J. said. "I'm ready for some civilized living for a while.

"And a great big hamburger."

Jackie nodded. "I'll second that."

Despite his fatigue, Ryan laughed.

"I need a group hug first," he said. "And I need it to last a long, long time."

He looked around as he squeezed. He saw that guardians had vanished.

"If the wolves were still around, I'd hug them too," he said. "Believe me, I would."

CHAPTER FORTY-ONE

"Good ol' Kendall might not be too happy about us getting the seats of his van all wet and muddy," Jackie said as the soggy trio sloshed toward the parking lot.

They walked hand-in-hand-in-hand, with Ryan in the middle.

After regaining their strength, they had climbed to the arches and found the keys. Fifteen minutes later, still dripping and squishing, they were nearing the van. It sat on the far side, near the edge of the woods. Sunlight sparkled on puddles all over the lot.

Ryan remembered what he had seen in the van—the "souvenirs." Once again, he realized how many children had died at the hands of that beast.

"If there's any justice in the world, good ol' Kendall is long past caring," he said. "He either drowned in the cave or was battered to death on those rocks. Either way, the world's a much better place."

Suddenly realizing how serious he sounded, Ryan smiled and squeezed the hands of the women he loved.

"Tell you what, though, we'll run it through the car wash—with the windows open. We could all use a good rinsing before we rejoin polite society."

Jackie spied a glob of mud on the side of Ryan's shorts. Quickly she picked it off and flicked it on his nose. "Speak for yourself," she said. "I, for one, don't need a bath."

Dropping Ryan's hand, she struck a glamour pose and swung her dark, wet hair about. Water sprayed both father and daughter.

"I have a natural beauty that even storms and floods can't hide. Don't you think?"

Ryan looked at P.J. "Maybe that mud puddle over there will do a better job of hiding it. What do you think?"

All three were intoxicated with fatigue and joy and feeling a little goofy.

P.J. pretended to be shocked. "How could you suggest such a thing? We both are supermodels."

She pushed out her hip and posed as well.

"All right, then," Ryan grinned. "You'll be first!"

He lunged for P.J.

"No!" she squealed and tried to run.

Mud and gravel, however, had turned her sneakers to leaden weights. Ryan scooped her up in his arms and carried her to one of several large puddles in the lot.

P.J. put her arms around his neck and pulled close. "No, no," she giggled. "I'll be good, I promise. No more water right now. Pleeassseeee."

"What do you think about this one?" he asked. "No, not quite the right shade of muck for your complexion, I think."

He transported her to another. "Now, this one. This one seems appropriate for a natural beauty such as yourself."

"Noooo," she cried. "Not that one. I'll have you arrested. I know the deputy sheriff."

Ryan shook his head. "For bathing my dirty daughter? My, oh my, what kind of punishment does that carry?"

He bent at the knees and extended his arms as if to drop P.J. in the puddle.

"Dad! Look! Someone's coming!"

An old blue pickup truck came bouncing through the ruts of the gravel lot. It parked between the trio and the van. Ryan carefully put P.J. back onto her feet.

"Stay close," he said.

He saw a large, bearded man in the driver's seat, but glare on the windshield kept him from seeing if anyone else was in the pickup.

As the man stepped out of the pickup, his velvet cape burned crimson in the late-afternoon sun.

P.J. squealed with delight.

"It's Sir Ted!" she said. "He's a friend."

Ted bowed grandly from the waist. "My, lady," he said.

At the same time, a small boy with black hair and brown skin came around from the other side of the pickup.

"And Miguel"

P.J. ran to the boy and hugged him.

Jackie feared the worst. Had Stallings escaped after she left him with Miguel?

Ted saw her look of concern.

"Fear not, auburn-haired defender of the law," he said.

He returned to the driver's side of the pickup and pulled out a tall man with white hair. Well, it would have been white if it had not been covered in dirt. His face also was stained, as were his khaki trousers and polo shirt. Blood dripped from the splinter wound in his left leg. His hands were tied behind him.

"Did you lose this?" Ted said with a huge grin.

He shoved the Colonel toward Jackie.

"He tried to charm his way into my truck so he could steal it and leave me dead and bloody by the road.

"But I was too clever for his attempted deceit and dispatched him with my walking staff.

"Then I found Miguel. He told me where we could find you."

Ted then looked toward P.J. "And I have something for the Princess of Wolves. If all of you would be so kind as to follow me."

Back at the truck, he pulled up the tarp on the bed. Six men lay in the bottom. They were bound hand and foot. They also were gagged.

"I had not learned of the evil until Miguel told me," Ted said. "But when I saw one of those guards chase this lovely child and try to shoot her, I knew that I must intercede.

"For the past couple of days, I've been out collecting the Colonel's minions. I believe that I finally have the entire set."

"Wow!" said Jackie. "That's great work. Want a job? We're going to need a sheriff, as well as a couple of new deputies. I see a couple of the old ones in there."

Ted held up his hands in protest.

"Oh, no," he said. "You, I suspect, will be the new sheriff, and a very good one at that. As for me, well, I probably wouldn't be so good at law enforcing since I'm not always so law-abiding myself."

On a hunch, Jackie glanced at his feet. They were at least a size 13. And he was wearing Merrell hiking boots, the same type that left the tread marks along the highway.

"You wouldn't happen to be the one cutting down the billboards?" she asked.

P.J. and Ted both laughed.

"See?" the big man said. "I told you that you would make a good sheriff."

Ryan stepped forward to shake Ted's hand.

"I want to thank you for being a friend to my daughter and for all you've done for her," he said. "Now, we need to get these murderers into town and behind bars.

"I wonder if you'd do one more favor for us."

Ryan put his arm around Ted and they walked to the front of the pickup to talk.

CHAPTER FORTY-TWO

Sir Ted drove his pickup out of the parking lot. P.J. and Miguel had joined him in the front seat. Jackie and Ryan followed in the van, with Stallings on the floor in back.

"So you want to tell me why we're doing this?" Jackie asked as she drove up the gravel road. "Why split us up like this?"

"This is the van that Kendall used to kidnap P.J.," Ryan said. "Also, when I was going through it earlier, I found a box. It contains kids' clothes and shoes, stuff that he took from the ones he killed. I just couldn't stand the thought of P.J. riding in here again."

Jackie nodded.

"I understand," she said. "Being in here just about makes me sick at my stomach. With all of this evidence, it's almost too bad that Kendall isn't around to stand trial. Maybe we'd be able to find out what he did with the bodies. Then the poor parents of those children could get some closure."

Ryan rolled down his window. "That's the only reason that he should be alive. You know, I don't believe in the death penalty. But if ever anyone deserved it, he does."

Jackie gestured toward the back with her right hand.

"He deserves it, too," she said. "Because of him, dozens, maybe hundreds of people are dead. I can't even begin to understand how anyone could do anything so horrible."

Hands and feet tied, Stallings had managed to push himself against the side to sit up.

"You're both fools," he said.

"Illegal aliens, especially the Mexicans, are ruining this country," he said. "I was doing a public service."

Ryan looked back. "Of course, you didn't do it for the money."

Stallings' ice-blue eyes glared at him. "That was just a side benefit," he said. "I would have done it for free.

"Western Europeans are what made this country great. Everyone else is turning us into a third-rate world power. Anyone who doesn't believe that is fooling himself."

Ryan raised an eyebrow. Then he looked over at Jackie. "Of course, that's Western European *men* you're talking about, isn't it, Colonel?"

Jackie pounded Ryan on the arm in mock anger. Stallings, however, did not see the humor.

"We never should have let women vote, or be soldiers or deputy sheriffs, for chrissakes," he said. "Haven't they been one giant pain-in-the-ass? Especially one of them in particular?"

Jackie grinned broadly into the rearview mirror. "Coming from you, Colonel, I'll consider that a compliment."

Just then the van lurched to the right. The sudden shift nearly jerked the steering wheel out of Jackie's hands. Quickly she lifted her foot from the gas pedal. As she gently pressed the brake, she guided the van to the side of the gravel road.

"Uh, oh," she said as she turned off the ignition. "Doesn't sound good."

Intersection with the paved county road was still a hundred yards up the hill. Jackie and Ryan saw the pickup turn left and disappear. On the smoother blacktop, Ted likely would pick up speed and quickly increase the distance between them.

Ryan was certain that he had nothing to worry about. What harm could it do if they fell a little behind the pickup? But this realization made him nervous anyway.

He stepped out of the van, walked around the van door, and crouched by the flat, front right tire. "Too late" was scrawled in red on the rubber.

In a flash, he was back inside.

"Drive!" he yelled. "Drive!"

Jackie looked in shock toward Ryan. "Why? What's wrong?"

"Go!" he yelled. "We have to catch them! Now!"

The deputy restarted the van. Looking toward Ryan, she saw total devastation in his eyes.

"I'm going," she said. "Just tell me what's going on."

Jackie pressed the gas pedal as hard as she dared. The van bounced toward the intersection.

Ryan knew that they never could catch the pickup, no matter how hard Jackie pushed the van. Still, they had to try. They had no other option. If only Ted would look in his rear-view mirror and see that they weren't behind him.

"Kendall is alive," Ryan said. "He put a hole in the tire, probably with his knife. He made it small enough so the tire wouldn't go flat too quickly. Then he left us a message with his blood."

CHAPTER FORTY-THREE

"Ohhhhh, I'm in heaven," P.J. said as she rode between Ted and Miguel. She leaned her head back against the seat and closed her eyes.

For a week, she had slept on the ground and sat on rocks. Now her poor, tired bottom was resting on a cushioned seat. Even better, the truck had just left the bumpy gravel and turned onto a smooth, paved road.

She lifted a heavy eyelid and looked over at Miguel. His eyes were closed, and he was leaning against the door. If he wasn't asleep, he was giving a good imitation.

"How far to town?" she asked Ted.

"About thirty minutes," he said. "Go ahead and take a nap if you'd like. I'm certain that you must be exhausted."

P.J. shook her head. "No, that's all right. Does the radio work?"

Ted turned the knob both right and left. "I'm afraid not," he said. "But I'll happily sing for my lady if you'd like. How about 'Greensleeves'? It's one of my favorites."

The girl laughed. "No, no, please. I'm afraid that you will sing as badly as you howl."

Ted laughed too. "Point taken."

They rode in silence. Warm sunshine made the interior of the truck even more cozy and comfortable. P.J.'s head drifted against Ted's arm as she slipped into sleep.

* * * * *

Suddenly the crunch of breaking glass jolted P.J. awake. It fell onto her head and shoulders as something wet sprayed her in the face. She opened her eyes and saw red.

Blood!

A heavy weight toppled onto her, and she fell toward Miguel. Sir Ted! Someone had killed Sir Ted! Blood gushed from a gaping wound in his neck. It poured onto P.J. It dripped on the floor. It splattered the windshield.

Miguel screamed and screamed.

The truck lunged to the right and almost went off the shoulder. Two arms reached in through the broken window and pulled it back onto the road. A bright red tattoo adorned one of those arms.

A leg with a black boot followed. It shoved and shoved until Ted's body was squeezed into the floor.

Then Crater Kendall climbed inside. He slowed the truck and pulled onto the side. He looked over at the blood-covered girl and boy.

"Happy to see me?" he said.

His shark-like eyes glittered.

P.J. pushed and kept pushing—until she realized she had no place to go. Miguel was lifeless, probably in shock. His body blocked her escape through the passenger door.

Kendall laughed. "At last, just the two of us. Or it will be as soon as I take care of your little brown buddy. No wolves to protect you now. No father to get in the way."

P.J. finally found the door handle. She pulled and pulled again. But the door wouldn't open. Frantically, she found the lock and popped it up.

Now her blood-covered hand kept sliding off the handle before she could open the door. She wiped it on Miguel's shirt. Deep sobs wracked her body.

Kendall grabbed her arm. But it, too, was slippery with blood. With one mighty effort, P.J. pulled free of his grasp and opened the door. Miguel tumbled out first, and she fell on top of him.

P.J. struggled to her feet. She was awash in blood. Only her right side and a small portion of her right leg were not drenched. She grabbed Miguel's arm, hoping to bring him to his feet. But she couldn't do it. He was as lifeless as a rag doll.

Then Kendall was beside her. He knocked her away as he lifted Miguel with his left hand.

"This probably isn't necessary," he said. "But just in case…"

He slashed the boy's throat and tossed him down against P.J. More blood spurted onto the girl.

"Now, it's your turn," Kendall said. "Only I'm going to take my time with you."

He lifted her close to his face and smiled. His hateful, black eyes devoured her.

* * * * *

Even the worst nightmare had difficulty awakening P.J.

Totally exhausted, she quickly had fallen into a deep, deep sleep. As Kendall held her close, she fought to escape the horrible dream, but her heavy head held her back. Finally, heart pounding, she opened her eyes. They were wild and fearful. Her fists were clenched.

To the right, Miguel continued to sleep against the door. To the left, Ted hummed quietly as he drove toward Parkland.

P.J. swallowed hard. She fought to slow her breathing.

A nightmare. Just a nightmare, she told herself.

But her other dreams had been more than dreams. What if this one were as well? Was it a warning?

P.J. grabbed Ted's arm, and he jumped with surprise.

"We have to stop," she said. "Right now."

Ted grinned. "Need a bathroom break?"

P.J. shook her head. "No. It's not that. Just stop the truck right now. Please. It's important."

Ted pulled to the side. P.J. shook Miguel. He yawned and stretched. The three stepped onto the road.

Ted looked back toward the intersection. "I don't see the van," he said. "I hope nothing's wrong. We'll go back and check."

Miguel started toward the back of the pickup, but P.J. pulled him toward the front. Together, they joined Ted near the driver's door.

"First, let's check the back," P.J. said.

Ted put his hands on his hips. "What's wrong with you, Wolf Princess? Those villains are secure, believe me."

He saw the worried look on her face.

"All right," he said. "We'll look."

P.J. pulled Ted's walking stick from behind the seat. "Don't forget this," she said.

At the rear of the truck, Ted scratched his head at what he saw. "Now that is strange," he said. "I'm certain that I didn't leave that tailgate down."

P.J. touched his arm. "Just check under the tarp, please. And be careful."

Ted handed his stick to the girl. She pulled Miguel a few feet back with her.

"Okay," he said. "Here goes."

He loosened the tarp on both sides and pulled it back. As he did so, P.J. grabbed Miguel's hand. She was ready to run and take her new friend with her. She was certain that Kendall was hiding there.

"See? Same old six criminals," Ted said. "And they're all still gift wrapped. But I can check each one if you'd like."

P.J. edged closer. Her eyes carefully scanned the bed. She, too, saw only the six. No Kendall. No danger.

"No, that's all right," she said. "A bad dream just made me a little edgy. I feel a lot better now. Let's go back and find Dad and Jackie."

Ted smiled. "Sure thing, my lady."

P.J. and Miguel walked around to the passenger's side of the truck as Ted closed the tailgate and re-attached the corners of the tarp to the truck.

"Sorry to wake you," she said to the boy. "I know how tired you are. Me too."

Miguel smiled. "No problem. Soon we will be able to sleep in real beds."

Stick still in her hand, P.J. climbed in. Miguel followed and closed the door. They waited for Ted. When he didn't appear, they looked back through the rear window. He wasn't at the rear either.

"Oh, no!" P.J. whispered. "Oh, my God, no!

"Miguel, get out of the truck and run!"

She reached across the boy and opened the door. Then she pushed him out. He fell, and she fell on top of him.

"Run!" she yelled.

She pulled herself up with Ted's stick and ran back toward the intersection. Miguel followed.

"What is it? What's wrong?" he cried as he hurried to catch her.

Crater Kendall slid into the driver's side and closed the door. He reached across and closed the passenger door.

"What's your rush?" he yelled.

The big man had been easy to get rid of. Kendall simply had reached out from under the truck and tripped him. Then he had beaten the man's head against the pavement. That would leave a nasty stain for the county road crew.

Now, what to do? He simply could drive away and forget all about this Hell hole where he had been stung by bees, chased by wolves, and nearly drowned in a cave. He had lost all his money. His brother had been killed by that double-crosser Stallings. And he had managed to rape and kill only one child — that kid in the orange trunks — during the past month.

He needed another one, and soon.

And he really wanted the girl. He wanted her not just because of her sweet young body and her perky little breasts. He wanted her because he had been so close to having her so many times, and each time, she had escaped.

He wanted her because she had defied him, and he could not live with that.

So, he would not drive away. He would not flee to some other town in some other state. He would not tuck his tail between his legs and slink away like a cowardly dog. He would not do that even if it meant he could live many more years and enjoy many more children.

He wouldn't even waste time running the truck back and forth over the body of that stupid man in the cape.

Kendall shifted the truck into drive. He spun the wheel hard to the left and went after P.J. The tailgate flew open, and one of the men fell out onto the road.

First, though, just a slight detour to take care of the Mexican. Kendall floored the gas pedal and steered the truck onto the bumpy shoulder after the boy. Two more men bounced out of the truck. One moaned and struggled to free himself. The other lay lifeless.

Kendall grinned as he closed in on Miguel. He stuck his head out the window.

"Hey, Colonel!" he yelled. "No charge for this one!"

The boy ran away from the road and down a steep slope onto unfenced pasture. The truck jolted after him, the last three bodies tumbling out behind.

Miguel looked over his right shoulder just as Kendall closed in. He swerved at the last second but wasn't fast enough. The truck clipped his leg and sent him flying into the tall grass off to the left.

"Ooooh, I'll bet that hurt!" Kendall laughed.

Running over the boy's body once or twice would be fun, too, but he didn't want to waste the time. He was too close to the girl. He was too close to finally having her with no interference from anyone.

Kendall looked ahead, searching for his final target. There she was, not far away. But he wouldn't hit her with the truck.

Oh, no, he thought. Don't want to ruin that fine young body. I want to keep it neat and sweet.

He would run her down, though. He would keep chasing her until she collapsed from exhaustion. Then he could take his time with her.

*   *   *   *   *

As she ran, P.J. looked over her shoulder. She saw Ted's body lying by the side of the road. She saw Kendall hit Miguel with the truck. Both still could be alive. They also might be dead. Except for the blood, this was as bad as the nightmare.

She looked forward again, put her head down, and pumped her legs as hard as she could. But no matter how fast she ran, she couldn't escape a truck. She would be next.

Only Kendall would do worse things to her than he did to Ted or Miguel.

The truck came straight at her now. As she ran, P.J. saw that tall grass turned into woods up ahead. Kendall couldn't chase her with the truck in the trees. But she'd never make it that far.

Pulse pounding in her ears, P.J. remembered what her father said when he taught her to ski.

"If you really want to do this, you have to put your heart into it," he had said. "Skill is important, but heart is everything.

"Failure is only a temporary condition—unless you give up."

Well, she had heart. And she would not give up. She had too much to live for, including a father who loved her and a wolf family who would die for her.

One of them already had died for her!

Possibly so had Sir Ted, that funny but brave man who had captured all of Stallings' men.

And the man who had killed them now was coming for her. He also had murdered Miguel's parents and little sister and maybe even Miguel.

Fear turned to anger as P.J. ran, the walking stick still clutched in her right hand. She heard the truck closing in, and she felt herself slowing down. Unfortunately, rage could not fuel her tired body. It needed water and oxygen and, most of all, rest.

As she stumbled closer to the woods, P.J. noticed that pasture didn't suddenly shift from grass to woods. It gradually changed. She passed small trees scattered here and there.

And rocks! Just a few at first, but more and more as the forest neared. Bigger ones, too.

Maybe big enough to stop a truck.

Or if not stop it, at least buy her a few seconds. That's all that she'd need.

P.J. ran straight toward the biggest rock she could see. The roar of the truck's engine grew louder and louder behind her. She could almost feel death at her heels. She expected the pickup to smash into her at any second.

But it didn't.

Going full stride, P.J. leaped to the top of the rock and then was off again. Over her shoulder, she heard metal strike granite. The sound of the truck's engine grew farther and farther behind her.

"All right!" she said and raised her left fist.

Now she scanned the ground as she ran. Finally, she found what she was looking for.

Earlier, Kendall would have caught her if she had paused for even a second. Now she had time to pick up the softball-size rock in her left hand.

Then she ran on until she found a spot with large rocks on both sides. P.J. turned and planted her feet as the truck bore down on her. She might be dead tired and half-starved. But she still had heart.

And she still had the best throwing arm on her softball team. She threw the rock.

It hit the windshield squarely. Hundreds of tiny lines spread out like spider webs from the impact spot. Then the safety glass crumbled into a million tiny pieces.

Temporarily blinded, Kendall swerved, and the truck slammed into a large rock to the left of the girl.

For what seemed like forever to P.J., the truck sat silently. Finally, she heard coolant dripping onto the ground from the cracked radiator. She watched pieces of glass fall out of the windshield frame.

And she saw the driver's door open.

Kendall stepped out. He staggered as he knelt to pull his hunting knife from the sheath at his ankle. He did not see P.J. running toward him. The last thing he expected was for his victim to become the attacker.

When he stood up, P.J. was crouched and waiting. Swinging mightily with Ted's walking stick, she struck him squarely in the stomach. The knife flew out of his hand.

As Kendall crumbled to his knees, she swung again as if she were hitting a waist-high fastball. Only this time, she connected with the back of his head.

The man in black toppled face-first onto the rocky ground.

P.J. Conners not only had the best throwing arm on her school's softball team. She also was one of its best hitters.

P.J. leaned on the stick, closed her eyes, and breathed deeply. This would be a Fourth of July that she never would forget.

When she looked up, she saw her father and Jackie running toward her from the paved road.

EPILOGUE

Prompted by a dream, P.J. suggested that the wedding take place at the mouth of the cave.

"Your father and Jackie will be happy together no matter where they marry," Grandfather wolf said. "But the Old Ones would be most pleased if they would be joined in this special place, and the cave always would be a welcome refuge for your family."

From her time there with P.J., Jackie knew the cave to be a magical place and immediately agreed. More a traditionalist and not yet introduced to the Old Ones, Ryan required persuading.

"Wolves can't go to a church," P.J. said as the three sat on the top of the sandstone arches.

They looked out across the valley at the colorful fall foliage.

"We have to have the wedding outside so they can come. They're family too, you know," she added.

Jackie nodded.

"Autumn is a great time for an outdoor wedding," she said. "And if it rains, we can always move the ceremony inside the cave."

Ryan rolled his eyes and raised his head to the heavens. "Yeah, right. I want to be in that cave when it rains again."

As if they had been planning months for this, Jackie and P.J. displayed perfectly synchronized pouts. They were of heart-wrenching proportions.

Ryan raised his hands in surrender.

"Okay, okay," he said with a smile. "We'll get married at the cave. And the wolves can come. But I draw the line at bats. If they are in the cave, they will have to leave until this is over."

* * * * *

Bats did not attend the October wedding between Ryan Conners and Sheriff Jackie Novak. Neither did Mam Ma Jennings, who had moved into a nursing home, nor her daughter Cathy, who had joined a religious cult in Arkansas after news became public about the crimes committed by her husband and Crater Kendall. Both were in jail, awaiting trial for crimes that likely would put them in prison for life.

But Sir Ted was there. He had recovered completely from his injuries. He wore his cape and floppy hat, of course, as well as clean jeans and a bright green tee shirt. The shirt featured a black billboard with a red circle around it and a red line across it.

Also, he brought his three small sons with him. With their blond hair and overalls, they appeared identical.

Miguel attended too. He still walked with a slight limp from his broken leg but soon would be back to full health. Federal authorities had allowed him to stay in the United States and live with relatives.

And, of course, the wolves were there, all except for Bert, who had given his life in defense of his family. Because of the flash flood, his body was never found. Ryan, Jackie, and P.J. put a small wolf-shaped plaque on a tree near the cave in his memory.

Arthur and Guinevere intended for their clan to watch the wedding from the bluffs above the cave. But Moe, now a lanky adolescent, would have none of it. He crept down to a tree near the side of the cave. From behind it, he stared with huge and curious eyes.

P.J. saw him and winked. Moe pulled back and then peeked out again.

Other wolves watched too. They stood all about the sand bar, invisible as the wind. They always would be there to protect the cave, the Old Ones, and now the family being united there.

Inside the cave, the Old Ones celebrated the union. But only P.J. heard their flutes and drums, as well as their bestowing of good wishes. Looking into the blackness of the cave, she saw an old man in buckskins materialize.

The Indian smiled.

"I am proud of you, wolfchild," he said. "You and your father have triumphed against great odds and now are together again, as you should be.

"Also, you have a woman who loves you both as much as your mother did. She will be good for you, and you for her. You will have a good life together."

As her Grandfather faded and vanished, P.J. watched her father and Jackie exchange vows. She looked to the top of the bluffs and down to the tree near the cave, where Moe gazed intently. She glanced over at Sir Ted, who seemed to have something in his eye.

Yes, P.J. decided with a smile, Grandfather was right. She and her family would have a good life together. And as she watched Ryan and Jackie kiss, she discovered that she, too, had something in her eye.

ABOUT THE AUTHOR

Robert U. Montgomery is the author of 15 books for adults and children. Most of them focus on animals and the outdoors. This is his second novel about wolves. The first was *They're Back!* His three-book set of illustrated children's mysteries teaches young readers about nature and encourages them to go outside and explore. Other books include *Fish, Frogs, and Fireflies: Growing Up with Nature* and *Pippa's Journey: Tail-Wagging Tales of Rescue Dogs*. Montgomery contributed to the International Bestseller *Bright Spots: Motivation and Inspiration to Light Your Path in a Changing World*.